Outstar

"This book has something for everyone: not sex scenes, a sexy hero with a tragic past, a smart and compassionate heroine, intrigue, danger, and Regency London at its most decadent!"
Romantic Times

"*Simply Sexual* by Kate Pearce is one of the most arousing and enigmatic historical novels I have read this year."
Romantic Junkies

"Intelligent characters, complex emotions and a plot that engaged my emotions to a rare high. Very highly recommended."
Two Lips Reviews

"Can you say HOT? Well it doesn't get much hotter than *Simply Sexual.* From the first scorching page to the last, Kate Pearce takes you on a wild ride of sex and suspense, keeping you guessing until the very end."
Simply Romance Reviews

PLANET MAIL

"This book is so hot I suggest several drool rags and a working air conditioner."
Euro Reviews

"The scenes in *Planet Mail* were some of the hottest and most erotic that I have ever read."
Just Erotic Romance Reviews

"Wow! This story is a veritable inferno of heavily sexual delights."
Coffee Time Romance

EDEN'S PLEASURE

"Any story that can drain me emotionally as well as sexually is rare indeed, and *Eden's Pleasure* does both."
Just Erotic Romance Reviews

"An exceptional erotic romance."
Love Romances

"Sizzling . . . the reader will wonder why the pages of the book do not burst into flames."
EcataRomance

Books by Kate Pearce

SIMPLY SEXUAL

SIMPLY SINFUL

SIMPLY SHAMELESS

SIMPLY WICKED

SIMPLY INSATIABLE

SIMPLY FORBIDDEN

Published by Kensington Publishing Corporation

SIMPLY SHAMELESS

KATE PEARCE

APHRODISIA

KENSINGTON BOOKS
http://www.kensingtonbooks.com

APHRODISIA BOOKS are published by

Kensington Publishing Corp.
119 West 40th Street
New York, NY 10018

ISBN-13: 978-0-7582-3220-5
ISBN-10: 0-7582-3220-9

First Kensington Trade Paperback Printing: May 2009

10 9 8 7 6 5 4 3 2

Printed in the United States of America

This book is for Lorraine Kalajakis, the first person to read one of my romance novels and tell me I had the talent to succeed. It's also for Louisa Edwards, Robin Rotham, Mel Francis, Lili Feisty, and Maria Geraci who make writing, and even critiquing my stuff, such a pleasant experience. I love you all!

1
___

Dover, January 1801

"Sir, if you get any closer to the lady, you will be inside her gown, instead of merely slobbering over it. Might I suggest you move away?"

Helene's gaze flew to the softly spoken gentleman who sat opposite her in the crowded coach. At least, she assumed he was a gentleman. His face was obscured by the brim of his tricorn hat, but his drawling tone and elegant, though somewhat grubby attire proclaimed his high-ranking status in life.

The fat curate sitting next to her straightened abruptly and removed his hand from her thigh. His pudgy face turned puce as he struggled to sit forward.

"I am a servant of God, young man. How dare you imply I was doing anything untoward to the lady?"

"I'm not implying anything, sir. I'm stating a fact. Move away from her, or I'll eject you from the nearest window."

Helene shuddered as she contemplated the snow-covered landscape outside the coach. No one in their right mind would choose to be out today. The curate had better keep his groping hands to himself. She smiled. If the man hadn't intervened, she'd planned on using the three-inch pin from her hat to pink the curate's fleshy fingers. It was a surprisingly effective weapon.

She stole another glance at her unlikely savior, caught the suspicion of a smile, and nodded in return.

"*Merci*, monsieur."

He touched the brim of his hat with one gloved finger. "You are welcome, ma'am."

His English accent held a hint of foreign places, of secrets to be explored, of mystery. The other passengers on the dilapidated coach faded into the background as Helene focused on the man across from her. He sat at ease, one elbow braced against the side of the swaying coach, his other hand tucked into the pocket of his greatcoat.

Beside her, the curate harrumphed his displeasure, but his hands stayed in his lap, conspicuously folded around a worn prayer book. Helene closed her eyes as weariness overtook her. She'd been traveling for three days and had yet to reach her destination and the enticing prospect of a new future. She touched the tarnished silver locket at her throat. Images of her family, of Marguerite and of the past, threatened to overwhelm her. She had to succeed in London. It was the only way to make sense of her life.

The air inside the coach was stale and fetid, but no one complained. Outside, the wind howled across the barren fields. Rain lashed against the windows, occasionally rattling them as it turned to hail. Helene wiggled her cold feet and knocked against something hard. The gentleman opposite her had stretched out his legs until his boot tips were even with her toes. She studied the gleaming leather, wondered where his valet was, unable to believe that such an elegant man cleaned his own boots.

A muffled shout from the coachman and the blast of his

horn made Helene sit up. Were they due to stop, or had the coachman decided not to go any farther in such awful conditions? She clenched her fists and felt the pull of the old kid leather against her knuckles. She wanted to put the past behind her and move on. Another delay suddenly seemed unbearable.

The coach slowed and then stopped. A door was yanked open, and a blast of freezing air sliced through the stale atmosphere. The coachman lowered the scarf wrapped around the bottom half of his face. "All out, ladies and gents. We've got to change the horses again. You've time for a quick drink and a bite to eat before we go on—if we go on."

Helene waited until the other five passengers disembarked before she slid along the seat and anchored herself against the door frame, ready to jump down. She almost squeaked when a hand cupped her elbow.

"Allow me, ma'am."

She looked straight into the face of the young man who had sat opposite her. His eyes were a pale hazel brown that almost matched the tanned color of his skin. Was he indeed English or from a different land altogether?

"Thank you, sir."

She ducked her head to avoid both a flurry of snow and the intensity of his gaze. Why was he being so helpful? What did he want? Helene chided herself for her instant distrust. Although she had reason to know that most men were bastards, she shouldn't judge a stranger for simply wanting to help her.

He kept hold of her hand as they headed for the small picturesque inn, only releasing it when they stepped into the narrow hallway. Helene moved away to rearrange the hood of her cloak and bonnet and to pat down her hair, which was in complete disarray.

She became aware of her companion waiting behind her, seemingly oblivious of the chattering passengers who milled around them. With strange reluctance, she turned toward him. There was nowhere to go but back out the front door or past him into the noisy taproom beyond.

He bowed low, hat in hand. "May I be so bold as to introduce myself? I'm Philip Ross. Acknowledged black sheep and second son of a minor baronet, with slender but tantalizing hopes of a real title one day."

He straightened, a smile on his lips, as if he wanted her to know he jested. She guessed he was about twenty, not much older than her. His dark brown hair was tied at the nape of his neck with a black bow. Under his heavy cloak, he wore a simple thick overcoat, black breeches, and a matching waistcoat.

Helene curtsied in return. "I'm Madame Helene Delornay."

His gaze swept her conservative brown gown. "Delaney, eh? Is your husband Irish?"

"My husband is dead, monsieur, and, no, he wasn't Irish. It's Delornay. The name comes from the town of Lorme in the province of Livernoi."

He grimaced. "Of course, you are French. I've been away from England for so long that my ear for accents has obviously disappeared."

"It is of no matter, monsieur." She smiled at him. She'd practiced the lies so often that they came easily to her lips. To her surprise, he frowned.

"I can only apologize for your loss, too, ma'am, and express regret for being insensitive enough to remind you of it."

She shrugged as he gestured toward the crowded taproom and offered her his arm.

"He died over a year ago. I am used to being alone."

He paused to look down at her. "If I might be so bold, you seem a little young to have been both married and widowed."

Helene dabbed daintily at her nose with a lace-trimmed handkerchief. "I am eighteen. My husband was much older than me. We were married for less than two years."

"Still, you must have been but a child."

Helene raised her eyebrows. "I was old enough, monsieur, to know exactly what I was doing."

"Really." He held her gaze, a skeptical challenge in his hazel eyes. "I'm sure you are right, ma'am."

He drew out a chair for her and then sat opposite, his hands folded on the scarred table in front of him, his dark head bent toward her. Despite the hubbub around them, she could hear every word he said with perfect ease.

"Thank you for aiding me in the coach."

He glanced over his shoulder at the fat curate, who sat by himself drinking a mug of ale in the corner.

"That man should be ashamed of himself."

"Why?"

"Because he took advantage of you!"

She glanced at his flushed face. "He simply acted like most men do when they see a woman traveling alone."

"Are you suggesting this has happened to you before?"

Helene stifled a bitter laugh. He was obviously an innocent who still believed in honor and the code of a gentleman. Why did she have to be the one to disabuse him of his idealistic notions?

"Women traveling alone, especially widows, are seen as fair game."

He frowned. "Because they are vulnerable without a man?"

She held his gaze, too tired to humor his ignorance any longer. "Because they've had a man before and must want another in their bed."

He blinked. "I hadn't thought of that."

Helene sipped at the tepid coffee a harried serving maid placed in front of her.

"Isn't that why you decided to champion my cause in the coach? Aren't you expecting to benefit from my undying gratitude?"

His expression changed, became as arctic as the weather outside. Beneath his charm, she glimpsed the iron will of the man he would become. "You believe I would take advantage of you like that?"

Helene raised her eyebrows. "Why not?"

He stood up and bowed. "I beg your pardon, ma'am. I'll remove myself from your presence just in case I forget myself and force you to bed me before we get back on the coach."

His stiff outrage might have been amusing if Helene hadn't been so tired or so certain that he meant every word. She took a slow breath.

"I'm sorry."

He'd already turned away from her and didn't stop moving even after her soft apology. She finished her coffee, winced at the awful taste, and resolutely set her thoughts on London.

Helene hesitated long enough at the entrance of the coach for the slammed door to catch her rear and propel her forward. Her lone traveling companion made no attempt to help her regain her balance as the coach lurched on its way. She settled herself and her belongings on the seat opposite Philip Ross.

Where was everyone? Had they all decided it was too dangerous to continue on the way to London and stayed at the inn?

She attempted a smile at her silent companion. "It seems we are the only two people desperate enough to travel in a snowstorm to reach our destination."

He stared at her, all the good humor gone from his face. "Am I supposed to reply to you?"

Helene frowned. "If you wish."

He glanced around. "But we are alone. Aren't you afraid I'll try and force you or something?"

Helene sat up straight. "Mr. Ross, I apologized for my remarks. I was tired and perhaps a little overcautious."

"A little?"

She held his gaze. "Perhaps I have good reason to be wary, monsieur, but I should have given you the benefit of the doubt."

He shrugged, the motion fluid. "Perhaps you are right. I have been away from England for five years. I've forgotten some of the more peculiarly quaint notions about women traveling alone."

His world-weary airs, despite his obvious youth, made Helene want to laugh. She felt herself relax.

"I have no knowledge of this country either, monsieur. This is my first visit."

He grinned, his teeth white against his tanned skin. "Then perhaps we should forgive each other and start afresh?"

She smiled back at him, grateful for the reprieve, glad to have found someone she might gain useful knowledge from.

"I would like that."

His smile died and he leaned forward, his expression intent. "And what if I told you, in the spirit of honesty and friendship, that you were right to be wary of me?"

"Monsieur?"

"That like most men, I do desire you and that I would be delighted if your gratitude extended to a night in my bed."

Despite her extensive experience with men, Helene simply stared at him. She licked her lips. "I would thank you for your honesty and politely decline."

He leaned back, and the meager lamplight illuminated the perfect angles of his face. "You don't feel it, then? This attraction between us?"

"Not really. Lust is usually a male problem, I believe."

He took hold of her hand and squeezed it hard. "*Lust* is perhaps too harsh a word. I'd rather call it an instant attraction, a desire to know you better, a—"

"An opportunity to bed me."

She was deliberately blunt, curious to see how he would

react to her coarse use of language. Would he retreat? To her surprise, part of her hoped he wouldn't.

He studied her, his thumb massaging the palm of her hand through her worn glove. "You are very direct."

"I've had to be."

She tried to pull back her hand, but he held on.

"Then perhaps I can be equally frank. I want you. I want to run my hands through your glorious blond hair and hear you cry out with pleasure while I come deep inside you." He paused to bring her hand to his lips and kiss her fingers. "Am I being too honest for you now?"

Helene realized she was shaking her head. Her body stirred at his words, the images implanted in her mind with the clarity of cut glass. How long was it since she'd felt the skin of a young man against her own, a healthy man, a man who desired her?

"I value honesty," she whispered.

He tugged on her wrist, drew her across the narrow gap to sit beside him.

"So do I."

He unbuttoned her glove and kissed the soft skin on the underside of her wrist. She shivered as his tongue flicked over her vein. She'd never felt like this with a man before, this sense of illicit heat and excitement, the thought that she could choose to have him if she wanted, rather than simply be taken or sold or forced.

He pulled off her glove, kissed his way around her fingers, and drew her thumb into his mouth before releasing it with a soft pop.

"I want you, but I would never take what wasn't freely offered."

"I understand." *Mon Dieu*, was that her breathy voice? She cleared her throat. "It is unfortunate, then, that we are both in such a hurry to get to Town."

He sighed, his expression suddenly remote. "Ah, yes, London and my future. I'd almost forgotten."

"You do not wish to go to London?"

"I have no choice. My duty to my family demands it." He shrugged, the gesture as eloquent as any Frenchman. "I've been brought all the way back from India to save the family name."

"I have no family."

He grunted. "Lucky you."

She folded her hands in her lap. "Believe me, it is not easy being alone in the world. You should be grateful that your family cares about you and wants you back."

"They don't care about me. I'm the official black sheep, the one shipped off overseas to make something of himself when all else failed." He glanced up, must have seen her puzzled expression, and laughed. "It's a tradition in England among the upper classes."

"To force their children to do their duty?"

"To force their children to obey them and sacrifice everything for the glory of the family name."

His bitterness surprised her, and she touched his sleeve, anxious to change the subject.

"I'm going to London to start a new life."

"And I'm going to London to live my brother's."

"I do not understand."

He retreated, one arm along the back of the seat. "My eldest brother died, and I have to marry in his place."

"Marry a woman you haven't even seen before?"

"Oh no, I've seen her. She grew up with our family." His smile was unpleasant. "My father is her guardian. Anne has a tidy little fortune, you see, and the vague hopes of a title. My father is reluctant to lose her wealth, seeing as he's been living off the income from her estates for years."

"The poor girl."

Philip stiffened. "What about poor me?"

Helene studied his indignant face. "In truth, I feel sorry for both of you, but you could still cry off. She has no such choice."

He sighed. "I suppose you're right. I've been so busy feeling sorry for myself that I've forgotten how wretched she must be."

"Did she love your brother?"

"William? I doubt it." His smile reappeared. "If she showed a preference for either of us, it was probably me."

Helene patted his hand. "Then you have the ability to make her content and make your marriage a happy one."

His face fell. "But I don't want to be content and marry someone I already know. I want so much more." He held her gaze. "I want to meet someone at a ball, instantly fall in love, and be horribly rejected so that I must take to wandering Europe in search of a new love."

"Whilst sampling a succession of willing ladies along the way, I presume?"

Philip smiled. "Perhaps that would be part of my recovery."

Helene laughed and he reluctantly joined in. She couldn't quite believe she was jesting with him, flirting even. Within the tight confines of the coach, she felt freer than she ever had before. What would it have been like to grow up with such confidence in the future? To dream of such things as true love or happiness?

His smile dimmed. "But I will have none of those things. My destiny is set in stone, and I cannot escape it."

Helene let out her breath. Perhaps she wasn't the only one whose life wouldn't follow a path to happiness. At least her future was finally in her own hands, her destiny hers to make.

"I'm sorry, monsieur."

He squeezed her hand. "Not as sorry as I am, believe me." He cleared his throat. "And what of you? Why are you traveling to London?"

Helene considered him. How much should she reveal? He

obviously considered her a lady, and she was enjoying the experience too much to shatter his illusions.

"I am meeting with my trustees to consider my future."

A half-truth, but enough, she hoped, to content him.

He glowered at her. "Don't let anyone force you into another marriage."

"I can assure you that will not happen."

"Well, whatever happens, make sure you are well provided for."

Helene fought to conceal a smile. "Now you sound like my grandfather."

He leaned closer and brushed her lower lip with the tip of his gloved finger. "As I said, I don't feel particularly grandfatherly toward you."

She swallowed hard as his warm spicy scent filled her nostrils. "We have already agreed, have we not, that our business in London prevents us from exploring any of your fantasies."

His thumb rubbed against her lip. "I don't remember saying that. I would love to know some of your fantasies, especially if they include me, naked in your bed."

She pictured him there, all lithe elegance and long tangled limbs, and wondered if his skin was tanned all over.

He leaned closer and nipped her ear. "I learned a lot in India."

"About commerce and trade?"

His lips brushed her cheek. "About sex, about how to pleasure a woman until she screams."

"With pain?"

He chuckled, his warm breath close to her ear. "Not quite. Closer to ecstasy, I think."

Helene tilted her head away from him so that she could look at his face. "Most men are not known for being considerate lovers."

"In Europe, perhaps. But in India, it is a requirement, and I have studied hard to become proficient."

Despite her cynicism, his arrogance was almost impossible to resist. Her body stirred at the thought of having him over her, inside her, possessing her.

With a start, she blinked and moved away. Had she no sense at all? Opening her legs to the first man who showed interest? Where was all her newfound self-respect and her promise never to allow herself to become dependent on a man's goodwill again?

She straightened her bonnet and risked a glance at Philip. His hazel eyes were heavy-lidded, his erection obvious even through the thickness of his breeches.

"I'm sure your new wife will appreciate your skills, monsieur."

"I'm sure you'd appreciate them more."

"What do you mean?" Helene felt her cheeks heat. Had he realized she was not what she seemed?

He looked surprised at her icy tone. "Only that I think we would deal well together in bed. My future wife is a virgin and unlikely to wish to explore the kind of sexual satisfaction I now crave."

"You can teach her everything she needs to know."

He cupped her chin. "I'd much rather teach you."

Helene closed her eyes as he leaned closer, and her world abruptly turned upside down.

2

"Damnation!"

Philip Ross swore as the carriage lurched to one side, careened down a slope, and finally came to a shuddering stop. From his position, he guessed the body of the coach now lay on its side. *His* body was on top of Madame Helene Delornay. With a grunt, he braced his arms against the seat and levered himself off her.

"Are you all right?"

She stared up at him, her face a pale blur in the darkness.

"I'm not sure I can move."

She sounded faint, her breath coming in short gasps. Philip took her hand and felt the irregular flutter of the pulse at her wrist.

"That's probably because I knocked the wind out of you." He smiled encouragingly. "Just concentrate on breathing for a moment while I listen."

He craned his head and stared up at the outline of the door above him. He could only hope the coachman and horses were unharmed and likely to come to the rescue before more snow fell and buried them for good. Above them, horses whinnied, harnesses jingled, and someone was shouting orders. How far had they fallen? Were they even visible from the road? He tried to stand, wedging his feet against the seat, and jiggled, the door latch. It refused to work, and he cursed under his breath.

"Do you think we will get out of here?"

He shifted his gaze down to Helene. Her arms were wrapped around herself, and she was shivering so hard her teeth were rattling. He frowned.

"Are you hurt, madame?"

She shuddered and looked away from him. He fiddled with the clasp of the door again, more violently now.

"If I can't open the door, I'll kick out the window and we can get out through there."

She laughed, the sound wild and high, like a gathering squall at sea. "Fancy to have lived through a bloody revolution and then die in a stupid carriage accident. Perhaps there is a vengeful God after all."

A bang on the other side of the carriage door saved Philip from answering.

"Are you all right, sir?"

"We're fine, although the door is jammed."

"Stand back, then."

Philip crouched down next to Helene as a hefty boot crashed through the carriage window, sending splinters of wood and glass raining down on them. He drew Helene against him, shielding her from the worst of it, giving her the protection of his broad back.

The coachman's grim face stared down at him.

"Is the lady able to move?"

Philip nodded and maneuvered himself around until he could grasp Madame Delornay around her trim waist. With all his strength, he held her up toward the burly coachman, who caught her under the arms and hauled her through the narrow opening. Philip boosted her from below, gained a mouthful of frilly petticoats for his trouble, and followed her out.

The coach was beyond saving. Two of the wheels were smashed off their rims and lay at an awkward angle to the carriage body. Philip raised his gaze to the newly scarred bank down which the coach had slithered and let out his breath. They were lucky to have stopped where they did. Below them lay an ice-covered stream and jagged rocks.

"We passed a small inn about half a mile down the road, sir. You and the lady can seek shelter there for the night."

"Thank you."

Philip shivered as he followed Madame Delornay and the coachman up the slippery bank. His hands shook, whether from cold or shock he didn't care to guess. Snow at the top of the embankment was trampled and muddied, the horses' huge prints already being covered with fresh snowfall. The coachman hesitated beside the horses. Philip waved him on.

"You're needed with the livestock. I'll take care of the lady."

"Aye, I am, sir. Thank you. Just follow our tracks down the hill, and you'll be sure to find the inn."

Philip watched him vault onto the back of one of the horses and grab the lead rein of another. He turned to his silent companion and offered her his arm.

"Madame?"

She tucked her gloved hand into the crook of his arm and kept pace with his slow stride. He headed for the least muddy side of the road that ran alongside a copse of trees. After the brush with disaster, his senses seemed more alive, more aware of everything around him. He glanced down at her face and saw some color had returned to her cheeks. Snowflake flurries floated down and melted on her skin.

"It seems that all our plans have gone awry."

She grimaced. "At least we didn't die in there."

He squeezed her hand. "You were afraid of that? It would've been most unlikely."

Her breath clouded in front of his face as she turned to look at him. "I've learned that the most unlikely things happen all the time."

He studied her blue eyes, saw the shadows in them, and stopped walking. He touched her trembling rosebud mouth with the tip of his gloved finger.

"Like now, you mean?"

"Monsieur?"

She raised her chin to look at him, her expression puzzled.

"We are trapped together until the morning; no one knows where we are or can come and find us. Don't you find that interesting?"

She continued to stare at him and then smiled. The beauty of it made Philip blink.

"I hadn't thought of that. For the first time in my life, I'm absolutely free."

He slid his hand around her neck and brought his face down to meet hers. "Free to share my bed? Free to let me inside you?" Even as his cock expanded, his heart seemed to slow as she considered him.

"*Oui.*"

"That's *yes,* isn't it?" he asked, his mind moving too slowly for his growing needs. "Tell me it's yes."

Her lips answered him, her mouth soft and fierce against his, her breath flowing into him. He groaned and licked the line of her lips, seeking admittance, and groaned again when she let him inside the warm cavern of her mouth. She kissed him back, her tongue entangling with his until he drew her tight against him.

With a growl, he opened his greatcoat and pressed the whole length of her body against him. She was much shorter than he was, and his engorged cock rubbed against the hard busk of her gown. Without breaking the kiss, he picked her up until his shaft met the softer curves between her legs.

After five months of almost complete celibacy on a sailing ship, he was far too ready to come. Her hand fisted in his hair, almost dislodging his hat. He strained against her, wishing he could simply pull up her skirts and fuck her right there in the snow. But she was no dockside whore; she was a lady who honored him.

Using all his resolve, Philip lowered her to the ground. Her lips were swollen, her blue eyes soft with desire.

He cleared his throat. "We should walk to the inn."

She smiled again. "It would certainly be more comfortable."

He stroked a wayward curl back from her face. "For you, definitely. At this moment, I don't care about anything other than getting inside you."

Her smile faltered and she touched his cheek. "Then perhaps we should hurry."

Mon Dieu, he was beautiful, his hazel eyes full of lust, his cheeks stained red with the rush of his desire and the cruel cut of the wind. She wanted him, his vibrancy, his life force, and his body. In her troubled life, she'd learned to savor the swift moments of pleasure and hold them close. After the horrid shock of the carriage accident, their night together would be a perfect memory to carry with her into her new life.

Helene took his arm and, laughing, they slipped and slithered down toward the inn settled in the curve of the road. Smoke poured from the chimneys, and the scent of fresh manure and horses rose to greet them as they tramped through the cobbled courtyard.

A warm blast of beer-scented air welcomed them into the taproom. Helene shivered as Philip drew her tight against his side. A thin woman with graying hair appeared at the doorway and bobbed a curtsey.

Philip cleared his throat. "Good afternoon, ma'am. I'm Mr. Philip Ross. I require a room for myself and my wife. Do you have anything available?"

"That we do, sir. I'm Mrs. Gannon. I heard about the carriage accident from the coachman; such a terrible thing to happen. Are you and the lady both well, sir?"

Helene managed a quick nod and a smile in the landlady's direction and then looked down again. In her threadbare garments and patched boots, she scarcely looked the part of a gentleman's wife. Mrs. Gannon was sure to notice it even if Philip didn't.

"I'll bring you up some supper on a tray shortly. That's all you'll need tonight after the shock you've had." Mrs. Gannon continued talking as she led the way up the stairs. "Just put your wet clothes outside the door, and I'll have them back to you in the morning. My husband will try and retrieve your baggage from the coach."

"We'll do that. Thank you, Mrs. Gannon."

Helene found herself pushed firmly inside the room as Philip shut the door behind him. Moments later, the key turned in the lock, and he pulled her into his arms. He rained kisses all over her face and neck as he struggled to untie her bonnet and strip her out of her cloak. His fingers were freezing and clumsy against her heated skin.

"God, I need you." He turned her until her back was against the door. "I need to be in you right now."

She didn't stop him, her hands working just as busily to push off his hat and outer clothing. Before she could start on his waistcoat, his cold hands were under her heavy skirts, parting her thighs, lifting her against the door. He kept kissing her even as she worked on the buttons of his breeches. She'd never felt like this before, this heat, this desperate need to have a man inside her right now before cold reality reasserted its grip. His icy fingers delved between her folds, rubbed and fondled her into sudden intimate wetness.

Seconds later, the crown of his cock pressed against her entrance, and she gasped at the sudden pressure. Here was truth; here was the thick physical evidence of his lust. Would it be different this time because she wanted him? He paused, hands rigid on her thighs, breathing ragged, his hips barely moving. He leaned his forehead against hers.

"Take me inside; please, take all of me."

Helene deliberately relaxed her muscles and he slid inward. His passionate groan made her even wetter. He grabbed her buttocks and thrust hard, pressing her into the unforgiving door with every long upward stroke. She gripped his muscled arse with her heels and gave herself up to his rhythm, his enjoyment, his need for her.

"Come with me."

He changed the angle of his thrusts, bringing his weight onto her most sensitive bud, building her desire along with his. She strained and clung to him with a wild abandon she'd never allowed herself to feel before. But this was her night, her stolen chance to experience something entirely for herself, and she intended to enjoy every minute of it.

His rhythm faltered then grew faster and more frantic until she no longer had any control over his movements, could only hold on and experience the fury and frenzy with him.

"God, I'm coming."

He started to withdraw but she held him deep. The strength of her own climax squeezing his cock took her beyond common sense, beyond reason and care. He managed to pull out, his seed still pumping in a wet hot stream down over her belly and thighs. With a groan, he buried his head on her shoulder and set his teeth on her skin.

Helene closed her eyes and enjoyed the sensation of his

weight slumped over her. His heart thumped against hers, the sound as audible as his breathing. The silver buttons of his waistcoat pressed into her soft flesh. He licked her neck and drew back.

"I'm sorry. That was hardly a good display of my so-called skills, was it? I'll try and do better next time."

He released her buttocks and allowed her feet to slide down to the ground. Her legs shook as she tried to straighten them, and she had to hold on to him for balance. With a chuckle, he picked her up and deposited her in the chair closest to the fire. She stared up at him as he stripped off his waistcoat and drew his shirt over his head. His chest was as tanned as his face, his brown nipples visible through the light sprinkle of dark hair.

He was slender, his muscles well defined and his stomach flat. With a grin, he pulled off his boots and took off his breeches and smallclothes to stand naked before her. A pulse settled low between her legs as she gazed at him. Such a handsome man, his cock already thick and full for her.

Without taking her eyes off him, she tugged at the lace fichu around her shoulders and dropped it to the ground. With a groan, he came down onto one knee, his gaze riveted on the upper swell of her breasts.

"Let me help you, madame; let me see you."

She shivered as he searched out the pins that held her bodice and skirt together, his fingers sure and deft as he worked.

"You may call me Helene, if you wish."

His slow smile was intimate. "And you may call me Philip, as long as you say it in that enchanting French way."

She shrugged, letting the bodice of her gown fall away. "It is the only way I know how to say it."

His hands slid around her waist and urged her forward. She stood and allowed him to peel off her sodden skirts and petticoats, leaving her in wet stockings, stays, and a linen shift. He sat back on his heels and stared up at her.

"You are beautiful, Helene."

Part of her hated his saying that, the comment inevitably being followed by a man's possession of her body. When she was younger, she'd fantasized about being ugly, wondered if her life would've been different. As she matured, she realized her beauty was yet another weapon to be wielded at her discretion. And yet, she believed Philip. She could see it in his eyes and through the reverence of his touch.

"Lift your leg."

He cupped her heel and placed her foot on the arm of the chair, displacing her shift, leaving her open to his gaze. To her surprise, he didn't immediately shove something inside her but continued to ease her damp filthy stocking down her leg. His concentration aroused her, made her shift in the seat. He kissed her knee and then her ankle as the stocking joined the growing pile of clothes on the floor.

Without asking, he put her left foot up onto the other chair arm and worked her stocking down her cold flesh. She studied his bent head, the high arch of his cheekbone and long eyelashes. She stroked his bound hair and enjoyed the silken sensation against her fingers. He shuddered and let the stocking fall to the ground; his mouth descended and kissed its way along the line of her thigh to her sex.

"You smell of me, but not enough. Never enough." He licked her clit, the tip of his tongue as direct as a finger. "Before the end of the night, you'll be covered in my cum, my scent, my sweat, until you forget anyone else."

Even as her body gloried in his possessive words, Helene's mind considered them carefully. Would he really be able to make her forget herself? Make her think only of him? God, she hoped so. Her past sexual encounters were nothing to be proud of. She would give a lifetime to forget them. It was a novel experience to have a man intent on her pleasure as opposed to one expecting her to entertain him.

His tongue swirled around her clit, dipped into her plump folds, and parted the swollen lips of her sex. She could smell his spicy scent mingled with her own. Open to him like this, she could only allow his touch. She gasped as his fingers followed the path of his mouth, adding pressure, teasing, probing until she writhed against him, her fingers tangled in his long hair.

He raised his head to smile at her, the faint stubble of his beard shining with her moisture, his lips swollen.

"You are very quiet."

"I am too busy enjoying myself to talk. Surely that is a compliment to your skill?"

"But I want you screaming and begging, remember? One of the things I learned in India was that most men have no idea what a woman hides between her legs." He smiled at her. "Apart from the obvious, of course."

"That is certainly true."

He leaned forward and swirled his tongue around her clit. "One of the Indian women who tutored me in the sexual arts told me that women not only taste like oysters but have a pearl concealed in their plump folds as well."

Helene gasped as he traced a circle around her clit and then flicked it with his tongue.

"Once I understood that, I was far more able to please a female lover."

He hooked his finger upward and forward and sucked on her clit at the same time. Caught between the two firm pressures, she teetered on the edge of a sharp climax. A moan escaped her as she spasmed with pleasure, gripping his head to hold him there. He fought free and emerged to grin at her.

"And then she taught me how to do that. Much better, but I'm hoping for more."

"And will you scream too?"

His expression intensified. "I intend to. It's impossible to drive you wild without taking myself there as well."

She gave him a superior smile, aware of his cock nudging the inside of her thigh, leaving a trail of precum on her skin.

He frowned. "What?"

"You've never wondered if any of the women you've bedded pretended to experience ecstasy?"

He knelt up and began to unlace her stays.

"I would know."

His confident tone amused her. "You would not."

His fingers strayed over her full breasts, teasing her nipples as he removed her stays and shift. "We'll see about that. Stay there."

He gathered all the clothes and headed for the door, giving her a fine view of his slim buttocks and long legs. Helene remained on the chair, her body open to him, her nipples already tight and anticipating his touch.

When he returned, he sank down onto his knees in front of her again and sighed. "It seems that I have a lot to prove to you about my lovemaking skills. Are all Frenchwomen so demanding?"

She found herself smiling down at him. When had sex ever been fun for her? This lighthearted banter and amorous teasing, this . . . connection? He knelt between her legs, cupped her breasts, and carefully thumbed her nipples. Situated as she was, right at the edge of the chair, his furred stomach rubbed against her wet sex with every ragged breath she took.

He leaned closer and let his lips brush her flesh. She tensed as he circled her nipple with his tongue and then sucked it into his mouth. Helene closed her eyes. He was so careful of her pleasure, so willing to bring her joy. She let his body slide against hers as he suckled each breast in turn, so wet now and so hot that she wanted him again.

His cock lengthened and fitted itself between her splayed thighs, the side of his shaft moving between her swollen pussy lips, pulling his foreskin down to expose the thick, wet purple crown. She tried to lift her hips to engulf the head but couldn't manage it.

"Please . . ."

He lifted his head, his hazel eyes narrowed with passion. "Not yet, Helene. I haven't finished with you."

She caught the black ribbon and untied it, allowing his hair to settle around his shoulders. Such a beautiful man. Such an innocent in so many ways. Memories of all the faces that had come before him rose to taunt her. With all her resolve, she shoved the images away and concentrated on the texture of Philip's hair and the pull of his mouth on her breast.

His hand curved over her hip and then inward to slide between their heated bodies. She shivered as he delicately fingered her clit, circling it with the tip of his finger, making her strain against him. He kissed the space between her breasts and then the gentle swell of her stomach before burying his face back between her legs.

She was already swollen from his lovemaking, and her flesh yielded instantly to the pressure of his mouth and fingers. Pleasure spiked, made her gasp and call his name, made him laugh low against her sex and drive her even further along an unknown path of delight. Her focus narrowed to the play of his fingers, his mouth and the exquisite sensations unfurling within her. She climaxed again, desperate now to feel him inside her.

"Please, Philip, I want you." She almost couldn't believe her own words. Had she ever begged a man to fuck her and meant it?

When she opened her eyes, he held his dripping cock in one hand, his thumb massaging the thick flesh of his shaft. He guided his cock between her legs until the crown was inside her and stopped. Helene licked her lips as he considered her.

"As you said, how will I know whether you really come for me when I'm inside you?"

She stared down at his cock, silently urging him on. She

wanted to cry when he withdrew until he was barely inside her at all.

"How will I know, Helene?"

"Because I will scream your name?"

His smile was both tender and full of sexual anticipation. "But you could pretend to do that, couldn't you?" He stroked her swollen clit until she shuddered. "How, Helene?"

She simply stared at him, her mouth dry, her body poised on the edge of the unknown.

His smile disappeared and was replaced by shocking raw need. "Because inside you, I'll feel you gripping and releasing my cock like a fist, making it well nigh impossible for me to pull out in time when I come."

With one swift thrust, he filled her and she obliged him, climaxing with a force that blinded her to everything but his body and her response to it. He arched his back and bit down hard on his lip as she convulsed around him, his shaft a thick unyielding presence deep inside her.

"I'm still not sure I have this right."

Helene closed her eyes as his fingers played with her nipples, drawing them into tight sensitive buds. She swallowed hard.

"Trust me, you do. If I experience any more pleasure, I think I'll die."

"Isn't that what the French call it anyway? *Le petit mort?*"

He kissed her gently and began to move his hips, shallow upward strokes that made her gasp. She gripped his muscled forearms and dug her nails deep as another wave of satisfaction crashed over her.

He pulled out, and his cum flooded her belly and pooled on the chair beneath her. He kissed her throat and sat back on his heels, breathing hard.

"Next time, I want to stay in you longer." He stroked his now-flaccid cock. "Damnation, I wish there was a way to gain satisfaction without having to withdraw." His gaze was direct. "I want my seed in you."

"You do not." Uneasily, Helene counted the days since her last monthly course. "I have something in my baggage that might help—if it ever gets here."

He drew away from her, his expression careful. "You have sheepskin condoms?"

"Don't men use those to protect themselves against disease? I have something to protect *myself*."

Despite the sudden nervousness in her stomach, she met his gaze full on. Had he realized she was not what she seemed? She hated the thought that he might turn away from her in disgust. There had to be something she could say.

"My husband's children from his first marriage did not want to dilute their inheritance. My widow's portion depended on my making sure it didn't happen."

Mon Dieu, another lie, but what else could she say? Her sense of happiness and well-being dissipated.

Philip got to his feet and stretched before looking down at her. "I'm sorry."

"For what?" Helene wrapped her arms around her knees and retreated farther back in the chair, anxious to avoid his piercing stare.

"For making assumptions about your character when I hardly know you. For bringing the outside world into our refuge." He shoved his hand into his hair. "This is our time away from reality. The only time we can really be ourselves, and I had to ruin it."

She met his impassioned stare, amazed that he felt the same as she did and that he had the ability to put her yearning into such eloquent words.

"We are never truly free."

His shoulders drooped. "I know, but I wanted it to be different for us tonight."

Helene stood up and walked to him. His seed clung to her

thighs, and his scent covered her own. She already owed him so much. She stroked his back and encircled his waist with her arms.

"If this is a dream outside of time, then we make the rules, *oui?*"

"I suppose so."

She rubbed her cheek against his warm skin. "Then perhaps we should simply enjoy each other?"

He sighed. "I would like that."

She went up on tiptoe to kiss his luscious mouth. "I would too."

He slid his hand into her hair and deepened the kiss until his cock nudged her belly again. Helene felt an answering quiver in her sex. To have such a young vigorous lover was a revelation. His fingers tightened in her hair.

"Let's go to bed."

3

Philip thanked the maid, shut the door, and returned to the bed, balancing the supper tray in his hands. The steaming bowls of beef stew, fresh crusty bread, ale, and apple pie gladdened his heart. Food on the ship had been plain at best, inedible or infested at worst. And although he'd loved the spices of India, it was a pleasure to come home to the more simple things in life.

He halted by the side of the bed and stared at Helene, who dozed beneath the well-rumpled covers. Her blond hair was tangled, her skin a delicate shell pink from the roughness of his unshaven chin. Despite her disarray, she reminded him of the porcelain figurines on his mother's mantelpiece.

They'd coupled all night in every conceivable position and found a closeness that had so far eluded him in his life. Her body craved his with an intensity that humbled him. Even as he studied her, his cock rose in anticipation.

With a groan, he set the tray down on a small table and climbed between the sheets. He tickled Helene behind the ear.

"Are you hungry?"

"For you? Always."

He chuckled. "Not this time. I meant for food."

Her nose twitched as she caught the scent of the feast in store for them. She yawned. Philip leaned across to plump up the pillows and pull her into a sitting position. Her breasts came into view over the top of the covers, and he stared at their rosy tips. His cock grew even more.

Helene brushed the hair out of her eyes and accepted the mug of ale he handed her. She shuddered as she drank and then put her cup down.

"English ale is so weak. How can you prefer it to wine?"

Philip toasted her with his mug. "Because I'm English?"

Her smile made his heart clench, made him want to cover her with his body and protect her from every ill. There was something fragile beneath her astonishing beauty that called to him at a primitive level.

"Whereabouts in London are you staying, Helene?"

The question escaped him before he considered the implications. He cursed himself for a fool as her face became guarded. Why couldn't he just accept the here and now? Why did he have to spoil it? He finished his ale, poured himself another cup, and then balanced the tray of food on his knees.

"Eat, you must be hungry."

To his surprise, she took him at his word, eating with a serious thoroughness that made him question whether food had always been freely available to her. The thought of her wanting for anything made him curiously angry. He focused his gaze on her hands, not wanting her to see his unguarded expression.

With a soft curse, he encircled her left wrist with his finger and thumb, making her drop her bread. He turned her arm over to display the rough marks on her inner wrist.

"Who hurt you?"

"Why do you ask?"

She went quiet, her breathing so shallow he wondered if she

might faint. He squeezed her flesh, felt small bones flex and yield beneath porcelain skin.

"I've seen the scars manacles make on skin before."

She sighed. "My family was caught up in the revolution. I was imprisoned for a while."

Philip simply stared at her as he grappled with the appalling images her simple statement brought to life. Despite his exile in India, he knew all too well the horrors that had accompanied the French Revolution. Helene wrenched out of his grasp and clasped both hands to her breast. She retreated to some private place he sensed he would never be allowed or able to enter.

She took a ragged breath. "I do not wish to talk about it. I survived and I wish to move on with my life."

Philip nodded. She was only eighteen. He might complain, but what had her short life been like, compared to his indulged and cosseted existence? He felt far too inadequate to ask about the suffering mirrored in her fine eyes.

He picked up his ale. "Then here's to life."

She glanced at him, her expression still distant and wary. He reached across, handed her back her mug of ale, and raised his eyebrows. To his intense relief, she managed a tremulous smile. His heart softened, melted, and came to rest at her feet.

"Life," she said, raising her mug.

Philip smiled back and returned his attention to his plate, reasoning that if he could fill his mouth with food, he was less likely to say anything stupid. And as soon as Helene finished eating, he'd show her exactly how far he was willing to go to remove the hurt from her gaze.

Much later, when the room was a series of shadows and distorted gloomy shapes, Helene stirred in her sleep. The old feather bed sagged in the middle and made them a perfect nest. Behind her, Philip lay on his side, one hand buried between her legs, the other cupping her breast. His half-erect cock nestled between her buttocks. She felt more comfortable with him than with any other man. His deep appreciation of her was evident in everything he did. He worshipped her body, he freely *shared* himself with her, and she gloried in every new sensation.

If she'd met him in her former life at a ball or some other social occasion, would she have felt like this? This instant connection and strong sexual attraction? She'd changed so much that she no longer trusted herself. Bitter experience had replaced her former romantic dreams. Nothing was ever as good as it seemed, and yet here she was, wrapped in a man's arms and at peace for the first time in years.

She smiled into the darkness. His scent bathed her now, the exotic smell of spices and his seed as familiar as her own cream. Had she ever allowed herself to lie entwined with a man without wanting to rid herself of the physical reminders of yet another unwanted sexual encounter?

"You're awake."

She slowly opened her eyes as Philip nuzzled her neck.

"I suppose I am."

He chuckled, the sound muffled against the nape of her neck. "I keep imagining I'm back on the ship again. I woke up because everything wasn't moving."

"The voyage from India is very long, *n'est-ce pas*?"

"Aye, five to six months on average." He squeezed her breast. "And no women passengers to flirt with. Can you imagine that?"

"I cannot imagine how you survived without sex for that long."

He laughed again, the sound sleepy and intimate. "There were some avenues I explored—unconventional ones, I might add."

She placed her hand over his as he slowly fingered her nipple. "Such as?"

"You are a curious minx, madame. I hesitate to shock you."

She almost laughed. "I don't think that is possible."

He sighed and settled himself against her, his breath warm on her cheek. "From my first day aboard the ship, one of the men who served in the passenger cabins made it clear to me that if I was interested in a sexual tryst, he would be happy to oblige."

Philip kissed her shoulder. "I, of course, politely declined his offer, telling him I had no interest in men. But as the voyage progressed and my hand became the only means of satisfying myself, I began to see his proposal in a different light."

Helene arched her back against the growing swell of Philip's cock, felt the first wetness of his precum soak into her skin.

"I found myself lingering in my cabin to watch him perform the simplest tasks. I loved the way he laid out my linen, the tight stretch of his breeches over his arse as he made my bed. He was a handsome man, too, with long black hair and a gold earring in each ear.

"One morning, about three months into our voyage, I met him in one of the narrow corridors between the state rooms and the kitchen. A roll of the ship threw me against him, and he caught hold of my arms. I didn't step back. I let my body press his into the wall, felt his erect cock grind against mine."

Helene shivered as the tip of Philip's thumb worked its way inside her back passage.

"When he licked my lips, I almost came in my breeches. . . ."

"And how did that make you feel?"

He groaned and rocked against her, his precum making his cock slide easily between her buttocks. "Hard, horny, and desperate, if you really want to know. Two days after that, I deliberately met him again outside the tiny storeroom. He shoved me inside the room and went down on his knees. Before I could even speak, he had my cock in his mouth and soon my seed was pumping down his throat."

Helene slid her leg up over Philip's thigh and anchored her foot on his hip, leaving her sex open to his questing fingers, her arse ready for the first penetration of his cock. He pressed against her, withdrew, and then returned, his cock now slathered in oil and precum.

"God, I let him do that to me every night in my cabin, my hands in his hair, holding him against me, making sure he took every drop of my cum." He moaned and undulated his hips against her. "And then he offered me his arse and showed me how to grease my cock to get inside him. And God forgive me, I took him on his hands and knees, over my table, in my bed . . ."

Helene closed her eyes as he worked his way inside her. She climaxed almost immediately, erotic images of Philip fucking the unknown man with all the concentration and finesse he had given her floated through her mind.

"I would've liked to see you together."

He bit her shoulder. "I would've liked that, too, as long as you were naked and so aroused you made yourself come with us."

"And did you give him the same liberties?"

Deep inside her, Philip's cock twitched and swelled as he gave another long, slow thrust. "I took him in my mouth . . . I enjoyed that."

He gripped her hips as he pumped hard against her buttocks, his breath hot and harried on her neck, his fingers digging into her flesh as he came. His final words were whispered so quietly she almost missed them.

"I was ready to let him fuck me, but the voyage was ending, and he was called away to other duties."

"You were surprised by your lust for this man."

He shifted behind her. "At first I was horrified, but then I felt no shame, only a deep need to be fucked, to be taken, even if it was by another man."

Dreamily, Helene considered his words. Here was a man who might understand that love came in different disguises. A man who might love her despite her past. She eased away from him to the edge of the bed. What on earth was she thinking? She had a new life to plan, a new future. The last thing she needed was to throw herself into Philip Ross's arms and beg him to keep her there forever. Had she learned nothing?

"Helene? Have I disgusted you with my story?"

She opened her eyes and focused on the soft candlelight as it flickered beside the bed. She hated the dark and always insisted on a light. It meant the faces of those who had fucked her were all too memorable. But at least it kept out the decaying ghosts of those who were no longer able to fuck anything at all.

"I'm not shocked, Philip. In truth, I found your story arousing. It is unusual to find an Englishman with such liberal sexual views."

He laughed. "Perhaps I should start a new kind of gentleman's club to instruct my fellow Englishmen in the erotic arts. What do you think?"

She stared at him for a long moment as his words swirled around her head. She would love to be in charge of such an establishment. To show men how women should be treated in bed, to explore the sensual delights Philip had revealed to her.

"Helene?"

She blinked and refocused on his face.

"Are you sure I didn't offend you? You seem distant."

He came up on his elbow to study her. His hair hung around his face, softening the hard, clean lines of his cheekbones.

She sighed. "I was thinking about tomorrow."

"We agreed not to think too hard."

Helene grimaced. "I know, but it is difficult. I have enjoyed this time with you"—she gestured at the untidy bedchamber—"this space, and this idyll."

He crawled toward her, his expression intent, his hazel eyes level with her own. "Our time is not over yet, madame. I have plenty more pleasure to give you before the morning." He slid his knees between her thighs, opening them wide, and shoved his cock deep. Helene moaned as her exquisitely sensitive sex absorbed his thick fullness.

"I promised to make you scream, Helene, and I'm a man of my word."

She reached for his shoulders, but he drew her hands over her head and held them there as he pumped into her. She could only move with him, watch him take her and make her his own. His expression was savage, his intention to possess her all too obvious to a woman of her experience. For the first time in her life, she allowed herself to imagine what it might be like to be loved so completely.

He pulled out, crawled up her body, and slid his cock into her mouth, groaning as she took him deep in her throat.

"God, I love you sucking my cock."

She drew back and used the tip of her tongue to torment the slit on the pulsing crown, swirled her tongue around the head until he cried out. With a growl, he jerked back and knelt between her thighs, plunging his shaft back inside her pussy in long hard strokes.

Her climax took her by surprise, sending her spiraling into ecstasy with a suddenness that made Philip come too. He barely managed to pull out in time, and his hot cum spilled on her belly. He continued to hold her close, his hips still moving in the rhythm of love.

Helene bit her lip as his now-familiar weight settled over her. He'd reminded her that even the ecstasy of his lovemaking was all too brief a joy in a life that might end tomorrow. She'd lost too many of the people she'd loved to ever believe such perfection could last. Her fingers tangled in his damp hair, and she fought back tears. For the first time in years, she found herself praying, but whether her prayer was for forgiveness for daring to hope or for a miracle, she couldn't tell.

* * *

Philip risked a wary smile at Helene over the coffeepot. She was all calm politeness, but something had changed. Something indefinable but vital had slipped through his fingers during the cold unknown hours of dawn while they slept. A knot of tension formed in his gut as he studied her.

He couldn't stand to part from her. The realization held him frozen in shock, his cup half raised to his mouth.

She wore her own clothes again. The patched and worn garments of a lower-class woman. He put down his cup. It didn't matter to him. He was prepared to buy her anything she ever desired.

"Would you like some more coffee, Philip?"

"No, I thank you."

Abruptly he stood up and started to pace the room. Helene put the coffeepot down and watched him carefully, a small frown creasing her forehead.

He turned to face her. "I can't go through with it."

"With what?"

"The marriage to Anne, the whole stepping into my dead brother's shoes."

"Tell your father when you see him. Perhaps you misjudge him and he will understand."

Philip fought off a shiver. "He will never understand. For him, duty to your family is almost as important as duty to the king and God."

She bit her lip. "I do not know how to help you, *mon ami*."

He held her gaze. "Yes, you do. Marry me."

She blinked rapidly, her face paling as she stared at him.

"I . . . cannot do that."

"Why not?" Anger rose, displacing the fear. *He was proposing marriage, goddamn her—why wasn't she smiling?* "I promise I'll be a good husband."

"That's not the point. You hardly know me; we are not of the same social class, or even the same nationality."

He stalked back to the table and leaned over her. "I *know* you."

She gazed back at him, her beautiful features composed. Her mouth quirked up at one corner and fueled his gathering incomprehensible rage. "Philip, you know my body. Sex doesn't make a marriage."

He stared down at her, his breathing harsh. "I want you; you want me. Isn't that enough?"

"Not for me."

He pulled back as if she'd hit him. "I am not good enough for you? Who is waiting for you in London, the king?"

Pain flickered across her face, and she gripped the arms of her chair harder. "That is not what I meant. You are young; you have the whole world to discover. If you want to get out of marrying your Anne, just tell your father the truth. You do not need to pretend to fall in love with me just to give yourself an escape route."

He glared at her over his shoulder. "She is not my Anne."

Her cool logic cut at him, reduced him to a raging impotent child. He moved away to pace the floorboards again. How dare she turn him down?

"We can go to Gretna Green, get married there."

"And how will we support ourselves when your father cuts off your income?"

He swung back to face her, his rage dying as he studied her beautiful face. "I think I could love you, Helene."

She stood up so violently her coffee cup fell to the floor and shattered.

"You have no right to do this to me!"

"What the hell are you talking about?"

She thumped her fist against her breast. "I have plans; I have a new life awaiting me. I cannot deal with this, this . . ."

"Stupidity? Me falling in love with you is stupid?"

"I didn't say that!" She briefly closed her eyes as if she

couldn't bear to look at him. "You can't love me. I won't allow it."

He held her anguished gaze, his smile wretched. "You think I have a choice in the matter?"

"We all have choices. Yours are already clear. Go home to your family, marry the girl you are supposed to, and forget all about me."

His throat ached, and he took an unsteady step toward her. "I can't do that. I want you and only you. I don't care about your background or the fact that you are a widow. I just want to marry you."

She worried her lip so hard she drew blood. "You can't."

"Why not? I know that you care about me." He placed his hand over his heart, mirroring her gesture. "I know it *here.* Tell me what I can do to make things right for us."

She shivered violently and lifted her chin. "I am not what you think."

Philip drew an unsteady breath. "You are the woman I love."

"I am a whore."

He opened his mouth to reply and shook his head as words finally escaped him.

"It's true. I've bedded more men than you could ever imagine. I spent two years in the Bastille servicing the guards and two years as an old man's mistress. I am a whore."

He still couldn't speak; his throat was so constricted. She sat back down, her features composed; only the fine tremor in her folded hands displayed any hint of inner turmoil.

"Are you suggesting that what we shared was a fake, a sham? That I was just another customer to you?"

She inclined her head the merest half inch. Rage bubbled and boiled inside him again, and he picked up his coat and hat.

"Madame, you are good in bed, but not that good. I know when a woman is pretending and you . . . you were not."

She raised her eyebrows, and he caught her chin in his hard fingers. "You didn't have to pretend with me. Say it."

She swallowed hard, her tongue moistening her lips. "Perhaps I am not only a whore but a brilliant actress."

He gazed into her blue eyes as the pain in his heart threatened to fill his whole chest and then crawl up his throat. "You lie. If you choose to pretend we mean nothing to each other, have it your way. But I know the truth. I *know* you."

Her eyelashes fluttered down, concealing her expression. In a savage motion, his fingers curled around her neck. The pulse at the curve of her throat pounded like a trapped animal. With all his control, he let her go and stepped back, dug his hand into the pocket of his greatcoat, and drew out his purse.

"How much?"

"What do you mean?" she whispered.

He jingled his purse. "How much do I owe you for our night together?" She looked away from him. "If you are a professional whore, surely you have a regular charge?"

"*Va chez le diable*, Philip!"

He stuffed his purse back into his pocket with shaking fingers and waited until she looked at him again. The mixture of desolation and anger in her eyes probably reflected his.

"You see, you can't charge me, can you? Because you know we shared more than a business transaction or a slaking of lust. We shared each other's souls." He put on his hat. She flinched away from him as if expecting a blow. Sadness ate at his anger. "It's a shame you are too afraid to trust me. I expect one day you'll realize what you let slip through your fingers, and I hope you'll feel as empty and wretched as I do today. Good day, madame."

She didn't speak, didn't even look at him as he headed for the door, shoving his half-packed bag out with him. He slammed the door shut and leaned against it. His mind refused to function properly as he strained to make sense of the silence behind him. Thoughts tumbled erratically through his mind. He should hire a horse, get to London as quickly as possible, and marry whomsoever his father wanted.

He closed his eyes. What was the point in doing anything else? Helene might think him a romantic fool, but he knew love when he found it. He also suspected he was unlikely to ever meet its like again.

Helene held her breath as the door shut behind Philip and his baggage. In the sudden silence, she stared at the back of the door. Was he still out there? What was he waiting for? For her to beg him to return? She'd hurt his pride, that was all, nothing more. He'd simply been upset when she'd ignored his ridiculous marriage proposal.

A moan escaped her tightly clamped lips. *Mon Dieu*, it hurt to breathe. In her soul, she knew he'd meant every word. Part of her longed to run after him, to fall into his arms and find happiness. But she couldn't risk it, couldn't allow herself to be used and discarded again when he realized his mistake. And his family would make sure he realized what a colossal mistake she was.

She got slowly to her feet and bent over like an elderly woman with the pain of his leaving, with the pain of denying him. Images of his face when she'd told him what she was, the shock he'd tried to hide, his gallant offer to love her anyway. She didn't deserve such love; she was already beyond redemption. Everyone who had truly loved her was dead.

Tears fell down her cheeks as she crawled back into bed and buried her face in the sheets. She could still smell him, his scent as familiar now as her own.

London would have to wait until the next passenger coach came through. She had people who were depending on her to succeed. She needed to mourn again, to rebuild her strength and try, if it was possible, to forget Philip Ross had ever existed.

4

One last time, Helene checked the address on the battered piece of parchment clutched in her gloved hand. Was this imposing house on St. James Square really the residence of Viscount Harcourt-DeVere? It seemed far too large for one family. The last time she'd seen the viscount, he'd been in rags and manacles, trying to avoid a beating from the guards at the Bastille. Accused of spying for the English, escape was his only option, and Helene had been glad to help him.

She swallowed her sudden nausea and mounted the steps, which gave her an elevated view of the square and the deserted garden in the center. The trees in the central area were bereft of leaves and frosted with ice. A large brass knocker shaped like a church bell loomed in her face. It took all her strength to raise it and let it fall. She almost turned and retreated down the steps when the door abruptly opened.

"May I help you, ma'am?"

The man she assumed was the butler was dressed in somber black that contrasted strongly with the whiteness of his wig and his pale thin lips.

Helene lifted her chin. "I wish to speak to the viscount. Is he at home?"

The butler regarded her for a long moment. "Do you have an appointment, ma'am?"

"I do not, but the viscount told me that if I ever visited London, I was to seek him out immediately." She offered him the scrap of parchment. "He gave me his direction and told me to bring him this."

The butler took the parchment, bowed, and opened the door. "Perhaps you might care to wait in the small morning room while I inquire as to the viscount's whereabouts?"

Helene was too grateful he hadn't shut the door in her face to worry about her less-than-enthusiastic reception. She followed the butler through the shadowed marbled hall and into a room facing the front of the house. Heat from a diminutive fireplace embraced her as she entered the oak-paneled room. She took off her gloves and held her hands out to the flames.

A clock ticked loudly on the high mantelpiece, eventually grinding and wheezing to strike a single note to signify the quarter hour. Helene paced the room, her nerves too on edge to allow her to sit.

"Madame?"

She turned to find the butler at the door.

"The viscount will see you now."

"Thank you."

Helene gathered her courage and followed the butler down another long shadowed corridor to an imposing set of double doors. A footman opened the doors to reveal a man sitting at an opulent desk, quill pen raised in his hand as if he was just about to write something. His hair was almost gray, his face aristocratic, and his gaze held a hint of wariness.

"Madame Delornay?" The viscount got to his feet and bowed, his silver-gray eyes fixed on her face. "I apologize if I can't quite place your name. Perhaps you can remind me of where we became acquainted."

Helene dropped him a deep, respectful curtsey. "My lord, you might remember me better as Helene."

He dropped his quill pen, and two patches of color stained his cheeks. He picked up the small piece of parchment from his desk and reread it.

"Good God, Helene from the Bastille? Have you carried this with you for all these years?"

To her surprise, he came around the desk, took her hand, and brought it to his lips.

"The woman who saved my life. How could I ever forget you?"

She attempted a shrug. "Hardly that, my lord. I merely helped you escape from your cell."

He chuckled. "And if you hadn't done that, I wouldn't have gotten very far, would I?"

She met his gaze and smiled into his eyes. "I am simply glad you survived, sir."

His expression softened. "I'm more surprised that you did, my dear. Your appalling existence in the prison was not conducive to survival."

She felt her cheeks heat as she remembered being fondled by one of the prison guards while they chained the viscount to the wall and beat him.

"I managed to find a way out. I'm not proud of how I did it, but in truth, I had no choice."

He used his fingers to raise her chin and look into her eyes. "You are alive, *ma petite*. You should never regret that."

He placed her hand on his arm and led her over to the fire, where two large wing chairs faced a comforting blaze. He helped her into a seat and went back to the door to speak to the footman stationed just outside.

"Please make yourself comfortable, Helene. You seem fatigued. I've ordered some tea for us while I hear the rest of your story."

Helene gripped her hands together in her lap to stop them from shaking. The viscount seemed to be an honorable man. But how much of her story would she need to reveal to gain his support? In the heat of his escape, he'd promised her anything her heart could desire. She fought a bitter smile. But so had Philip, and that had scarcely ended well.

The viscount returned and settled himself in the chair opposite her. His gaze swept over her dark gown and the black silk ribbons of her bonnet.

"It is only three years since I last saw you. Have you married, then, my dear, or God forbid, are you widowed?"

"Neither, sir. I decided it would be safer to travel to England dressed in mourning garb than as a single woman."

Not that her disguise had done her much good. It certainly hadn't deterred Philip Ross or saved her heart from being broken.

She took a deep steadying breath. "I was hoping you might help me start afresh here in England. I have no desire to continue the life I've been forced to live."

The viscount reached across and patted her knee. "I can assure you that will not happen. Over the past few years, I have met several gentlemen who benefited from your help in the Bastille. I am sure they will be as interested to hear that you have survived as I am."

Helene managed a smile. "As I said, sir, I was only a small part of the undertaking. Your thanks really belong to the others who risked their lives to get you to the coast."

The viscount leaned forward, his expression gentle. "They were adults who knew the risk of their involvement. You were only a child."

"Not really, sir. I stopped being a child when I was separated from my family."

"Excuse me for asking this, but are they all now deceased?"

Helene swallowed hard. "Yes. I watched them being taken away one by one to their deaths." She shrugged. "My father thought to save me from such a fate. Sometimes I wished he'd allowed me to die with them, rather than trading me to the guards to be used as they wished."

The viscount made a stifled sound, shot to his feet, and started to pace the room. Helene tensed as he swung around to face her, his piercing silver eyes fixed on her face.

"I apologize, *ma petite*. The thought of you enduring such an existence and yet risking so much for complete strangers makes me want to find the Bastille guards and choke them with my bare hands."

"But I wanted to die, monseigneur. It seemed a perfect way to accomplish my goal."

"Yet you survived and here you are."

"Yes, here I am."

He nodded slowly. There was a tap on the door, and a footman entered bearing a large silver tray. A maid followed with another tray filled with afternoon delicacies. Helene's stomach grumbled, and she felt herself blushing.

"I hope you are hungry, my dear. My cook will be very disappointed if you don't at least sample her cakes and pastries."

He poured her some tea and handed her a plate filled with food. Helene regarded the spread dubiously. Since Philip's abrupt departure, she'd experienced great difficulty keeping food down at all. With a murmur of thanks, she rested the plate on her lap and sipped at her tea, allowing the warmth of the brew to settle in her stomach.

The viscount sat down and helped himself to a selection of pastries before turning his attention back to Helene.

"Will you tell me how you escaped the Bastille?"

The directness of his manner reminded Helene of Philip. Were all English aristocrats so used to being obeyed that they assumed all their questions should be promptly and honestly answered?

"As I said, sir, I'm not proud of what I did, but at the time, I could see no other course of action open to me."

His smile was full of stark memories. "Do you think I will condemn you? I experienced the horrors of your existence for only a few days. In your place, I believe I would've done anything to escape."

Helene was emboldened by the unexpected flow of sympathy. "Shortly after you left, I realized I was pregnant, and I was, quite frankly, terrified."

"Hardly surprising when you are fifteen and alone, my dear." He paused to pour himself more tea. "Did you have any idea who the child's father was?"

She bit down on her lip. "I had no idea. I . . . had no choice as to who bedded me, or how many . . ." Her hand shook so badly that tea spilled over the side of her cup, scalding her fingers. The viscount leaned across, took the cup away from her, and set it on the side table.

"I'm sorry to bring back such unpleasant memories for you. If this is too difficult, we can leave it in the past."

"No, sir." She raised her gaze to meet his. "I would like to share my story with someone who might understand, someone who will not judge me."

He handed her his handkerchief and sat back. "Then please continue."

"I also realized if the guards found out I was pregnant, my child was unlikely to survive." Helene took a deep breath. "So I decided to find a man who could get me out of the prison for good."

"A wise decision. I only wish I'd been there to help you."

"Thank you, sir, but *I* am glad you had escaped."

His slight smile made her feel a little better.

"One of the new regime's elderly lawyers was quite taken

with me, so I flirted with him and persuaded him to buy me from the guards."

"And you were successful."

"I was. I also convinced him to bed me, and I pretended the child was his."

The viscount's smile held no hint of condemnation, only wry approval. "I can only applaud your ingenuity. He would not marry you, though?"

"Unfortunately, he had a wife, but he was rich enough to set me up in my own apartment and to arrange care for me throughout my pregnancy."

"A good choice, then."

"Yes, apart from the fact that he wouldn't let me keep the baby."

The viscount stilled. "What became of the child?"

"My daughter was sent to a local nunnery that cared for orphaned and abandoned children. My lover agreed to pay for the child's upkeep until she reached a marriageable or employable age."

The viscount sighed. "I suppose, in the circumstances, that was the best you could hope for."

Helene tried to smile. "Even though I do not know who her father was, Marguerite is still my child. I was not allowed to see her after she was taken from me. I write to the nunnery once a month to inquire as to her health, and they are kind enough to write back with the barest of information. As far as I know, she is thriving."

She risked a direct glance at the viscount. "I had hoped to have her with me in England, but now I am not so sure."

He frowned and put his cup and empty plate back on the tray. "Why ever not? I'm sure we can arrange something." He gestured at her untouched plate. "Now, please eat. You are far too pale."

Helene looked down at the delicacies heaped on her plate and tried to swallow.

"My apologies, monsieur, but I feel a little nauseated."

She clamped a hand over her mouth as her vision dimmed and a roaring sound thundered through her head. The last thing she remembered was the viscount's concerned face as she slid bonelessly to the floor.

Helene came to in a pretty feminine parlor decorated in soft yellows and greens. Over her head, a woman gave orders to an indistinct number of people who seemed to mill around the room. She thought she heard the viscount's deep voice and strained to see his face. A soft hand on her brow stopped her from moving too far. Her feet were raised on a cushion at the other end of the cozy chaise lounge, and a lavender-scented shawl was tucked around her.

"Are you feeling better now, madame?"

Helene opened her eyes fully and gazed into the face of an exceptionally beautiful woman she assumed must be the viscount's wife. She struggled to sit up.

"I feel much better now. I apologize for behaving so inappropriately."

The viscountess smiled. "I hardly think you passed out deliberately, madame. I'm only glad my husband had the presence of mind to bring you to me."

Helene glanced around and saw the viscount in the doorway. He bowed and ventured closer.

"I apologize for not realizing how exhausted you were. Forcing you to retell such a harrowing story so soon after your arrival was not well done of me."

"I am absolutely fine, sir, and perhaps I should be leaving before I cause you any further embarrassment." She couldn't believe the viscount had taken her to his wife. She was hardly the sort of company a noble lady of the *ton* would expect to entertain in her private parlor.

The viscountess frowned and stood up, smoothing the creases from her silk dress. "Surely Madame Delornay is staying with us, my dear? It's the least we can do for her, seeing as how she saved your life."

"Of course she is. I could not permit anything else." He bowed again to Helene. "Please, madame, be our honored guest, at least for the night. I intend to gather a few of your friends here tomorrow to discuss your plans for the future."

Helene was too tired to argue. In her haste to get to the viscount, she had made no arrangements to stay in London and carried all her possessions in her large carpetbag. Uncertainly, she turned back to the viscountess and found her smiling and nodding.

"I would be delighted if you would stay. My sons are away at school at the moment, so I would appreciate some company."

Helene found herself smiling weakly in return.

"Thank you. That would be wonderful."

5

When Helene awoke the next morning, it was with a sense of unreality. She slipped out of the massive bed and went to the window to peer through the curtains. The bright and sunny bedroom she'd been placed in was on the same floor as the viscountess's suite and faced the private garden and the mews at the back of the house.

The tranquility of the setting reminded her of the house where she had grown up in the countryside near Versailles. She'd almost forgotten how it felt to live in luxury, to wake without fear, with the sense that nothing could go wrong in her world as long as her parents loved her.

A knock on the door had her scrambling back under the covers. The door opened to admit a maid dressed in a blue and white checked uniform, a tray balanced in her hands.

"Good morning, madame. I'm Betty."

"Good morning." Cautiously, Helene returned the maid's cheerful smile.

"I've brought you some hot chocolate and warm water to wash in." She placed the tray on a table by the side of the enormous bed and whipped off the cover. "His lordship asks if you could meet him after breakfast in his study but that you should take your time."

Helene gazed at the maid as she whisked about the room, opening the curtains and pouring water into a porcelain bowl decorated with roses to match the water jug. The girl's expression was so open and cheerful that she made Helene feel old, and yet they were probably a similar age.

"Would you like a bath, madame?"

"That would be nice."

Helene watched curiously as she opened another door and disappeared inside. After a short while, the scent of roses and a few wisps of steam filtered through to the bedroom.

Betty popped her head around the door. "Won't be long, madame. I'd already arranged for the water to be heated."

"Thank you," Helene called as she reached for her hot chocolate and carefully took a sip. Her stomach did a slow revolution, and she hastily set the mug down again.

"Her ladyship thought you might like to borrow some of her clothes, seeing as your luggage has been delayed. I'll set them out on the bed while you bathe, madame."

What luggage? Helene appreciated the viscountess's inventiveness and got out of bed. She clutched on to the pink silk bed hangings as a wave of nausea rolled over her.

"Are you all right, madame?"

Helene opened her eyes to see the maid staring anxiously at her. For a second, she struggled to remember the words she needed in English.

"I'm fine. Thank you for your help. I'll have my bath now."

The breakfast parlor was deserted, so Helene was able to eat the dry toast and sweetened tea her stomach demanded without anyone commenting. After the third cup, she felt better and began to appreciate the intimacy of the small paneled room.

Family portraits and landscape paintings adorned the walls, including one of identical twin boys whom she guessed must be the viscount's absent sons.

A stack of neatly folded newspapers sat in the corner of the sideboard beside the toast rack. Helene's fingers itched to read one. Many men, including her previous protector, considered reading about the current bloody political climate too injurious for women's fragile minds. Helene had always hated that attitude and had read everything she could get hold of. After a quick glance around the room, she picked up the *London Times* and settled down to read.

The clock on the mantelpiece chimed the half hour, and she looked up. Most of the dishes on the sideboard had been taken away, and she hadn't even noticed. As she carefully folded the paper back into its original shape on her lap, an all-too-familiar name leapt out at her. She started to read the narrow column in the society announcements section. When she finished reading, the paper slipped through her suddenly nerveless fingers.

So Philip Ross had married his father's choice of wife after all. . . . Had her cruel rejection pushed him into such a momentous decision? Or had he simply regretted his moment of folly with her the second he was reunited with his family? No doubt, secure within his family's approval, he was on his knees thanking God for his lucky escape.

Her last hope, her last romantic fantasy, withered and died and was replaced by smoldering anger. Despite sending Philip away, she still felt betrayed. She'd denied her feelings for him and let him go for all the right reasons. Had Philip justified his hasty change of heart by reminding himself that she had told him to go? Had it made him feel better about his abrupt marriage?

Unsteadily, she wiped a single tear from her cheek. There was no room for sentiment now. She had to be brave and put her foolish notions of being rescued behind her. Philip had only behaved like most of the men in her life: taken what was offered and moved on. Why shouldn't she do the same?

Helene picked up the paper, folded it carefully, and got to her feet, hands clenched at her sides. Whatever the viscount offered to do for her, it was imperative she was her own mistress. But what skills did she have to make her way in the world? She'd managed to stay alive through the hell of the Bastille; she'd learned how to flatter men and make them happy in bed.

Perhaps those much maligned skills would save her now. It was time she turned the tables and used her abilities for herself. The faint glimmering of an outrageous idea flowed through her mind as she made her way to the viscount's study. Perhaps she did have something to thank Philip for after all. It was definitely time to discuss her future with Viscount Harcourt-DeVere and ascertain exactly how grateful he intended to be.

To her surprise, there were several men gathered in the viscount's study, and they all stood up and smiled at her. The viscount came around his desk and led her to a chair in the center of the room.

"My dear, I'm not sure if you remember these gentlemen, but please allow me to introduce them all to you."

Helene focused on the youngest of the men and nodded. "I recognize the Duke of Diable Delamere. How are you, my lord?"

The duke inclined his head; his handsome face still bore the marks of his suffering. "I am well, madame."

"And your daughter?"

"She is well too." His smile was crooked. "She misses her brother but . . ."

Helene held his gaze. "I apologize, sir. I wish we had been able to save your son as well."

He straightened and bowed. "Madame, there is no need to apologize. You risked more than most people would ever do to warn me about my wife's devious plans." He closed the gap between them and kissed her hand. "I owe you my life and my sanity."

"*Merci,* monseigneur." Helene's eyes filled with tears. "I only wish I had been able to do more."

He released her hand and stepped back into the shadows, clearly unwilling to display any emotion in such a public place.

The elderly man standing next to him cleared his throat. "Madame Delornay, we haven't actually met before. I'm Lord Derek Knowles. You saved my wife, Angelique. Do you remember her?"

Helene was almost relieved to turn away from the duke and allow him some privacy.

"I do indeed, sir." Angelique had almost died of a fever during her time in the Bastille. Helene was delighted to hear she had prospered. "Is she well?"

Lord Derek's face brightened. "She is." He fumbled inside his coat and handed Helene his large gold watch. "I had a portrait of her commissioned just this year."

Helene opened the delicate gold clasp and studied the miniature portrait of the woman on the inside of the case. Angelique wore a red gown, her prematurely white hair arranged in formal braids tight to her head. Her smile was breathtaking. The artist had caught her uncrushable spirit, the strength of which helped her survive the Bastille and the horror of imminent death.

Helene handed the gold watch back. "Thank you for showing me this. Your wife looks to be in far better health than I remember her."

"Indeed. She was but skin and bone when she returned." Lord Derek smiled benevolently. "When you are settled in, my dear, I'm sure she'll insist on visiting you herself. She has never forgotten you, and I know she will rejoice at your escape."

Helene glanced at the third man, who was leaning against the desk, his arms folded as he watched her. Something about his long lean frame seemed familiar, but she couldn't remember exactly when they'd met.

He bowed. "Madame? I'm Lord George Grant."

She smiled at him. "I hardly recognized you without the beard and long hair."

Amusement animated his smile and twinkled in his brown eyes. "The life of a spy is never easy, madame, especially a captured spy. I was not at my best when we first met."

"Neither was I, sir."

He held her gaze, his brown eyes steady. "But we both survived to see another, prettier day, didn't we?"

The viscount chuckled. "You're scarcely pretty, George, and Madame Delornay was always beautiful to me."

"She was an angel."

Helene found she couldn't look away from Lord Grant's eyes. He understood her; they all did. They knew what she had been, and yet they still saw the best in her. Tears pricked at her throat.

"You are all too kind, gentlemen. I only did what was necessary."

"You did far more than that." The viscount looked around the room. "And now it is our turn to make sure you will never want for anything else in your life." He sat forward. "We have agreed to buy you a house in whatever part of the country you prefer and give you a yearly stipend that will be increased when necessary."

Helene took a deep breath and allowed the silence to settle around her. Did she have the nerve to propose her pathetic plan to the powerful men surrounding her? What if they thought she had run mad and refused to help her at all? Was it truly worth the risk?

"It is more than I expected, gentlemen, much more. I assumed you might help me find some employment, not offer me such a secure future."

The viscount raised his eyebrows. "You are too modest, my dear. You saved our lives and the lives of those we love. How could we offer you anything less? You will have enough money to live comfortably for the rest of your life."

Helene contemplated her hands, which were twisted together in her lap. Could she ever settle down in this foreign country and pretend to be what she was not? Would any amount of money be large enough to make her forget the abuse of her body and the destruction of her innocence?

She thought of Philip Ross, his hands on her skin, showing her that lovemaking didn't have to be a chore or something to be endured. He'd also taught her that there was power in the sexual act for a woman. Her shocking idea stirred to life again in her brain. Could she use that knowledge to change her life around? Did she have the determination to take her past and finally make sense of it?

"Madame? Are you feeling well?"

She looked up at the viscount and saw the concern in his eyes. "I am fine, sir. I was just contemplating my future and how I should respond to your generous offer."

"You are not thinking of turning us down, are you?"

"Oh no, sir." She gathered her courage. "I was just thinking that it might be more interesting if we went into business together instead."

"Business? What kind of business?" Lord George Grant said.

Helene hesitated again, and the viscount smiled at her. "My dear, whatever it is, please tell us. We are hardly likely to object or be shocked by any suggestions you might have."

"I'm not quite sure of the details yet, my lord." Helene closed her eyes. Perhaps it would be better to just blurt it out. "I think it will involve the erotic carnal arts."

The viscount raised his eyebrows. "The erotic carnal arts?"

"Yes, sir. I recently met a man who reminded me that the English are not known for their skills in pleasuring their partners."

"That is true, madame, but I fail to see how—"

"I would like to offer discerning patrons a place to learn these arts, improve their lovemaking abilities, and explore new sexual possibilities." Helene smiled cautiously at them all. "I would like to own a pleasure house like that."

The viscount frowned. "My dear, as we said, there is no need for you to—excuse my directness—go whoring again."

"I would not be whoring, sir. I would be offering a very expensive and discreet service to a limited amount of customers."

"An exclusive brothel, then, but I still don't see—"

Helen kept talking as the idea took further shape in her mind. "No, sir, more of a private club, like a gentleman's club, where each member has to be approved and pay a yearly fee."

"But why would anyone want to do that when they can go to a thousand bawdy houses and pay almost nothing?"

"Because we will be offering something unique. We will offer our members the opportunity to take part in any sexual fantasy they can imagine or watch others exploring their own fantasies."

"Oh, I say." Lord Derek Knowles cleared his throat. "Are you quite sure you wouldn't prefer a nice little cottage in the countryside?"

"I think we should allow Madame Delornay to do anything she damned well likes." The Duke of Diable Delamere suddenly straightened and scowled at the other men in the room. "If this is the life she chooses, I will support her decision. At least she will be in control of her own destiny."

"Thank you, monseigneur." Helene inclined her head to the duke.

"A pleasure, madame, and might I say that your premise intrigues me on a personal level as well?" There was a wicked glint in the duke's pale silver eyes. "I think I might well become your first . . . member."

"After me, Delamere." The viscount rose to his feet. "There are a lot of details to be worked out, but I have no issue with Madame Delornay doing exactly as she pleases." He glanced at the other two men, who both nodded in agreement.

"I suggest we set up a partnership, giving Madame Delornay forty percent of the business, the rest shared between the four of us." He smiled at Helene. "And as this young lady is obviously as tenacious as she is beautiful, we will also offer her the opportunity to buy back our shares in the enterprise when it becomes successful. Are we all agreed?"

A chorus of agreement greeted his question, and Helene briefly closed her eyes as a wave of thankfulness enveloped her. She didn't believe in God any longer—how could she after all the destruction she had witnessed? But she did believe in fate and the strength of her own will.

If she could be successful at this, she would never want for anything again. Strange that it was Philip Ross's erotic lovemaking that had given her the ghost of an idea. At the thought of Philip, she remembered her more pressing problem.

"I appreciate your faith in me, gentlemen, and I promise I will not let you down." She took a deep breath. "But there is one issue that means I will have to put our plans on hold for about a year." She sighed. "It also means I won't be able to have my daughter back to live with me yet."

The viscount's smile dimmed. "Madame?"

Helene stood up and faced them. "I'm pregnant."

6

December 1819
Eighteen years later . . .

Helene slipped out of bed, careful not to disturb the young man who lay sprawled across the silken sheets. Lord Thomas Roebuck had been too drunk to perform last night. In truth, he had *come*, but not in the appropriate place and not by offering Helene the slightest hint of pleasure. She sighed as she surveyed his luscious naked buttocks. So much promise and yet such a disappointment.

No doubt he'd forget his failure and boast of his conquest until either his friends tired of hearing him or he found another woman willing to put up with his inadequacies. She was tired of tutoring young men in the erotic arts and had begun to appreciate having her bed to herself.

She made her way into her dressing room and contemplated the gray leaden skies outside her window. Winter was closing in. It was her least favorite time of the year. The exposing of the bare bones of the trees and the unforgiving hardness of the earth made her think of death and the past. With a shake of her head, she dressed in a light corset and an old gown she could lace up herself. Sitting at her dressing table, she ignored her pale reflection in the mirror and quickly put up her hair.

The large clock in the main hallway struck six, echoing around the empty space as she walked down the back stairs to the basement. In the kitchen, Madame Dubois was already awake and working hard. Two scullery maids were busy preparing the fruit and vegetables bought fresh from the market that morning. The aroma of fresh coffee and croissants wafted across the kitchen to tantalize Helene's senses.

"*Bonjour*, Madame Dubois."

"*Bonjour*, madame. *Comment-allez-vous?*"

"*Je suis bien*, madame, *et vous?*"

"*Bien aussi*."

Madame Dubois flicked a cloth over the scrupulously clean pine table and motioned Helene to sit. Within seconds, Helene's mouth was full of warm chocolate and the buttery layers of flaked croissant. She sighed and sipped at her coffee. Madame Dubois made the best croissants in London and made sure Helene had one for breakfast every day. Over the years, Helene had employed a lot of French émigrés who had fled the successive regimes on the other side of the channel. Madame Dubois had been with her for the longest time, and Helene hoped she would never leave.

Rising from the bench seat, Helene murmured her thanks, put her mug and plate in the sink, and took her apron off its hook. She doubted any of her aristocratic clients would recognize her in this dull garb. Each morning she liked to take stock of her business from top to bottom. If some of her employees thought her a little eccentric, none of them dared say it to her face. In her mind, she was responsible for every little detail, and success was in the details. She had learned that lesson well over the past eighteen years.

She took a deep breath and climbed four flights of back

stairs to the very top of the house, under the attics, where the smaller, more private rooms were situated. Here, where the ceilings were lower and the hallways narrow, the scent of sex and cigar smoke hung heavily in the air. Helene checked four of the small intimate bedrooms and then headed for the more public area.

For once there was no one lying asleep on the floor, or worse still, chained to the wall. Helene frowned. It also appeared that all the equipment had been put back in its proper place. Whips, gags, chains, masks, and leather straps all hung in their allotted spaces on the black-painted walls.

Helene picked up her skirt to avoid a dark stain on the floor. There were patches of blood and other bodily fluids on the plain wooden boards, but that was to be expected. Clients who liked to hurt each other, or to be hurt themselves, would be disappointed in their evening's play if a little blood wasn't spilled. The servants who cleaned the upper floor were paid higher wages to ensure their complete discretion as to what and whom they saw in these rooms. No future Prime Minister or Lord of the Admiralty would want it known that he liked to be dominated by a woman, tied up, or fucked by a man.

Helene stepped into the second room and found one of the manservants already cleaning up.

"Good morning, Michael."

"Good morning, madame." He bowed, his face pink. She noted his shirt wasn't tucked in and that his uniform was rumpled.

"I thought I'd make a start on the rooms, madame, seeing as how I was here quite late myself last night and all that."

Helene studied his expression. "Did you enjoy yourself?"

He met her gaze without shame. "Yes, madame, I did."

"Then all is well. Thank you for your efforts, but don't forget to go and get something to eat and rest before your next shift."

He grinned at her and picked up a bloodied flogger someone had left underneath a chair. "I will. And, madame? Thank you for giving me the opportunity to work on this floor. I feel quite at home here already."

Helene inclined her head. "I'm pleased to hear that, Michael, but remember, even though you are a servant here, no one can force you to do anything you don't want to do."

"Yes, madame."

Michael licked his slightly roughened lips and glanced down at the flogger. He stroked the leather tails and shivered, a dreamy smile on his face. Helene left him to his task. She had a talent for spotting the particular sexual interests of both her paying clients and her staff and had sensed Michael's curiosity about the more extreme sexual acts early on in his employment.

She retraced her path and went down a flight of stairs, checking the dust on the spindles as she descended. Michael was happy and so were most of her clients. In her establishment, they had complete privacy to indulge themselves as they wished with other consenting adults. She never recruited prostitutes of either sex from the streets, and nothing as vulgar as money ever changed hands between her customers and staff. Everyone who worked for her came with a personal recommendation, and every client was obliged to maintain the standards of the house or their membership was revoked.

She paused to survey the largest salon on the third floor. Most of the rooms leading from this hallway were for private fantasies or more intimate lovemaking. They were distinct from the more public rooms below, where almost anything could happen and usually did. Those rooms were for the voyeurs and exhibitionists. The ones of this floor were for the connoisseurs of sexual passion and erotic desire. Helene tweaked a damask curtain into place and retied the sash. Not that she was judging any of the preferences expressed by her clients. It was not her place to form an opinion; she simply provided the most erotic and exotic sexual experiences the very rich could ever desire.

Helene sighed as she walked through the rooms, righting a chair, moving a floral arrangement to a different table, retrieving a lost silk shawl and mask. When had her joy in her accomplishments turned into dreariness? She had achieved her aim. She partly owned and managed the most discreet and successful pleasure house in the city of London. Her waiting list was three years long, and membership was more difficult to obtain than vouchers for Almack's or admission to White's.

She paused in the hallway and listened to the silence around her. The house was deliberately designed to conceal noise and create a sense of intimacy for her patrons. This morning it felt too quiet and too empty. Helene gripped one of the door frames until her fingers whitened. What was wrong with her? She sounded as jaded and out of sorts as her old friend Peter Howard.

Was he right? Did every man and woman come to realize that all the sexual opportunity and pleasure in the world didn't make up for that loneliness, that empty bed, that lack of companionship? He'd certainly reduced his visits to her establishment since he'd found love.

"For goodness sake, Helene!"

In an effort to rally herself, she said the words out loud. They sank quickly into the deadening silence of the walls and thick pink carpet.

"I am not alone. And I can have any man in London with a snap of my fingers!" Helene demonstrated the snap and walked through to the main landing. "I refuse to turn into the kind of woman who walks around hallways talking to herself."

"But you are talking to yourself."

Helene gasped and peered down into the gloom of the open stairwell. Lord George Grant grinned up at her from the circular entry hall two stories below. His black hair was windblown, his cheeks red with cold, and his brown eyes sparked mischief. At forty-five, he was still a very attractive man. Helene leaned over the banister, hand to her heart.

"You wretch, you startled me. I didn't realize anyone was there!" She started down the stairs, hands held out to him. "I didn't even know you were back in London! How are you, *mon ami*?"

Lord George took both her hands in his and kissed them.

"I'm well, thank you, busy with all this diplomatic nonsense with France but glad to be home for a few weeks."

She linked her arm through his and drew him toward the back of the house. "Come and talk to me while I answer my correspondence—that is, if you have the time." She hesitated. "Have you been home to your family yet?"

"To my loving wife, you mean?" He shrugged. "As far as I know, Julia's still busy fucking Lord Lambdon. I doubt she'd be pleased to see me at six-thirty in the morning."

Helene patted his hand. "I'm sure your daughter would appreciate your company, though."

Lord George threw himself into a chair and looked up at her. "Dammit, Helene, you're not my conscience. Of course I'll go and see Amanda. She's the only reason I stay married." He glanced at her under his long eyelashes. "Of course, if you wanted to marry me, I'd be out of this chair and pounding on the door of my solicitor's office in a second."

"I don't intend to marry anyone."

He sighed. "I know, but it doesn't stop me hoping."

Helene tried not to smile as she rang for some refreshments, then sat at her neat desk. Her leather journal lay on the blotter. She opened it at the correct date and read through the already lengthy list of tasks she needed to accomplish before the day ended. A notation on the following page caught her eye. Tomorrow was the twins' eighteenth birthday. She had sent them a substantial sum of money and her usual letter full of lies.

With a sigh, she shut the book and returned her attention to Lord George. Of all the original founders, George was the one who had the most to do with the day-to-day running of the business. He dealt with the bank and relayed Helene's monthly reports to the other partners, who no longer wished to attend the meetings. He was one of the few men in London she hadn't slept with and actually trusted. Since Philip Ross, she'd learned never to bed men she genuinely liked. Friendship was far too precious to mix with the uncertainties of sex.

A knock on the door brought not only their tea but also the morning post. Helene smiled as Oliver, her newest footman, managed not to spill the tea or drop the letters. He'd been with them for only a few weeks, but he was already starting to put on weight and regain his confidence. One of the other servants had found him starving and beaten in the street after being thrown out by a brothel catering to men and had brought him to Helene.

George accepted a cup of tea and sipped at it, his expression thoughtful. Helene sorted through her mail, pausing when something caught her interest.

"There is a letter from Sudbury Court. Isn't that Lord Derek's country house?"

"Aye, it is." George sat up. "I wonder what the old goat wants."

Helene frowned at him, broke the black wax seal, and scanned the single sheet. Her hand flew to her cheek.

"*Mon Dieu*, this is horrible."

"What?"

"It is from Lord Derek's solicitor." Helene stared at George. "They are both dead from the smallpox. Lord Derek died quickly. Angelique seemed to have recovered but succumbed to an infection of the lungs." She managed to pass him the letter. "Here, read it for yourself."

Lord Derek had always been a staunch supporter of hers. His wife had been Helene's friend. Images of the vibrant woman she had helped rescue from the Bastille crowded her mind. Despite the harsh rules of society, Angelique had insisted on claiming Helene as her friend. They'd spent many hours together speaking their native tongue, sharing secrets and happier memories. Most women tended not to like Helene.

"It seems the whole house caught the smallpox from the new kitchen maid." Lord George gave a disgusted sigh. "You would've thought they would have tried out Jenner's vaccine."

Helene dabbed at the tears on her cheeks. "Lord Derek was always a little skeptical of science, wasn't he? He preferred to place his trust in God." She swallowed hard. "At least they are together. At least neither of them is left to mourn alone."

George studied the letter. "It seems they were buried in some haste as well."

"Not that I would have been welcome at the funeral anyway." Helene tried to smile. "But I would've liked to have paid my respects. Perhaps we can go and visit their graves. I would love to say good-bye properly."

He met her gaze, his expression serious. "Of course we will go. I'd be delighted to escort you." He frowned. "I wonder who will inherit his property and his title. They had no children, and he is the heir presumptive of his uncle, the Earl of Swansford."

"Trust you to be thinking such mercenary thoughts on such a dreadful day."

"I'm not being mercenary, Helene." He tossed her the letter. "Unless Lord Derek bequeathed the shares back to you in his will, whoever inherits the estate inherits fifteen percent of your business."

Helene put the letter back on the desk and smoothed it with her fingers. "I hadn't thought about that. I've been meaning to ask Lord Derek to sell me back his stake for years, but he always seemed so thrilled to be involved in something so scandalous."

George finished his tea and set the cup down. "I wouldn't fret about it. You still own seventy percent of the business, so whatever happens, you have a controlling interest."

Helene fixed him with a sharp stare. "I would own even more if you allowed me to buy back your share as the Duke of Diable Delamere and Viscount Harcourt-DeVere have done."

His face darkened. "They don't need the income this place generates. I do. Former gentleman spies and diplomats aren't paid very well, you know."

"I know and I apologize." She sighed. "I suppose I'll just have to contact the solicitors and discreetly try and buy the shares back through them."

George got to his feet and stretched. "That might take a while, my dear. An estate that complex won't be sorted out overnight."

"I realize that, but it will probably be easier to deal with a lawyer than with the new heir."

George chuckled. "It will surely be one of the more unusual inheritances a man might receive. A title *and* part ownership in a brothel."

"It's not a brothel, George."

He winked at her as he headed for the door. "I know. And now I am off to take breakfast with my daughter and steal her away from her lessons for a few hours before I fall into my lonely bed."

Helene nodded. "If there is a memorial service to be held in London for Angelique and Lord Derek, will you escort me there?"

He bowed. "If my wife doesn't expect my escort, and somehow I doubt that she will, I'm at your service."

Helene waited until the door swung shut behind him before resting her now-aching head on her hand. Sometimes George still surprised her. His lack of distress over a man and his wife he had known for almost twenty years seemed cold. In the last few months, since his wife had taken a lover, he'd seemed to grow even more distant and cutting. It was as if by shutting off his emotions for his wife, he had shut down everything soft inside him as well.

Helene took a moment to copy the address of the Knowles's solicitor and set the letter to one side. She continued to sort the mail, removing the latest Ackermann's journal to read later. Under a flyer about a miracle cure for baldness, she discovered a slim letter in a familiar hand. The signature scrawled across the corner of the letter was too hard to read, and the red seal was unfamiliar too.

She unfolded the single sheet and peered at the closely written script.

"Dear Maman, I am writing to inform you that I am married. Please do not interfere. Your daughter, Marguerite, Lady Justin Lockwood."

Helene stared at the note until the words blurred in front of her eyes. *What in God's name had Marguerite done?* She was only a child. Helene crumpled the letter in her fist. No, not a child anymore. She was twenty-one. Old enough to elope. Old enough to deceive her mother and evade the nuns who were supposed to care for her. It was Helene's fault. She should have insisted Marguerite come to live in England as soon as she had completed her education, not allowed her to stay on and teach.

Helene stood up and began to pace the small space, her hands clasped to her breast. She would have to leave for France immediately, find out where her eldest daughter had gone, and have the marriage annulled. She stopped walking. The name of the man Marguerite had married sounded both English and vaguely familiar. She snatched up the crumpled parchment and reread it.

Lord Justin Lockwood. An image of a dark-haired pretty-faced man formed in her head. Had he ever visited the pleasure house? Helene went into the back room of her office where she kept her records and hauled out some of the large leather client books until she found the one labeled *L–M*.

Wiping dust from the surface, she lugged the huge volume onto her desk and started her search.

"Ah, yes, here he is."

Her finger alighted on his name. Not a paid-up member, but he had been admitted as a guest on several occasions by Sir Harry Jones. It was unfortunate that he was only a guest. If he had been a member, she would have far more intimate information about him and his sexual preferences. Helene tried to picture his friend, Sir Harry, whom knew she had served in the military during the Napoleonic campaigns in Spain.

A sudden sharp image of the two men sitting close together in one of the salons came to Helene, and she slammed the book shut. She had to get to Marguerite. Lord Justin Lockwood was not the sort of man who should ever marry. He seemed far too interested in his best friend. A sudden commotion outside her door made her look up. Judd, her butler, flung open the door.

"I apologize, madame, but these two persons insisted on seeing you."

With a sense of shock, Helene stared into the determined faces of the young man and woman who had pushed their way past her butler. How on earth had they found her? The young man smiled without humor and sketched a bow.

"Bonjour. Aren't you going to wish us a happy birthday, *Maman*?"

7

"It isn't your birthday until tomorrow."

Helene's reply was automatic. She took a deep steadying breath. "Christian, Lisette, what are you doing here? You are supposed to be at school."

She leaned back and gripped the edge of the desk, desperate to feel something solid behind her. Something to hold her up after the series of shocks she had suffered that morning.

Christian shared a quick conspiratorial glance with his sister. "We decided we didn't need to go to school anymore. We used the money you sent us for our birthday to come and visit you instead."

Christian smiled again, but his smile was not meant to reassure. He took his sister's hand and guided her into one of the chairs facing the desk. Helene fought to recover her customary composure. If Christian meant to shock her into agreeing to anything he suggested by turning up so unexpectedly, he would have a battle on his hands.

"I repeat, what are you doing here?"

"Don't you know, *Maman*?"

"If I did, why would I be asking you?"

Christian nodded, his hazel eyes narrowed as he studied her. "Setting aside the fact that you have lied to us for years about your occupation and refused to let us visit you in England—"

Helene lifted her chin. "I am not accountable to you for my actions. I did what was best for us all."

"Best for you, you mean."

Helene released her grip on the desk and sat down behind it, needing a barrier between her children and herself. It was easy for Christian to stand there and condemn her, so easy for him to judge her and find her wanting. God, she did that to herself every day anyway; she hardly needed his help. Surreptitiously, greedily, she studied her son. The length of his legs and his height came from his father. His features and hair color from her.

"I refuse to argue with you about any of this until you tell me exactly why you decided to cross the channel and find me."

Christian sat down next to Lisette and took her gloved hand. Lisette was almost as tall as her twin, her hair a shade darker, her eyes a light golden hazel that reminded Helene of Philip.

"It's about Marguerite."

"I received this from her today." Helene found the letter she'd just read and showed it to the twins. "Apparently she has married. Did you know of this?"

"Of course we did. She left a letter for the nuns, and they came to tell us." Lisette leaned forward, her gaze as condemning as her brother's. "We guessed she had eloped, but we wondered if it was some scheme of yours."

"And that is why you are here? To accuse me of yet another crime?" Helene rubbed her forehead, where a headache threatened. "I find your ability to believe the worst of me quite depressing."

"The man Marguerite married is an English lord. We thought you might have sent him to Paris to meet her." Christian's gaze wandered around the room, his curiosity almost palpable. "Since she completed her education and flirted with the idea of taking vows, she's been helping the nuns teach the rest of us."

"I know that. It's the only reason I allowed her to stay at the school and not come to England as I wanted."

"You wanted Marguerite and not us?"

Helene sighed. "Marguerite is older than you. I wanted you two to complete your education before I made any decisions about your future."

Christian continued to talk as if Helene hadn't spoken. "Lisette and I noticed a change in her a few weeks ago. She was very distracted but not as if she were frightened, more that she was in her own little world. Then she stopped turning up for the lessons at all."

"Did she tell you she was leaving?"

Lisette shrugged. "The last time I saw her, she told me not to worry and that she was going to be very happy. The next day she was gone."

Helene smoothed the leather cover of the massive book in front of her. "I certainly didn't send Justin Lockwood to France. I was just checking my records to see if he was a client here, and I found his name as a guest. But he doesn't know of my connection to Marguerite. And why on earth would I want to encourage my own daughter to elope?"

"To relieve you of one of your burdens?" Christian said.

Helene bit down on her lip to prevent a hasty retort. The twins had a right to their grievances. She had allowed others to bring them up and had never been a proper mother to them. She always tried to remember that when they treated her with such contempt. Sometimes it was hard. Today, it was almost impossible.

"I was intending to leave for France today and find your sister." Helene stood up. "If you wish to accompany me, I would enjoy your company."

Lisette smiled for the first time. "We're not going anywhere."

"I beg your pardon?"

Christian stood, too, and looked down at her. "We've decided to stay and see the sights of London. I'm sure you'll allow us to live here with you, won't you, *Maman*?"

"But I'm going to France to search for Marguerite."

Christian shrugged. "We'll be here when you get back." He looked at her plain dress. "Do you double as the housekeeper as well as the brothel keeper?"

Helene stared straight into his eyes, hoped he could see the anger building in hers. To her relief, he was the first to look away. She opened her desk drawer and sorted through the neatly labeled keys.

"I have some guest suites in the other house. You are welcome to stay there for the night. Tomorrow I'll instruct one of my staff to put you up at a decent hotel and to find you a chaperone, Lisette."

Christian frowned. "What do you mean, the other house? We want to stay here, not in a hotel."

Helene moved toward the door, her head held high. "Despite appearances, this house is actually two buildings knocked into one. The back part is actually the house on the square directly behind us."

She nodded calmly at Judd, who had remained in the hallway, and walked down the staircase to the basement. She didn't wait to see if the twins followed her. The smell of roasting pork from the kitchen made her feel nauseous.

"This area joins the two houses together. Today you may eat in the kitchen or be served in your rooms." She passed the kitchen door, moved into the small dark courtyard that was lit by oil lamps, and opened another door into the rear section of the building.

"The guest rooms are up two flights of stairs. My private

apartments are on the lower level. You also have your own private entrance at the front of this house, which faces onto Barrington Square."

She paused at the top of the stairs in the wide cream-carpeted hallway. "I'll assume you wish to be next door to each other." Helene checked her key ring, unlocked the two doors, and went into the second room. She paused to light the fire and open the heavy blue drapes before swinging around to the twins.

"Do you have any luggage?"

Christian shrugged. "Someone from the shipping company will deliver it later today."

To Helene's satisfaction, her brisk no-nonsense attitude had obviously left him uncertain of how to proceed. She had no intention of arguing with him or Lisette about their unplanned arrival. Christian didn't know that she'd learned to make the best of a bad situation well before he was born. Her search for Marguerite was far more important than trading insults with the twins.

A few riotous weeks in London and then hopefully they would be ready to go back to France again or at least compromise on new living arrangements. Despite her misgivings, she had planned on inviting them over to visit her at some point that year. Well, that point had arrived, and once she had sorted out Marguerite's more pressing problems, she was more than ready to deal with the twins.

"Aren't you going to shout at us?"

Lisette leaned toward the fire, her slender hands held out to the blaze, her wary gaze on her mother.

"Why would I waste my breath? You are here, aren't you?" Helene opened the doors that connected the two suites and lit the other fire as well. "Perhaps after I find Marguerite, she will wish to visit with me, too, and I'll have all my family together."

Christian laughed, and the harsh sound reverberated around the room.

"Don't lie, *Maman*. We all know you don't have a maternal bone in your body."

Helene walked back to the door. "You know nothing about me, Christian. And that was my choice to make, not yours." She met his gaze. "Perhaps it is time for there to be honesty between us. Perhaps your visit will enable us to make something out of the bonds that tie us together."

Christian moved to stand beside his sister. "Perhaps we don't care what you want?"

Helene faced them and suddenly envied their closeness. "Then why did you come here?"

"As we said, to make sure you help Marguerite."

"If Marguerite wishes to be helped, I will help her."

"What do you mean, if she wishes?"

"She is twenty-one and old enough to marry without my permission." Helene shrugged. "If she is really set on this course, there is little I can do to prevent her from choosing her own husband."

"So what you are actually saying is that you won't do anything at all."

Helene studied her son's angry features. "You deliberately misunderstand me. But I promise you, if Marguerite wishes to get out of her hasty marriage, I *will* make it happen."

His sneer was like a slap in the face. "As if you have the power to help anyone."

Helene raised her eyebrows. "Yet, you came to me for help—remember that."

He stared at her, his expression as challenging as her own. Helene turned her back on him and walked to the door.

"I would still like to know how you found out exactly where I live. I doubt it was blind chance that brought you here."

Lisette took off her bonnet. "We received a letter from someone who said he was your friend."

"My friend." Helene ignored the angry glance Christian gave his sister and concentrated on Lisette. "What exactly did he say?"

"That you ran a brothel in Mayfair and that you were a notorious whore."

"And you chose to believe him?"

Lisette blushed. "But he was right, wasn't he?"

God that hurt. It was her own fault for lying to them, but in her own defense, she'd hoped to spare them the harsh realities of her life.

"I do not have time to explain everything to you now, but I'm certainly not a whore, and this isn't a brothel." She held Lisette's gaze. "Does it truly look like that to you?"

"I've never been in a brothel before, *Maman.*" Lisette stuck her lip out. "But you did lie to us. When you visited us, you said you were a housekeeper and that you couldn't keep us with you because your employer hated children."

Christian snorted. "She couldn't keep us with her because she was too busy with all her men."

"That simply isn't true. I was busy building my business, and, yes, it is not the sort of place any woman would want to bring up her children." Helene held out her hands in a placatory gesture. "I wanted you to have the security of a decent home, the advantage of an excellent education, and the opportunity to grow up with your sister."

"You didn't have to lie to us," Christian muttered, his hands deep in his pockets, his mouth turned down at the corners as he kicked at the tiled grate.

"I did, Christian. You were only children. I intended to explain everything to you when I visited this Christmas, just like I did with Marguerite."

"Marguerite knows what you really are?" He frowned. "That's probably why she ran away. And I don't believe you meant to tell us anything; you're just saying that to make us feel guilty for coming here."

Helene held his gaze. "I told Marguerite the truth when she was eighteen. I doubt she waited three years to decide to run away because of what I said."

"Why didn't she tell us, then?"

"Because I asked her not to. Some things are better heard from their source, don't you think? Otherwise they might be misunderstood. The writer of that letter obviously wished to cause trouble between us. And it seems he has succeeded."

Even Christian had the grace to look away from her. She was glad he retained that much of a conscience. Eighteen-year-old men were not renowned for accepting they might have acted too hastily. Even while she smiled calmly at the twins, Helene's mind worked furiously. Who could possibly have sent them such a letter? Hardly anyone knew of the twins' existence, let alone where they went to school.

Satisfied that she had at least made the twins think about their actions, Helene nodded and opened the door.

"I will send a maid to help you settle in and show you back to the main kitchen if you wish to eat there. Tomorrow you will move to a hotel." She fixed both of the twins with her hardest stare. "If I find out that you have entered the pleasure house or participated in any way in my business before I return, I will instruct my butler to put you on the next boat back to France. No exceptions, no excuses. Are we clear on that?"

Lisette looked affronted. "Why on earth would we want to see the workings of a brothel?"

"Exactly, my dear. Why would you? When I return from France, I promise I will sit down and discuss all these issues with you."

Neither of the twins looked convinced, so Helene curtsied and shut the door behind her. Her footsteps slowed as she reached the landing. Who exactly had betrayed her to the twins? Were they lying? Had Marguerite given them the information before she eloped? It might explain the coincidence of their arrival with

Marguerite's departure. Helene stared blankly at the portrait of a young slain cavalier on the facing wall.

It was true that she'd told the twins she was the housekeeper of an important politician and could not keep them with her. She'd never expected to be forced to defend herself about her deception. She'd assumed she'd tell the twins when they were ready to hear her out, as Marguerite had. But they were not as compliant as her eldest daughter.

She'd never quite understood why, despite her best efforts, the twins seemed to dislike her so much. Perhaps she'd tried too hard to make up to Marguerite for the horrific circumstances of her birth and neglected to show her love to the twins. She'd assumed they'd know how loved they were, but obviously that was not the case. And as twins, their closeness had seemed to exclude her from the start.

She almost turned back to demand more answers, but her need to get to Marguerite was stronger. The twins' appearance and all the questions surrounding it would have to wait until she returned.

8

"What do you mean, you couldn't find her?"

"Christian . . ."

Helene sighed as she untangled the salt-stained ribbons of her bonnet and placed it on the hall table. Judd helped her off with her cloak, pelisse, and gloves, bowed respectfully, and retreated to the basement. She turned toward the back of the house and made her way to her office, Christian at her heels. There was no sign of Lisette, a small mercy for which Helene was profoundly grateful.

Just as she sat down, Judd reappeared with a cup of hot chocolate, which he placed at her elbow. She smiled up at him.

"Thank you, Judd."

"You are welcome, madame. Cook says to tell you to come and visit her in the kitchen as soon as you have finished your work. She is worried that you haven't been eating properly."

Christian muttered something under his breath as Judd winked at Helene and patted her hand. Helene took a sip of the hot drink and almost moaned at the deliciously sweet flavor.

"Are you going to tell me what happened or not?"

Helene eyed her son, who paced the rug in front of her desk, hands clasped behind his back.

"Marguerite and her new husband are apparently traveling through Europe."

"Where exactly?"

"I have no idea. They didn't leave a detailed itinerary with the hotel staff."

Christian sat down with a thump. "Perhaps I should go after them myself."

"You are welcome to try. Did you ever meet Lord Justin Lockwood?"

He frowned. "I think I saw them together walking in the grounds of the nunnery one day, but when I asked Marguerite who the man was, she denied having been there."

Helene cradled the hot chocolate cup in her hands, enjoying the warmth seeping into her cold skin.

"It is unlike Marguerite to be secretive."

Christian snorted. "How would you know? You know as much about her as you do about me and Lisette."

Helene put down her cup. "Christian, I am tired. I have been traveling for over a week. The last thing I need is to be attacked the moment I walk through the door."

"What are we going to do now?"

Helene struggled to ignore both his rudeness and his refusal to acknowledge how hard she had tried to find Marguerite. She got wearily to her feet, pressing her fingertips to the desk to counteract the swaying motion of a phantom ship, and moved toward the door.

"I have . . . friends who, given time, will be able to locate Marguerite if she is indeed in Europe."

"Friends." Christian's expression was skeptical. "I cannot believe the sort of acquaintances you have, *Maman*, would be able to help us at all."

She stopped beside him. "Just because you find it amusing

to undermine and belittle me, Christian, do not assume that others do as well. I know more heads of state and leaders of government than you have hairs on your head."

He raised his eyebrows. "I never realized whoring could be such an exalted profession. Are you the king's mistress?"

"I am nobody's mistress but my own." With the greatest of difficulty, she forced her hands to unclench. "Good afternoon. Perhaps I will see you at dinner tonight."

He stared at her, a perplexed look in his eyes that didn't reassure her. It was as if he wanted her to fight with him, to show him that she didn't care for him at all. From her sparse knowledge of him, it seemed Christian was as tenacious as she was about pursuing his aims. She doubted he would be prepared to leave her house until he'd heard better tidings of his half sister.

Despair shook through her as she took the back stairs down to her apartment. She'd told Christian the truth. Marguerite had left Paris and was heading toward Italy with her new husband. No amount of gold or threats had made the information any better or any clearer. Marguerite had gone, and there was nothing Helene could do but call in a few favors from some of her more influential clients, then sit and wait.

In the privacy of her apartment, Helene sank down on a soft chair beside the fire and covered her face with her hands. At least Marguerite wasn't alone. From all accounts, the young couple had paid their bills and departed in style. Marguerite wouldn't have to face the extremes Helene had. Perhaps she would even be happy despite the secretive beginnings of her marriage.

Helene stared into the flames as she pictured her eldest daughter's dark hair, delicate features, and pale olive skin. Marguerite meant so much to her, a beautiful healthy child saved from the horrors of the Bastille. A thing of hope that had helped Helene survive.

It had been hard to leave Marguerite in the care of others.

Helene had justified her decision by telling herself Marguerite would be safer in France than with her. The turmoil of the years since her children's births had made removing them from the nunnery almost impossible. She'd regretted the necessity of that choice every day since, and now she felt even more of a fool. Was there anywhere in the world that was safe anymore? Helene closed her eyes and allowed herself to weep.

Four hours later, she studied her reflection in the long mirror in the first public salon. She'd chosen to wear blue silk, one of her favorite colors, in the hope that it might detract from the lines of tiredness stretching her skin and the shadows under her eyes. Diamonds glittered in her ears, around her neck, and on the heels of her shoes. Tonight she needed to look every inch the proprietress of an exclusive club rather than the distraught mother of a runaway bride.

"Helene, you are back." She turned to find George bowing in front of her. His inspection of her was thorough and ended at her face. "You look tired."

She sighed. "I've just spent an hour trying to create the illusion that I am twenty-five again, and you ruin it in one sentence." She placed her hand on his arm and allowed him to lead her toward the buffet table. "I've been busy."

"Judd said you had to go to France."

"Judd told you that?"

"Why? Was it meant to be a secret?" George paused as he handed her a glass of white wine. "We are still friends, aren't we?"

"Of course we are." She glanced up at him. "Did he also tell you about my guests?"

"No. That he kept to himself. You have guests?"

"The twins arrived, demanding I find their sister."

"Ah, so that is why you went to France. To find Marguerite and to take the twins back to school." He squeezed her fingers.

"No wonder you are tired. That must have been quite an ordeal."

"Worse than you think. The twins are still here, and Marguerite has eloped."

"Good God," George said. "Do you know who she married?"

"Some English peer, apparently."

"Oh well, then I suppose you'll let her have her way. No point in interfering if the girl has gone and gotten herself a title."

Helene took a step back so that she could look into George's face. His expression was calm, and he wasn't smiling.

"I'm not happy about it, George. In fact, I wanted to ask for your help."

He inclined his head, his eyes instantly full of concern. "Of course. What can I do for you?"

"You have contacts in all the embassies in Europe. I'd be grateful if you could find out exactly where Marguerite and her husband, a Lord Justin Lockwood, finally settle down."

"You think they might stay abroad?"

"Wouldn't you?"

His smile was relaxed. "Absolutely. In fact, I'd probably not return until I had my son and heir in my arms to soften the hearts of my parents."

Helene shuddered. "I have no desire to be a grandmother quite yet. I'd just like to know she is safe and well."

"You've decided not to chase after her, then?"

Helene shrugged and set her wineglass back on the buffet table. "If I can find out exactly where she plans to reside, I'll go to her then."

"A wise decision. If she feels you are intent on discovering her, she might keep moving. I'll certainly make some discreet inquiries for you at the various embassies."

"Thank you, George." She squeezed his arm. "You are one

of the very few people who even know I have children. I appreciate your help."

He kissed her fingers and then her palm. "It's hard to believe you are old enough to have a daughter at all, let alone two."

"Unfortunately, I find it all too believable at the moment. I will see you later, George. I must go and mingle."

She disengaged her hand and strolled toward the main red and gold decorated salon, where a stream of people had begun to pour through the double doorway. As she walked, she nodded at those who greeted her and kissed her fingers to some of the younger men. It seemed that in her absence, everything had gone well. Her staff was well trained, and Judd oversaw everything perfectly.

"Madame Helene."

A familiar voice and an even more familiar smile made her pause. A man emerged from the press of people and bowed. His golden hair glinted in the candlelight; his black coat and white linen were impeccably cut.

Helene extended her hand. "Gideon, how are you?"

"I'm very well and so is Antonia." He looked around the rapidly filling room. "She's here somewhere. I'll tell her to come and make her bow to you later." He beckoned to a tall gentleman standing just inside the door. "There's someone I'd like you to meet. My father asked me to sign him in as my guest."

Helene's gracious smile froze on her lips as the man walked toward her. The noise and chatter disappeared, leaving her in a frightening empty void of pure emotion. When their eyes met, she wasn't sure if she was offended or relieved by the total lack of recognition in his gaze.

"This is Mr. Philip Ross." Gideon smiled. "He's recently inherited some fancy new title, but to my shame, I can't remember exactly what it is."

Helene moistened her lips with her tongue. "Mr. Ross, you are most welcome."

"Madame."

He took her cold hand, enfolded it within his, and brushed his lips over her skin with stiff, unenthusiastic propriety.

"Are you staying in London for long, sir?"

"It depends. I have some business to attend to. I'm not sure how long it will take."

Hopefully not very long, Helene prayed. The Fates were definitely conspiring against her. Thank God the twins weren't around. She frantically checked the crowd. It would be just like them to sneak into the packed salon without her realizing it.

"Madame?"

She forced her attention back to Philip Ross, noticed for the first time that he wore the dark somber colors of mourning and that his face was dour and unsmiling. In contrast to the flowing locks of his youth, his hair was now cut brutally short, accentuating the hard angles of his cheekbones. Would she have recognized him if Gideon hadn't introduced him by name? He bore little to no resemblance to the laughing elegant man she remembered from eighteen years before.

She mustered a smile. "I beg your pardon, monsieur. Would you care for some refreshments?"

"No, thank you."

Helene caught Gideon's amused and speculative gaze. He'd probably never seen her quite so distracted before. She forced another smile. "It was a pleasure to meet you, sir. I hope you enjoy your evening."

Gideon looked disappointed. "But, madame, I promised Philip that as my guest, you would give him a personal tour of the premises."

"Did you?" Helene narrowed her eyes at him. "I'm sure Mr. Ross would rather spend his evening with you."

"On the contrary, madame. Who better to show me around than the woman who created such an unusual establishment?"

Helene glanced sharply up at Philip Ross, who appeared to

be smiling despite the dismissive bite of his words. She curtsied and raised her chin.

"I'd be delighted to show you around, sir. Gideon is right. I am extremely proud of this pleasure house."

He placed her hand on his sleeve and nodded at Gideon. "Thank you for the introduction. Perhaps I will see you at White's tomorrow."

Gideon bowed and winked at Helene. "The introduction was my pleasure. Madame Helene holds a very special place in my affections."

"Indeed."

There was no mistaking the sarcasm in Philip's voice this time.

Gideon raised his eyebrows. "I met my wife here. I'm sure madame will tell you all the details."

"I'm sure she will."

Gideon turned and went back toward the doorway, where a younger man stood waiting for him. Helene hid a smile as Gideon gave the youth a kiss on the lips. She cast a quick glance up at Philip.

"That is Gideon's wife. She sometimes likes to dress as a man."

Philip didn't even blink; if anything, his gaze became even frostier. "And they met here. How . . . interesting."

"Yes, it was quite romantic."

"I'll take your word for it."

Helene led him toward the far end of the salon so that he could see the whole room. To her right, a group of young women and men were engaged in a game of cards that necessitated stripping off various items of clothing. Screams and giggles arose from the table as one of the women slowly rolled down her stocking and tossed it and her silk garter onto the steadily growing pile of clothing.

"These are the more public rooms. My clients are able to enjoy a series of entertainments, participate in group sexual acts, and enjoy themselves without worrying."

"I can see that."

Philip's tone was scarcely encouraging, his face even less so. Helene faked a laugh. "You disapprove, sir?"

"Of course I disapprove. Such behavior is scarcely appropriate in public, is it?"

"It depends how you define 'public,' sir. This is a private club. People pay to belong to it and for the privileges it offers them."

"The privilege to behave like rutting fools."

Helene shrugged. "There is nothing wrong with that, is there? Sometimes we all need to be foolish."

"If you insist, madame."

The scathing glare he gave her ignited something fierce and low in her chest. How dare he stand there and judge her and her patrons? She raised her eyes to his, a challenge in her gaze.

"Perhaps you should leave now, monsieur. This is only the beginning of the foolishness. I would hate to shock you."

A muscle twitched in his cheek. "I doubt you will do that. Please, show me more."

"If you insist, monsieur."

She led him back through both of the large public salons, making sure he got a good view of the naked jugglers and the exotic dark-skinned woman performing the dance of the seven veils. He said nothing and his face betrayed no emotion. What had happened to turn him into such a dull stick of a man?

In the hallway beyond the two salons, Helene paused.

"Beyond the public areas are more secluded rooms." She gestured at the line of doorways. "On this floor, we cater to the more popular sexual fantasies."

"How do you decide what they are?"

His quiet question surprised her, and she glanced up to find him watching her intently.

"Over the years, certain scenarios have been requested by our patrons many times. I keep a list of those favorites. When people stop enjoying a particular scenario, we simply change the theme and introduce another from our list."

"How efficient."

"This is a business, sir."

Why was she so intent on impressing him? Not only had he forgotten her, but he was treating her achievements with utter contempt. What had he expected to find here? Hadn't Gideon told him exactly what she provided? Well, if she couldn't impress him, she'd make sure she shocked him right down to his conservative, fuddy-duddy—no doubt churchgoing—toes.

"Would you like to go into one of the rooms?"

It was a deliberate challenge, and she waited for his response with a calm smile.

"Why not?"

"Perhaps you would like to choose which room to enter. The themes are on the doors."

He glared down at her. "I'd rather you chose. You are the expert."

At random, Helene pointed at the third door on the left. The plaque on the door read BLIND MAN'S BLUFF. "Let's go in here, shall we?"

He followed her into the darkened room and took a seat next to her. She focused her attention on the center of the room, where an oiled naked man was being tied to a black-painted backdrop. A narrow white silk scarf covered his eyes. When the man's hands had been secured above his head and his ankles locked in place, a collective sigh of feminine approval echoed around the room.

Helene hid a smile as one of the women in the audience crept forward and began to touch the man. Soon, a sea of females surrounded him, sucking and licking his skin, kissing him on the mouth, caressing his erect cock.

Beside her, Philip Ross shifted in his seat. Did the erotic tableau arouse or disgust him? Helene couldn't tell in the half-darkness; all she could sense was the heat and tension radiating from him. She risked a glance at his profile and saw his gaze was fixed on the scene, his mouth a hard line. He shuddered as one of the women fell to her knees and drew the man's cock into her mouth.

"I refuse to watch such—"

He got to his feet and blundered toward the door. Helene followed him out as quietly as she could. She found him farther down the deserted hallway, his back to the wall, his hands clenched at his sides.

"Monsieur? Are you feeling unwell?"

He raised his head to stare into her eyes, and she experienced a moment of pure fear.

"How should I be feeling after being forced to experience such appalling behavior?"

"I'm not quite sure what you found appalling, sir. Everyone appeared to be enjoying themselves immensely."

"Apart from that poor man, beset by those harlots."

Helene allowed him to see her smile. "That 'poor man' has been waiting a month for that experience."

"Are you trying to tell me that he wanted to be used like that?"

She shrugged. "This is a house of pleasure, sir. If that is his notion of pleasure, then I can only offer him the opportunity to enjoy it."

"Ah, so those harpies are paid to pretend to enjoy him."

"Not at all. Everything offered here is a choice. No one is forced to do anything."

He snorted. "I hardly think any respectable woman would choose to behave like that."

Helene took his arm and guided him to the far end of the hallway, where there was less chance of them being overheard.

He turned to stare out of the narrow window, his shoulders set and his back stiff. Helene studied his rigid profile.

"You might be surprised what a respectable woman wants. Almost all the women in that room are titled ladies." She looked up at him from under her lashes. "I can only apologize. Perhaps I chose a room your wife would've preferred more than you."

"My wife would never stoop to such salacious behavior."

"Perhaps you should bring her here and see if that is true? You might be surprised."

He swung around to face her more fully. "My wife is dead. But I can assure you that such erotic displays would have shocked her immeasurably."

How terrible for you. It took all of Helene's resolve not to speak the words out loud. If Philip's wife had indeed been such a lady, it was no wonder he looked so repressed and unhappy.

She took a deep breath. "I apologize again, sir. I should not have mentioned your wife."

"Why not? I'm sure you've been wondering about her all these years."

"I beg your pardon?"

Philip shrugged. "You know who I am. Don't try and lie to me."

"Indeed I do, monsieur." Helene paused to gather her defenses. "I thought you must have forgotten me, and I hesitated to remind you of my existence."

His smile was almost a sneer. "How could I forget you? You haven't changed at all."

Helene touched her face. "That is hardly true. I am no longer eighteen."

His laugh was harsh. "Thank God for that."

"I'm not quite sure what you mean. I'm certainly glad I'm not eighteen anymore. I make far wiser choices than I did then." She swallowed hard. "I sincerely regret my comments about your wife. I did not intend to cause you pain."

"You did not intend to cause me pain."

His loaded words hung in the air between them, throwing her back to the nights they'd shared, the feel of his skin against hers, his laughter and the delights of their lovemaking. *Had she hurt him?* Helene focused her attention on his plain white cravat to avoid looking into his face.

"Why are you here, sir?"

"Because Lord Gideon Harcourt brought me and because I've often wondered if the infamous Madame Helene could possibly be you."

"I am infamous?"

He bowed. "You are renowned as the woman who can have five men a night and still be looking for another for breakfast. A woman who only has to look at a man to drive him to his knees and make him forget anything but having you."

"If that were true, I would indeed be an amazing woman. But I have learned never to listen to gossip." She tried to laugh. "And now that you have seen me, what will you do?"

He raised her chin with his finger. "Surely that depends on you?"

"I do not understand."

He bent his head until his mouth met hers and outlined her lips with his tongue. Before she could protest, he kissed her, backing her up against the wall while he ravaged her mouth. She responded from somewhere deep inside as his remembered texture and taste flooded her, taking her off guard and into a world of pure sensation.

She flattened her hands against the grooved wooden paneling to stop herself from touching him. She couldn't stop her reaction to his kiss, which was as immediate and heated as his own. His body pinned her to the wall from knee to neck; his cock was hard against her stomach.

When he drew back, she would've stumbled if he hadn't caught her arm and pushed her back against the wall. She watched as he retrieved his handkerchief and deliberately wiped the red stain of her lip color from his mouth.

"You did say that no one gets paid for engaging in sexual activity in your establishment?"

Unable to speak, Helene simply nodded. He tucked the handkerchief back into his pocket.

"Then perhaps you'll fit me into your no doubt already full roster for tonight."

A roaring sensation destroyed Helene's common sense. She stepped forward and slapped him hard on the cheek.

"I also said that everyone here has a choice to participate in sexual acts or not." She curtsied. "Good night, Mr. Ross."

He shrugged. "Let me know when you change your mind. I'm sure you'll run out of men soon."

"I wouldn't bed you if you were the last man on earth."

His eyebrows rose. "Is that a challenge? You should know better than to throw down the gauntlet like that."

"Good *night*, Mr. Ross."

Helene gathered her skirts and turned away from him, heading for the private areas of the house. She wanted to run from the cynicism and dislike on his face but refused to give him the satisfaction. How dare he appear and insinuate that she was in some way responsible for how he had turned out? If anyone had a complaint to make about the results of their night together, surely it was her?

Mon Dieu, the twins . . . She touched her fingers to her lips, remembered his possessive kiss, and shivered. Despite her annoyance, if he had kissed her for much longer, she would have entwined her arms around his neck and held him close. That would've been a huge mistake. With the twins being in the house and Marguerite's disappearance, she was far too vulnerable to deal with Philip Ross at the moment. Hopefully he had seen what he wanted and would now leave her in peace.

9

Philip Ross contemplated the remains of his breakfast and stared out of the dirt-encrusted window of the house on Hans Street he'd rented for the Season. Last night had not gone well. He'd recognized Helene before Gideon introduced them and had plenty of time to school his features into an expression of polite disinterest before he had to face her.

Helene had not been given the same advantage. He'd seen the shock in her eyes when they'd been introduced, enjoyed it even, although she'd been quick to mask it. He was surprised at the heat of the resentment that shuddered through him as he saw her in her element, presiding over her "house of pleasure," a fancy name for a brothel if ever he'd heard one. How dare she be so radiant when he was . . . Ruthlessly he pushed his self-pitying thoughts away.

He finished his coffee and reached for the pot to have more. How the hell had she remained so beautiful? His cock had responded before he'd even drawn a breath to speak to her. He groaned and shoved a hand through his hair. So many years since he'd seen her, so many memories that came flooding back as soon as he'd smelled her unique lavender-and-roses scent.

At least he was old enough now not to be led astray by his cock. Helene had taught him that lesson well. But he had kissed her, and the kiss, although meant to be an insult, had turned into something far more potent and enjoyable. She'd felt perfect beneath his hands, her body warm and pliable, her mouth deliciously sinful and inviting.

But then she was a skilled whore. He drank more coffee, wincing at the bitter dregs. She probably thought she'd seen the last of him, but she had no idea.

He pushed away from the table and went to find his hat and gloves. Madame Helene, or whatever her damned name was these days, was in for another shock.

Philip wasn't surprised that Helene kept him waiting for a good half hour before she agreed to see him. In truth, he'd wondered if she would see him at all and that he would eventually have to conduct his business with her through his solicitor. So much more enjoyable to see her face when he told her the situation.

He halted in the open doorway to stare at her in surprise. Her office was as businesslike as his own, with no feminine frills or furbelows to distract her. She sat behind a large neat desk, her blond hair drawn up in a severe coronet on the back of her head, her green dress as high-necked and demure as a governess's. A small pair of spectacles adorned the end of her nose, but she took them off when she saw him. She didn't get to her feet.

"Madame." He bowed.

"Mr. Ross." Her tone was icy. "What can I do for you?"

He took his time settling himself in the chair in front of her desk. She tapped the end of her pen as she waited for him to return his attention to her.

"Did you come to apologize?"

He blinked at her. "What?"

She leaned forward. "Did you come to apologize for your appalling behavior last night?"

"I wasn't aware that I had behaved appallingly."

"You insulted and mauled me."

"I did not maul you, and you kissed me back quite willingly."

Color flooded her cheeks. "I merely allowed you to kiss me because you gave me no choice."

"Liar." He favored her with a lazy smile, then frowned as she got to her feet.

"If you have finished insulting me further, sir, you may leave."

"But I haven't even begun."

She sighed and placed her hands flat on the desk. "What do you want, Mr. Ross?"

From the pocket of his greatcoat, he withdrew the documents his solicitor had given him.

"I'm not sure if you remember, but Gideon Harcourt did mention last night that I have succeeded to a title."

She remained standing, her expression unencouraging. "Am I supposed to be impressed?"

He unfolded the documents and smoothed them under his fingertips. "You certainly should be interested. I'm now Lord Philip Knowles."

He had the satisfaction of seeing the color drain from her face and to watch her sink slowly back into her chair.

"*You* are Lord Derek Knowles's heir?"

"That is correct, which means I'm also the heir presumptive of the Earl of Swansford."

"Do you expect me to congratulate you?"

He shrugged. "Not really. I'm more interested in your reaction to a certain set of papers my solicitor handed me concerning your business." He tossed the papers onto her desk and waited until she pulled them in front of her. "Take your time reading through them. I'm sure you'll agree they are authentic."

She looked up at him, one hand flattened over the documents. "I know they are genuine. I knew Lord Derek and his wife very well."

"You knew his wife?" He laughed. "And how did she react to your friendship with her husband?"

She held his gaze. "She was happy for me."

Something in her eyes made him feel ashamed of his unspoken assumptions. He shrugged off the uncomfortable feeling and returned to the matter at hand.

"The thing that interests me is how a respectable gentleman like Lord Derek ended up owning fifteen percent of a whorehouse."

"It is not a whorehouse. It is a private club." Helene looked down her nose at him. "And how it came about is none of your business, is it?"

"I can guess, though. How many men did you have to seduce to get what you wanted, Helene?"

Her smile was as sharp and cold as his. "I needed only four grateful men to succeed. That was enough."

"Only four? How admirable. Did you reward them all at once or individually?"

"Again, that is none of your business."

"And if I'd stayed with you, you wouldn't have needed any of those other men, would you?"

She looked at him then, her gaze dismissive. "You wouldn't have stayed long, Philip. You would've run back to your family at the first opportunity."

His fingers clenched on the arm of the chair. "We'll never know, will we? You didn't give me the chance."

"You married less than a week after you left me. I would hardly say that vouched for your constancy."

Anger threaded through him. "How dare you assume the moral high ground when you are the one who chose to return to whoring?"

She flinched as if he had struck her. "I did what I thought was best for both of us." She drew a deep breath. "Now, do you wish to discuss your inheritance or rake over old hurts?"

"I'm not hurting."

She stared at him again. "If you say so, Mr. Ross."

"It's *my lord*."

She bit down on her lower lip until he could see a speck of blood. "I would like to purchase the shares from you."

"What if I don't wish to sell?"

She frowned at him. "Why on earth would you wish to keep them?"

"Because, apparently, they provide me with a decent sum of money every quarter. Every nobleman needs ready cash."

Her hands gripped each other so hard he could see the whiteness of her slender bones. "I am willing to pay you twice their value."

"But I am not willing to sell at any price."

"Why?"

In truth, he wasn't quite sure exactly what he intended to do. He was far more interested in finding out how Helene intended to deal with him. The sight of her name on the legal documents had provided him with his first spark of interest since his wife's death over a year ago.

"That is none of *your* business." He shrugged. "Perhaps I can help you become more respectable. Turn this place into a center of culture and learning."

"It is a center of sexual culture and learning, and I have no intention of taking any advice from you at all," she snapped.

He raised his eyebrows. He was almost beginning to enjoy himself. "You have no choice. If you insist on denying me my legal right to meddle in your business, I will take you to court."

Her smile was infinitely superior. "I hardly think you'll do that. Think of your no-doubt spotless reputation. What man would wish to be associated with a business such as this?"

"But if I changed it into something more respectable . . . ?"

Helene shot to her feet. "I will not allow you to do this to me."

He leaned back in his seat to look up at her. "How are you going to stop me?"

"I intend to talk to the other shareholders. Between us, I am sure we can get you to see reason."

"Of course, the other shareholders. I'd forgotten about them." Philip got to his feet. "Perhaps you should do that and then we can have another discussion. But I give you fair warning: I am not going to sell."

"Why do you hate me so much?"

For a second, her composure deserted her, and he saw the anguish in her eyes. He shoved his hands in his pockets and focused his gaze on her desk.

"There's no need to be so melodramatic. I don't hate you. This is just a business decision."

"It feels very personal to me." She drew a quick breath. "Are you still trying to punish me for refusing your marriage proposal?"

"Did I really propose to you?" He faked a laugh. "I'd forgotten about that. I can't believe I was so stupid."

"If you were stupid, then surely you should be grateful to me for refusing your generous offer rather than bringing up old grievances and threatening me."

She searched his face as if trying to see the man he had once been. But he knew it was useless. That man had died long ago in the endless void of his marriage.

"As I said, it isn't personal." He faced her. "I own fifteen percent of your business, and I am entitled to my opinions about the way it should be run."

"You are entitled to nothing."

Her moment of weakness was past. The woman who faced him now was magnificent in her scorn.

"As I said, madame, we will see, won't we?" He bowed and retrieved his documents from her desk. "Good morning. I'm sure you'll be in touch."

He left her with a condescending smile that disappeared the moment he gained the street. Inside his carriage, he stared blankly out the window. His damned conscience pricked him. Helene didn't deserve such treatment. She had obviously managed to become successful without him. Was that what rankled? That she was happy and he wasn't? Had he ever been happy since he'd left her at that inn? He closed his eyes. What a mean-spirited man he had turned out to be.

It would be better for all of them if he sold her the shares and went back to the countryside. With his new rank and social obligations, it wasn't as if he didn't have plenty to do. His children might also appreciate a visit from him. They had yet to settle comfortably in their new home. He missed them far more than he had anticipated.

Helene stirred his senses, made him feel emotions he had long believed buried and gone. Her angry response to him, the power he held over her, made him feel alive. Even as he thought about leaving, he realized he couldn't. Helene Delornay had cast her spell over him again, and there was nothing he could do about it.

Why?

Helene collapsed back into her chair as Philip shut the door behind him. She covered her eyes with her shaking hands and concentrated on her breathing. Philip Ross owned fifteen percent of her business, and he had no intention of selling the shares to her. She felt as helpless as her eighteen-year-old self when Philip had crossed her path and irrevocably changed the course of her life.

Why was he doing this to her? He seemed to be enjoying himself. Had he really turned into the kind of man who held his grievances so close to his chest that he would wait a lifetime to get his own back? Had her rejection of him really soured his life so badly? Despite her reputation, she'd never seen herself as the kind of woman men could never forget.

Apart from his excess of morals, Philip seemed to have done remarkably well for himself by most people's standards.

Helene slowly opened her eyes. Was she going to let him wrest control from her again? He thought he had all the power, but he had no idea how hard she had fought to get where she was or what she was prepared to do to keep him away from her. Despite their differences, she had the twins to think of as well. God forbid they ever found out about Philip. She had to find a way to make him leave.

She would talk to the other trustees today and see if there was any legal way to buy back Philip's shares. Somehow she doubted it. The original agreement had been based on the men's high opinion of her, not Philip Ross's obvious disdain. She smiled to herself. If there was no legal way to get rid of Philip, she had a few interesting ideas of her own.

She patted her disordered hair back into place and headed out into the hallway. She couldn't sit and wait for disaster to find her. It would be better to go and see Viscount Harcourt-DeVere right away.

"Unfortunately, I don't think there is anything we can do, Helene. As you said, the agreement was made between friends who wanted the best for you. We didn't make any provisions for hostile shareholders." Viscount Harcourt-DeVere sighed. "Derek was a fool not to cede the shares back to you. I told him to do it on countless occasions."

Helene could only nod in agreement. She turned to George, who sat on the corner of the viscount's desk, his arms folded.

"Can you think of anything, George?"

He shook his head. "I'll have to read over the contract again, but I believe the viscount is right."

Helene frowned at them both and resumed pacing the Turkish red carpet. To her dismay, the Duke of Diable Delamere was in France and unable to attend the impromptu meeting. Although given his more arrogant nature, it was perhaps for the best. Philip Ross might find himself being forced into a duel. Despite the watery sunshine and a roaring fire, the study felt cold, and she shivered.

"There has to be something. I cannot allow this man back into my life."

"Back into your life?" George asked, his expression full of interest. "Do you already have an acquaintance with the new Lord Knowles?"

Helene reluctantly faced him. "I've met him before."

"At the pleasure house?"

She stared at George. She'd never told anyone the identity of the twins' father, and she had no intention of divulging it now.

"It must have been there. I hardly could've met him at Almack's."

George held up his hands. "There is no need to cut up at me. I'm on your side, remember? I don't want this idiot coming in and ruining our business either."

Helene took a deep breath. "I'm sorry, George. I'm just so worried about what will happen."

The viscount cleared his throat. "I can only apologize for sending him to the pleasure house to meet you. I had no idea he meant to be difficult. You still control the vast majority of the business, Helene. Despite his threats, there is little the man can actually do without taking you to court."

"He said he was prepared to do that if necessary."

"I'll make sure that doesn't happen, my dear. Despite my failing health, I still have a great deal of influence in legal circles, and the Duke of Diable Delamere has even more." The viscount turned to ring the servants' bell. "I'll also summon the new Lord Knowles to a meeting here with me and set him straight on a few matters."

Helene slumped into a chair. "That is very kind of you, but I'm not sure it will make much of a difference."

"You'd be surprised, Helene. I can make his transition to the peerage easier or a lot harder, depending on the actions he chooses to take."

"I appreciate your help." Helene got to her feet and walked over to the desk. Close up, she could see the lines of strain on the viscount's face, the pattern of ill health on his sallow skin. "But you must promise not to overexert yourself on my account."

He patted her hand, his so fragile now she could see the delicate curve of his bones within. "It is always a pleasure to help you, my dear."

Helene hesitated as he smiled into her eyes. "You would have no objection if I attempted to change his mind myself, would you?"

His eyebrows rose, and for a moment she saw a flash of his wicked younger self in his gaze.

"As long as you don't kill the man, I have no objections at all."

She bent and kissed his hollowed, papery cheek. "It will hardly come to that. But I can't sit by and allow him to destroy everything I've made for myself."

"Good for you, Helene." George applauded. "I don't think he'll know what hit him."

Helene smiled properly for the first time that day. "All I hope is that soon he'll be heading back to his new home at Sudbury Court as fast as his horse can carry him."

10

Philip Ross carefully knotted his cravat and pinned it in place with a single pearl pin. Jones, his valet, handed him a dull brown waistcoat and his favorite black coat.

"There, my lord. You look very nice."

Philip managed to smile his thanks. He looked like what he was—a man headed toward forty who'd allowed others to suck all the joy out of his life. He knew Helene had been shocked by his dour appearance. When had he stopped smiling and enjoying his life? When had he last laughed out loud?

His wife hadn't encouraged laughter. In her increasingly delicate health, she'd even found the laughter of their children too much to bear. After all, they had ruined her life, hadn't they? He'd hated that, hated that she'd forced them to creep around the house like scared mice for fear of upsetting her. His mouth twisted. Such a gentle tyrant, ruling the house from her sickbed, but a tyrant nonetheless.

Yet, tonight a quiver of anticipation thrilled through his veins. Helene had asked him to meet her at the pleasure house, and he was more than willing to accommodate her. In truth, he hadn't stopped thinking about the room she'd taken him into. The ecstatic groans of the man being pleasured had etched themselves into his brain, making him wake up hard, wet, and wanting, something that hadn't happened to him in years.

He slipped his card case and a bag of coins into his coat pocket. Somewhere, deep within his soul, he realized Helene might offer him his last opportunity to live again. The question was, what would she propose to him, and how high was the price?

Helene checked the public salon, pleased to see that everything appeared to be functioning perfectly. Her staff was not only well paid, but well trained. Despite the nature of the entertainments offered, they rarely had any problems with the guests. The opportunity to indulge their wildest sexual fantasies, coupled with the fear of being struck off the members list, meant that most people behaved.

Beneath her calm exterior, Helene realized she was nervous. In a fit of gallantry, George had offered to take the twins for a week's vacation to his house in Brighton. Helene had been glad to accept on the twins' behalf and, despite their protests, had packed them off bright and early that morning. She had a week of relative peace to deal with Philip Ross, unless there was news of Marguerite, of course.

"Madame."

She turned to find Philip behind her. The severe cut and style of his dark clothing brought a somber note to the lush scarlet and gold salon. He smelled of sandalwood and brandy, his face clean-shaven, his expression as grim as ever. Despite his lack of enthusiasm, or maybe because of it, Helene realized she looked forward to the challenge of mastering him. How long was it since a man had resisted her, and how long since she'd really been interested in bending a man to her will?

She smiled slowly and allowed her experienced gaze to

travel down his long lean body. Unlike many men his age, he hadn't succumbed to the pox or the overconsumption of food or alcohol. She remembered the feel of his body pressed against hers, the sense of great strength and hard muscles. If she did have to resort to fucking him to get her way, it certainly wouldn't be a hardship.

"Are you calculating how long I'll last in your bed?"

Helene blinked and brought her eyes back up to Philip's. "How did you guess?"

"From the lascivious look on your face."

She raised her eyebrows. "You don't like to be admired?"

He shrugged, the gesture almost awkward. "There is little to admire. I'm simply a country squire."

Helene squeezed his upper arm as if testing his strength. "A country squire who probably helps bring in the harvest, hunts his own game, and rides to hounds."

"I do those things."

"And that is why you are worth admiring. I don't believe there is an inch of fat on your body."

He stepped out of reach, his mouth a hard straight line. "What do you want, Helene?"

She fluttered her eyelashes at him. "Just to talk to you."

"Here?" His wide gesture took in the rapidly filling salon.

"My office, if you prefer it."

He bowed and she placed her hand on his arm and allowed him to lead her toward the relative peace and quiet at the back of the house. In the dense silence, the rustling of her cream silk flounced dress and single petticoat sounded loud. She had no idea how he would react to her proposal but found she was invigorated by the thought of making it. He was no spoiled young aristocrat willing to do anything she asked. It was almost refreshing to have a challenge.

Helene took the seat behind the desk and waited for Philip to sit down.

"I have a proposal for you."

His smile was bored. "I'm not selling you the shares."

Her answering smile was full of sweetness. "I was thinking more in terms of a wager."

"A wager?" He sat slightly forward, his hands linked together, elbows resting on his knees. "Between us?"

"That is correct." She raised her eyebrows. "Is it beneath your newfound dignity to bet?"

"That depends on the wager and the terms."

She saw the spark of interest in his hazel eyes that he couldn't quite conceal. Her hopes rose. Beneath that hardened, glacial exterior, surely some spark of the swaggering adventurer remained?

"I want you to spend the next thirty days working alongside me at the pleasure house. If you leave before that time period ends, the shares are mine."

"And if I accomplish this fearsome task, do you expect me to *give* you the shares anyway? I doubt you're offering to give me yours." He laughed. "It seems the terms are all to your advantage."

"No, my lord. If you complete your thirty days here, I will not take you to court to regain possession of the shares, *and* I will allow you to remain as a silent partner under my very particular conditions."

His expression darkened. "You do not have the resources to take me to court. Who would listen to you anyway?"

Helene held up a list of names. "Almost all the judges in London, half the House of Lords, and quite a few of our current Members of Parliament are fully paid-up members here. I'm sure they wouldn't look kindly upon a case that might result in the closure of one of their favorite clubs."

There was silence as Philip stared at the list and then at her. She kept her breathing slow and steady, her expression pleasant.

"What exactly would I have to do at the pleasure house?"

Helene shrugged, determined not to show any sign of triumph at his apparent capitulation in case he rescinded it. "At first you would accompany me and learn how the house operates. If you prove capable, I might even allow you to take over occasionally."

"You make it sound as if I'd be unable to perform your so-called duties." He pretended to sigh. "Although, you might be right. I'm not sure if I could bring myself to fuck all the men."

"Perhaps you could fuck all the women instead. They would probably enjoy it." Helene put the list back into the drawer and locked it. "And I don't fuck everybody. Only those who appeal to me or need tuition in the erotic arts."

"Which is most of the English aristocracy."

She smiled at him, and he almost smiled back before converting his amusement into a frown.

"There is more to running this establishment than sex. I scarcely have time to share my bed with anyone these days. Having an assistant to share my burdens might be amusing."

"So you want me to act like some unpaid servant for the next thirty days in your brothel."

"It is not a brothel, but basically, yes."

"And in return, you'll not take me to court."

She nodded and he slowly shook his head.

"The odds still seem weighted in your favor."

"How so?"

"You get to tell me what to do for thirty days."

"I get to show you what your investment is worth and how to run it if you wish to be involved in its future. What on earth is wrong with that?"

"Everything."

He got to his feet and started to pace the woven rug, hands behind his back. Helene stiffened as he pivoted in front of her desk.

"If I agree, I want something from you."

"What, my lord?"

"Your body for those thirty nights, so I will have some compensation for all my hard work."

Helene licked her lips as she imagined herself and Philip entwined, naked on her bed.

"As I've already told you, my body is not for sale."

"I'm not offering you money for it."

"You wish to use me, though."

"As you wish to use me for thirty days."

Their gazes locked, and neither of them seemed able to look away. "And if I refuse?"

"Then I will not accept your terms, and we will be back where we started."

Thirty days of being bedded by Philip Ross . . . Did he still make love with such wicked abandon? Somehow Helene doubted it. Could she inflame his lust, make him crave her as much as he had eighteen years ago? Did she even want to? She was a successful woman in her own right, mother to three children whom she still had to protect despite themselves.

"If I agree, you must promise not to hurt me."

"Why would I hurt you?" He returned to his seat and sat down, one long leg crossed over the other.

"Because despite what you say, I still sense you are angry with me."

His smile was dismissive. "You are mistaken. If I'm angry at all, it is because you have put me into this ridiculous situation."

As her temper started to rise, Helene got to her feet and moved to stand in front of him, hands on her hips.

"The situation is of your own making, my lord. If you were truly a gentleman, you would simply relinquish your interest in this place and walk away."

"Then perhaps I'm not a gentleman." He wrapped his arm around her waist and yanked her into his lap. She shivered as he kissed his way up from her shoulder to her neck. "And when I'm in your bed, I'm the only man in it."

"Are you saying I can't have any other lovers?" Helene stifled a gasp as his teeth settled over the pulse at the base of her throat.

"It seems only fair, doesn't it? You get my entire attention for thirty days and I get yours."

She jabbed at him with her elbow to great effect and slid off his lap. He didn't try to stop her, simply waited as she rearranged the bodice of her gown.

"Your nipples are hard."

"It is cold in here."

He raised his eyebrows. "What does that have to do with the fact that you are aroused?"

Helene retrieved her paisley shawl from the chair behind her desk and put it around her shoulders.

"Are we agreed, then? You will spend your next thirty days with me, and I will spend the next thirty nights with you."

He got slowly to his feet, his gaze fixed on her breasts. "And what happens if I don't turn up every day?"

"Then our agreement is null and void, and you give me your shares."

She waited impatiently until he nodded.

"I agree to your terms, madame. In thirty days, after we both complete our parts of the agreement, we can discuss the situation again." He smiled. "Perhaps by then you will be so enamored of my body and my business acumen that you will decide to make my involvement permanent."

"As I said, if you *insist* on retaining the shares, we will negotiate the terms of your minor involvement in my business." She glared at him. "Please don't imagine you will be handed control of everything I've worked for."

"Madame, rest assured, I wouldn't dare to assume anything about you."

Helene tried not to grind her teeth. If she had her way, he would be gone long before then. She dropped him a formal curtsey and held out her hand.

"Perhaps we should start right away and continue our tour of the house?"

Philip kissed her palm and placed her hand on his sleeve, his expression ominous. "What else is there? I assumed I had seen the worst of it."

Helene cast him a sideways glance as she mentally reviewed the evening's entertainment schedule. Where should she take him first? What would shock him most?

Philip tried to avoid staring at the three well-endowed naked women writhing on the large silk cushions behind the buffet tables. They were eating purple grapes and drinking red wine as they pleasured each other. It was difficult not to stare. To his right, several men had gathered to watch and comment on the performance. Watching the women didn't particularly arouse him, although such a blatant and public display of their sexuality did.

He felt like a man who had lived on a diet of bread and water for twenty years suddenly being offered all the exotic food he could eat. Part of him wanted to gorge himself; the saner part knew that such excess would probably kill him.

"My lord?"

He dragged his attention back to Helene, who had been explaining the financial implications of providing such a luxurious buffet every night. He stiffened as he registered the hint of sly amusement on her face. How dare she enjoy his discomfiture? She had no idea how difficult his marital duties had been. He caught the echo of his own thoughts. Of course she had no idea. She couldn't know that sex had become something to be avoided, something so foreign to his nature that for years he'd struggled to even maintain an erection.

"Monsieur?"

The amusement in Helene's blue eyes had faded, replaced by concern. Philip inhaled sharply, and her scent invaded his nostrils, a subtle blend of lavender and roses.

"Shall we proceed? The buffet seems to be more than adequate."

"Of course, my lord. I want to take you to the next floor now."

He glanced at the open double doors. "There really is more?"

"There are two more floors that are open to clients and not their guests, unless I personally approve them."

He averted his gaze from one of the naked women, who was beckoning to him, and fixed it on the stairs. A tall well-built footman standing by the newel post nodded to them as they passed.

"Good evening, madame." The redheaded freckled man had a thick Irish brogue.

"Good evening, Sean. I'd like to introduce you to Lord Knowles. As of now, he has entrée into all parts of the establishment, including back stairs."

Sean stared at Philip for a long time as if memorizing his face and then nodded. "Aye, madame. I'll tell me brother."

Helene nodded. "Any trouble this evening?"

"None, madame."

Helene smiled graciously as he bowed his head. Philip found himself nodding too.

"Is Sean placed there to prevent unauthorized persons from going upstairs?"

"Indeed he is. His brother Liam is just over there by the wall."

Philip observed the other hulking figure and could only admire Helene's security. Not many men would get by the two Irish brothers without a fight. They reached the second landing, and Philip looked around him curiously. The hallway looked remarkably like the one below. White paneling, thick pink carpet, and a distinct lack of noise. More doors led off it, and the salon at the end appeared smaller.

"This floor is for our more discerning patrons. Usually they reserve a room in advance with specific requests about what items they wish placed in it."

"Such as?"

Helene smiled. "Perhaps it would be better if I showed you one of the rooms that is already set up."

Philip found he was holding his breath as she slowly unlocked a door with the number ten on it. To his surprise, the room looked quite normal. Kindling lay ready to light in the grate, the large bed was covered in cream silk sheets, and the rest of the décor appeared quite ordinary.

He shrugged. "It all looks perfectly respectable to me."

"It is respectable." Helene walked across to the bed, and he followed, reluctantly admiring the swing of her hips and the way her silk dress outlined the long line of her thigh every time she took a step. She picked up an item that had been placed on the silk counterpane and showed it to him.

"Why would these people ask for golden ropes?" Philip swallowed hard, his throat suddenly dry.

"To tie each other up?"

Helene let the thin gilded cords swing in her hand. Philip couldn't take his eyes off them. He imagined being tied to the bed or the wall like the man he'd witnessed the day before, having to allow sexual acts to be performed on him, having no ability to say no. His cock twitched and thickened in his breeches.

"What if a person didn't wish to be tied up?"

"Then they probably wouldn't ask for these, would they?"

Helene put the ropes back on the bed and carefully straightened them before moving to one of the large cream-painted cupboards against the far wall. She opened the doors, and Philip struggled to breathe. Inside the closet was a selection of whips, floggers, cuffs, and other items he didn't want to identify.

"Of course, if they get bored with their chosen scenario, there are plenty of other toys to choose from."

He licked his dry lips as memories of his time in India flooded through him, memories he thought he'd forgotten. The smell of spices and sex, his oiled body writhing between two women as they pleasured his cock and his mouth . . .

He turned to face the door. "Are all the rooms on this floor like this?"

"Most of them. There are two public salons, as well, for clients to meet in if they choose. There is also a network of peepholes and narrow passages between the rooms for those who simply like to watch."

"And you allow that?"

She shrugged, the gesture making the puffed sleeve of her blue gown slide down over her shoulder. "The choice is made by the people in the rooms. They decide whether to open the peepholes or not."

Philip stared at her. If he had known of this place during the long barren years of his marriage, would he have come here and indulged himself? He'd avoided exploring his sexual options because of his fear of what Anne might do to the children if she heard any gossip about him. The idea of watching other couples fucking rather than participating himself might have saved his sanity.

He shrugged. "I can't say that any of this excites me particularly."

Helene closed the cupboard doors and hesitated, her hand on the ornate paneling.

"There is one other special room, but I'm not sure you will appreciate it."

"I thought you agreed to show me everything."

She sighed. "I did, but . . ."

"Show me." He marched across to the exit and opened the door. "I'm not a child who needs to be protected."

She followed him out of the room and headed for the far end of the hallway. At the end of the corridor, a green door read PRIVATE. He tried to open it and found it locked.

Helene brushed past him, her scent overwhelming his already aroused senses.

"Not that one. That leads down the back stairs to the staff and servants' quarters. Everyone who works here has a key. I'll give you one tomorrow." She gestured to her left. "This is the door I meant."

Philip studied the door. It looked exactly the same as all the others. A small white plaque on it read ALL YOU DESIRE.

"What is so special about this room?"

Helene leaned against the wall and lifted her dainty chin to look up into his face.

"It is different in that it is a place to express your deepest sexual desires."

"Isn't the rest of this bawdy house enough?"

"For some people, no. In the privacy of this room, you can share a secret sexual desire that might not be acceptable to your lover, or your wife, or even perhaps to yourself."

"So?"

"So the pleasure house will try and fulfill your request in the anonymity of that darkened room. You might not ever know the identity of the person who provides the service for you. It is a way of trying out a new facet of your sexual personality in a safe and discreet environment."

Philip folded his arms and leaned back against the other wall. "I still don't understand why anyone who pays to enjoy this salacious place would suddenly become too shy to express their sexual desires openly."

"Perhaps they just wish to try something once or experiment without hurting a loved one." She smiled. "Or perhaps it is something that is not considered at all respectable."

"Like what?"

She shrugged. "Kissing a member of their own sex? Trying anal play?"

He simply stared at her as all his blood deserted his brain for his cock.

"Those things are sinful."

"So?"

"You are an amoral, wicked woman."

She didn't even blink. "Yes, I suppose I am."

He straightened away from the wall. "I would prefer to see the rest of the pleasure house tomorrow."

Her gaze dropped to his tented breeches, and he fought an urge to grab her hand and press it to his throbbing cock.

"Then perhaps you would like to escort me back to my private suite?"

11

Helene watched a series of conflicting emotions flow across Philip's face. Despite his arousal, he was obviously not the sort of man to be led by his cock. In truth, he seemed to fight any signs that he was a normal hot-blooded male. For the first time, Helene considered his marriage. Had he been happy? Was his disaffection with sex because he'd been so much in love with his wife that he couldn't bear the thought of touching another woman? Her normal instincts about men seemed to have deserted her.

"My lord, do you wish to accompany me?"

He nodded and turned abruptly on his heel. She touched his arm and he shuddered.

"We don't need to go back through the salons. We can use the servants' stairs; it is much quicker."

She felt the heat of his uneven breathing on the exposed nape of her neck while she unlocked the door. Had she pushed him too far? And how would he react if she had? She hadn't seen him for eighteen years and had hardly known him even then. He followed her down the steep uncarpeted stairs, the barren decor a stark contrast to the luxury of the pleasure house. She always loved escaping into that world, the place where her hard work and organization made everything happen.

Eventually they arrived at her suite. She murmured a cheerful greeting to the footman stationed outside her door and a dismissal to her maid within. She left the door open for Philip, and he followed her inside. What would he make of her inner sanctum, the place that was hers alone? The color palette was neutral. A harmonious mix of cream white and gold in a simple style that soothed her at the end of her hectic days.

He paused in the center of the room, his hands fisted at his sides. "This is not what I expected at all."

"It is not?"

She draped her shawl over a chair and kicked off her high-heeled slippers, giving her toes some much-needed relief.

"I imagined it would be more . . ."

"Crude, tasteless, and sinful?"

He frowned. "I was going to say *colorful*, but any of the above words will do quite as well."

Ah, so despite his raging erection, he was back to being stuffy again. Somehow that made it far easier for Helene to deal with him. She strolled across to him, watched him tense as if for flight.

"Could you undo my gown for me? I can't reach the ties." She turned her back on him and stood still. It took only a moment for him to start on the task. His fingers shook like a virgin's whenever they brushed her revealed flesh. Helene fought a smile. Whatever had happened to him in the past, his sexual future was hers—at least for the next thirty days.

"It is done."

"*Merci.*"

She slowly turned to face him and allowed the bodice of her dress to fall to her waist. His heated gaze followed the downward slide of the silk. With a deliberate shimmy, Helene allowed the dress to drop to the thick carpet and stepped out of it. She wasn't particularly vain, but she knew she looked well for her age, her skin firm, her breasts plump and rounded, her derriere tight.

Philip licked his lips as she ran her hands over her corset and sighed. Her breasts were almost fully exposed and were lifted by the design of the shift to look as if they were cupped by a man's hands. The shift beneath her corset was fine lawn and did little to hide her skin or the fair hair at the juncture of her thighs. Blue ribbons held up her stocking just above her knee.

She let out her breath with exaggerated care. "I hate wearing a corset. They are so restrictive." She plucked at the strings. "Men do not know how lucky they are not having to follow such absurd fashions."

Without speaking, Philip spun her around and unlaced the corset, letting it fall to the ground. Helene stepped out of it, turned away from him, and went to her dressing table. She sat down, raised her arms and began to take the pins out of her hair. In recent years, many women had adopted shorter, more fashionable hairstyles, but Helene believed most men preferred a woman to have long hair.

She watched in her mirror as Philip took two halting steps toward her. Even if he didn't realize it yet, every time he returned to her side was an admission of his sexual interest and of his needs. She picked up her silver-backed hairbrush.

"Would you like to brush my hair for me?"

"Why?"

She looked over her shoulder at him. "Because my maid has left, and it is hard to see the tangles at the back when I do it myself."

He held out his hand, and she gave him the brush. She loved having her hair combed. It made her feel like a child again, made her remember her mother in a kinder light than her last memories of their days in the Bastille.

"Mmm . . . that's nice."

Philip still didn't speak. His gaze was directed downward, his hands steady as he parted her hair and carefully brushed from the roots to the ends.

She tried to catch his eye in the mirror. "You are good at this. Did you brush your wife's hair?"

He went still, and the bristles stuck in her hair, jerking her head back. Ah, things had definitely been awry between him and his wife.

"No." He put the brush on her dressing table and placed his hands on her shoulders. "Now enough of this posturing. I want you to suck my cock."

She met his angry stare in the mirror. "If you don't take your hands off me, I will scream."

"I'm sure your footman's heard you scream before. I'll wager he doesn't burst in here every time you have sex."

She held his gaze. "Take your hands off me, or you will find out whether he knows the difference. Jem is a champion boxer. I can assure you your encounter will not be pleasant."

"You asked me to accompany you to your suite." He released her and stepped back, thrusting his hands in his pockets.

Helene swiveled on the low stool to face him. "That is true, but I didn't agree to touch you, did I?"

A hint of angry red flushed his cheeks. "You owe me thirty nights of sex."

Helene allowed her hand to slide from her throat to the swell of her breasts, and toyed with the lace ribbon of her shift. His heated gaze followed her fingers.

"Your first *day* is tomorrow. And night follows day, *n'est-ce pas?*"

"So why did you ask me in here?"

She opened her eyes wide at him. "I simply asked you to escort me to my suite, did I not?"

A muscle flicked in his cheek and he bowed. "I can only

apologize for my error, madame. You must forgive me. A country bumpkin like myself didn't realize that when an experienced woman who runs a brothel invites a man into her bedroom and he helps her out of most of her clothes, she is not actually offering to have sex with him."

She offered him her most enthusiastic smile and clasped her hands to her breasts. "That's exactly right, my lord. I'm so glad you see the error of your ways."

He glared at her and headed for the door. "I'll be on my way, then."

She waited until he almost reached the door. "My lord?"

"What is it now?" He turned reluctantly as she got to her feet.

"Could you possibly open that drawer beside my bed and take out the things inside?"

He slowly exhaled. "Why can't you get them yourself?"

"But you are closer, my lord." She fluttered her eyelashes at him. "You do not need to bring them to me. Just place them on the bed."

"Oh, for God's sake . . ."

He yanked open the drawer with such force that the contents ended up on the carpet. Helene kept smiling as he bent to pick them up. Her book of erotic sexual positions had fallen open, so he couldn't fail to see what she read before she went to bed. Her thick pink marble diletto looked awkward in his big hands. She imagined him using it on her and found the idea strangely arousing.

"Just put them on the bed, my lord." He obeyed her, his face impassive, his hands steady. She blew him an airy kiss. "Good night, and remember I'll expect to see you at six in the morning. Meet me in the kitchen."

"Good night, madame, and good riddance."

His final words were muttered under his breath as he

marched toward the door and slammed it shut behind him. Helene let out her breath. Baiting him was a dangerous game, but she needed to test his limits, find his weaknesses, and work on them to send him packing. She had learned one thing: His marriage had been difficult. She scolded herself for the small twinge of satisfaction that thought gave her.

With a sigh, she wandered over to her bed and picked up her book to study the complicated sexual position portrayed in the engraving. What a shame it involved two women. Philip would never agree to that. In the past, if his interests hadn't changed, he'd been more interested in men. Helene closed the book with a snap. That was definitely something to consider in her campaign to oust him from her business.

Tomorrow night would belong to Philip. How would he repay her for her deliberate attempts to rile him? Anticipation rose in her and she smiled. At least she couldn't complain that she was bored.

Philip escaped down the hallway and then realized he had no idea where to go next. His cock and balls ached so badly that he wanted to scream. Damn Helene for playing games with him, and damn that ridiculous agreement he'd made. He should've just put her flat on her back and fucked her the moment he'd gotten into her room.

"Can I help you, sir?"

He stared into the face of Sean, the Irish footman he'd met earlier.

"I'm fine, thank you, but I'm still a bit uncertain of the layout of the house. How does one get to the peepholes on the second level? Madame was going to show me them but had to retire."

There was no flicker of surprise in Sean's gaze or any hint of condemnation.

"That's easy, sir. Take the back stairs up to the next floor, and look for a white door in the middle of the hallway that doesn't have a number on it. That's where you enter the passages, sir."

"Thank you, Sean."

"You are welcome, sir. Have a good evening."

Philip found his way up the stairs and emerged into the silent corridor, his heart thumping hard, his cock now painfully engorged. After a quick look around, he opened the unmarked door and slipped inside. Despite his fears, the narrow passageway was well lit and high enough to let him stand upright. He also noticed that above each peephole was the number of the corresponding room beyond. How efficient, how just like Helene.

He pictured her creamy skin, the moment when he'd revealed her corset and the hard pink tips of her nipples thrust through the lace. Despite all their years apart, he still wanted her. With a stifled groan, he made his way along to the peephole marked number ten. It was open and he leaned forward, trying to adjust to the new view of the room and the two people on the bed.

The golden ropes tied a naked, dark-haired woman to the bed by the wrists and the ankles, her legs spread wide. A man dressed in elegant gray evening attire stood over her, his gloved hands busy caressing her flesh as she writhed against the bonds. Philip swallowed hard as the man shifted his position, allowing Philip an excellent view of the woman's sex.

Philip rested his brow against the wall and ripped open his breeches. His shirt and underthings were soaked with precum, his balls high and tight against the base of his swollen shaft. The man in the room also unbuttoned his breeches and knelt between the woman's legs.

Philip held his breath as the man slid his hands under the woman's buttocks and began to fuck her. Philip worked his own cock into their rhythm, matched the man's grunts and groans with his own. After about ten hard strokes, Philip came. The man on the bed continued to move, lifting the woman into his thrusts, his buttocks tightening and relaxing with each forward motion.

Despite having come, Philip kept his hand wrapped around his cock and continued to watch. Had they heard him vicariously sharing their pleasure? Had the thought that someone watched them excited them? Or perhaps they didn't care, too engrossed in each other to notice anything other than the delights of the flesh.

The man groaned, went still, and collapsed over the bound woman. She kissed the side of his neck and nuzzled his ear as he shuddered and writhed against her. Slowly Philip withdrew his hand from his breeches and took out his handkerchief to wipe the evidence of his lonely passion from his fingers. How pathetic was he? Reduced to watching complete strangers couple to reach sexual completion. No wonder Helene found him so amusing. With her vast sexual experience, his humiliating lack of practice must be all too obvious.

Philip shoved the handkerchief down the front of his breeches and roughly cleaned himself. Despite his efforts, his damp buckskin breeches would cling to his shaft, showing all the other guests at the pleasure house exactly how he had enjoyed himself. Not that he cared what they thought of him. He cared only that he'd allowed Helene to raise his sexual passions to such a height that he had to find release or die.

As he rebuttoned his breeches and slowly straightened, he couldn't resist one last glimpse through the peephole. The man lay tied to the bed now, his cock already erect, and the woman straddled his chest. Philip felt an answering twinge in his own shaft and forced himself to step away. Pleasuring himself once showed a severe lack of self-discipline. Twice would make him as depraved as the others who flocked to fuck here.

As he made his way back to the door, he thought about Helene. Wondered if she was reading her salacious book and plea-suring herself with that monstrous dildo. His cock hardened in a single rush. Damnation, he was beginning to feel like his fifteen-year-old self again, constantly erect, terrified that his parents and schoolmates would notice and laugh at him. Despite the abrupt nature of his dismissal from England that year, he'd been almost relieved when his father had sent him overseas. At least in India, he'd been able to understand and deal with his bud-ding sexuality.

He paused to readjust his damp breeches. He'd wager he was the only man leaving the pleasure house with a still-hard cock. Helene wouldn't be happy about that at all. He slammed his hand against the panel and pushed the exit door wide, no longer caring if anyone saw him. How dare she be so comfort-able with her brazenly sexual nature? Surely she should have some shame or remorse for the path she had chosen?

Philip consoled himself with the thought that his next night would be spent in Helene's bed. Perhaps it was time to turn the tables on her, tie her to the bed and do what he wanted to her. He smiled at the salacious thought as he descended the main staircase and waited for a footman to retrieve his hat and gloves. The ornate clock chimed once and he winced. He had only five hours before Helene expected to see him again, and he was al-ready drained. He still had letters to write to explain his contin-ued absence from the estate and his children.

He tipped his hat to the butler and stepped out into the light drizzle. His rented house wasn't that far from the pleasure house, so he decided to walk. Strangely enough, the thought of returning to win a wager against Helene was far more invigo-rating than delving into the complex administration of his new position. He had a lifetime to acquaint himself with Sudbury Court and its tenants and only thirty days with Helene to sort out . . .

He paused at the curb to look both ways and then took a

shortcut across the square. What *did* he need to sort out with Helene? A woman from his past, a woman so far removed from him socially that to be seen in her company would subject him to the kind of gossip and innuendo he'd striven so hard to avoid during his marriage?

Soft rain gusted into his face, and he licked his lips. He'd lost himself somewhere. After his carefree existence in India and his weekend with Helene, something had gone terribly wrong. Was he a fool to believe he was redeemable? He jammed his hat down on his head. Thirty days with Helene was the perfect opportunity to find out.

12

Philip checked his pocket watch as he clattered down the slippery stone steps into the basement of Helene's house. The outer door stood slightly ajar, so he squeezed past the stacked baskets of fresh produce and five live hens in a flimsy wire cage. He hadn't anticipated his journey would take so long. To his amazement, even at this unlikely hour of the morning, the streets had been packed with tradesmen, farmers, milkmaids, and assorted children running around to God knew where.

The narrow hallway contained a coal hole, a door marked CELLAR, a laundry room, and another door, which he opened. A warm blast of air laced with the delicious scent of baking bread hit him in the face, and he slowly inhaled.

"Ah, there you are, Philip."

He blinked and looked around the large busy space. Since when had he given Helene permission to call him by his given name? A rotund woman, whom he assumed must be the cook, stood guard over the range. Two maids swept the floor and a third sat at the pine table. He stared again at the woman seated at the table. It was hard to recognize the fashionably dressed social butterfly of a few hours earlier. Helene's blond hair was covered by a plain lace cap. Her spectacles were set firmly on her nose. Even he recognized that her dress was at least ten years out of fashion.

"Madame Helene?"

She nodded and gestured for him to join her. He took off his hat and gloves and laid them on the bench beside him before taking the seat opposite her. Helene's hands clasped a thick earthenware bowl filled with chocolate; beside her lay a plate on which resided the remains of a chocolate croissant.

"Would you like some breakfast, Philip?"

"If we have time, madame; I am already late, and I would not want to keep you waiting."

She shrugged and sipped at her chocolate. "I haven't finished yet myself."

She turned to speak to the cook in rapid French. He watched, fascinated, as her tongue darted out to lick a drip of chocolate from her lower lip. Just like that, he was hard again, wishing her mouth would lick other things, wondering about the night they would share together if he survived his first day.

The cook placed a croissant in front of him, followed by a bowl of chocolate. He smiled at the cook, who didn't smile back.

"Thank you."

Helene watched as he took a mouthful of warm flaky pastry and slowly chewed.

"Madame Dubois makes the best croissants in England."

He nodded his agreement, too intent on eating to worry about his manners. Another croissant appeared, and he ate that one too. By the time he was finished, Helene was on her feet and tying an apron around her waist. Philip rose, too, and put his bowl and plate in the sink.

She looked up at him. "Are you ready?"

He shrugged. "As ready as I'll ever be."

"*Bon*, then we will proceed."

He followed her out a different exit, which took them into the main part of the building. She started up the stairs, and he followed her, pausing to catch his breath as they moved inexorably upward. On the final landing she paused, waiting for him to catch up. He struggled to breathe normally.

"What exactly are we doing, and why are you dressed as a servant?"

She regarded him seriously, her blue eyes huge behind her spectacles.

"I like to walk through all the rooms of the pleasure house every morning. It gives me a sense of how things are and what needs to be improved."

"You do this every day?"

"Of course."

"And why do you dress like this?"

"Most of my clients don't see servants, unless they want something, so for all intents and purposes, I can remain invisible if I happen to bump into someone. And, occasionally, I can discreetly aid any client who has forgotten to leave." She paused and laid her hand on his arm. "I didn't show you the third floor yesterday evening. It is the most extreme of the floors and not for the faint of heart. Perhaps you should wait here."

He pointedly removed her fingers from his sleeve. "As I said before, madame, I wish to see everything this place has to offer, not just the parts you deem suitable. I'm perfectly capable of dealing with anything you dare to show me."

She sighed. "Then if you wish to accompany me, I must have your word of honor that nothing you see or hear on this floor will ever be divulged to anyone outside this establishment."

He tried to see her face more clearly in the gloom and failed. What on earth was she hiding from him? His stomach clenched, whether in fear or anticipation he couldn't tell.

"I give you my word."

Helene opened the door and stepped into a narrow corridor lined with black-painted doors. Candle sconces lined the uneven walls; spoiled red wax had dripped and hardened on the bare wooden floor.

"What is in these rooms?" he whispered.

"The most extreme of sexual delights or your worst nightmares, depending on who you are."

"Can we look?"

Helene gave him a considering stare. "We are here to make sure that everything is running smoothly with our business, *non*? It is our responsibility to make sure that everything is in place." She slowly opened the first door.

Philip leaned in to get a closer look and then recoiled. "Good God, is that a rack?"

Helene moved across the small space and opened the black curtains and the window. A thin stream of light illuminated the unmade bed, red silk sheets tangled around a long-handled whip. The scent of blood and raw sex made Philip feel nauseous. The chains that dangled from the top of the upright wooden rack swung gently in the draught.

Helene walked back across to him. "The cleaning staff will remake the bed and will clean and put away any of the toys the clients played with. I just check each room every morning to make sure no one has been left chained or tied to the racks or the beds."

Philip gripped the doorframe. "How can you be so matter-of-fact about such inhuman acts?" He gestured at the rack. "Someone has obviously been brutalized, and yet you not only allow it on your premises but you also seem to condone it." He shoved away from the door. "I do not understand you."

She followed him out into the hall and left him fuming as she methodically checked the other three rooms, writing notes as she went. When she closed the fourth door, he grabbed her elbow.

"Are you going to answer me?"

"What do you want me to say? You have already judged and condemned me. Why don't you leave and save yourself from any further contamination?"

"I want to know why you allow this."

"Because there are some men and women who crave such excesses in their lives. Some of them can only function sexually if they are submissive or if they can dominate someone else. Surely you know this? You went to boarding school, didn't you?"

"But this is supposed to be a house of pleasure, not pain."

She met his gaze, her eyes calm and steady. "But what is painful to you might be pleasurable to another. You must remember that no one here is forced to do anything they do not want."

"I find that hard to believe. How many of your staff are coerced into indecent acts because they fear dismissal?"

"None, as far as I know. And if you doubt me, please ask them. They are free to say no to anyone here."

"Even you?"

Her blue eyes flashed fire. "I don't sleep with my staff."

"Apart from me, you mean."

She stepped away from him, her expression chilly. "That is an unfortunate consequence of our wager and has nothing to do with how I normally conduct my business."

He bowed elaborately. "If you insist, madame."

She swung around to glare at him. "I do, my lord. Now if you have finished lecturing me, perhaps we might get on?"

"Of course, madame."

He followed her down the short corridor into a larger open space and abruptly stopped. The walls were painted black and covered with an unthinkable display of floggers, whips, chains, masks, and other degrading paraphernalia. He swallowed hard as his gaze traveled around the room. The two beds were empty, the floor beneath his feet sticky with substances he didn't care to examine. Helene moved ahead of him, picking up discarded whips and toys and restoring them to their rightful place on the wall.

Suddenly she straightened, her hands on her hips. "Anthony, not you again!"

She disappeared into the second room, and Philip cautiously followed. She was in the corner kneeling on the floor, skirts spread around her as she murmured to someone or something in front of her. An answering masculine groan had him moving forward to look over her shoulder.

A man lay on the floor, his head in Helene's lap, his eyes closed, face bruised. Helene was busy removing the chains from his wrists as she muttered to him in rapid French.

She turned to look up at Philip. "Can you find his clothes? They should be nearby."

Philip took a quick survey of the room and saw a mound of clothing flung carelessly on the seat of a wooden chair. He picked up the garments, noticed the fine lawn and the exquisite cut of the breeches. This was no wounded servant but a gentleman. He took the pile back to Helene. The young man was sitting up now, his expression rueful, his swollen mouth half-laughing.

Philip dropped the clothes to the ground and stood back as Helene helped the man pull his shirt over his head and step into his breeches. She continued to talk to him, her tone affectionate and motherly, her expression concerned.

At last the man stood up and stretched. "I'm fine, madame. Really I am. I just fell asleep."

Philip cleared his throat. "Did someone hurt you?"

Anthony looked curiously at him. "What is it to you?"

"Because I believe madame underestimates the amount of coercion that goes on in a place such as this. I cannot believe that a young gentleman like yourself would willingly participate in such perversions."

Anthony's faint smile disappeared. "Then let me set your mind at ease, sir. I was not coerced, and I willingly—nay, happily—engage in perversion. Are you satisfied now?" He bowed to Philip and kissed Helene's hand. "Thank you for waking me up. I'll see you this evening."

Philip watched the young man leave and turned to find Helene watching him.

"Are you satisfied now?"

"That he was not forced?" He shrugged. "I cannot continue to believe what he denies, can I?"

Helene picked up the manacles that had bound Anthony's wrists and laid them over the back of a chair.

"In truth, he worries me. I find him up here far too often. I am beginning to wonder why he seeks such painful ways to relieve himself."

Philip stared at her. "Are you saying I'm right?"

"*Non.* Just that Anthony is seeking the wrong things for the wrong reasons and that it will not end well."

"All the more reason to shut down this level of the house."

"Is that what you would do if you owned this place?"

"Absolutely."

"And then where would people like Anthony go? Probably some place where no one looked out for them, where they might be abused or killed. Is that any better?"

Philip tried to muster his arguments but found it hard to do so when faced by Helene at her magnificent, indignant best. He looked around the room at the discarded whips, smelled the blood and the heavy scent of sex.

"I cannot see pleasure here."

Helene came to stand in front of him and slowly backed him up against the wall.

"Are you sure about that?"

She gripped his wrists with both of her hands. "Imagine being naked and manacled to this wall. Imagine being blindfolded and not knowing who will touch you, how they will touch you, and whether you will like it or not."

He shuddered as she stood on tiptoe and kissed his chin. "Imagine hands on your flesh, making you hard, making you want—"

"I would not want . . . that." He swallowed hard as his cock thickened.

"Are you sure, Philip?" God, her voice was so seductive. "How can you say so unless you have tried it?"

He forced his eyes open and pushed her away as his memories threatened to overwhelm him. "I can assure you I would not enjoy sex with pain."

She studied him, her expression calm. "Perhaps I should explain that it is a condition of our agreement that you experience everything the pleasure house has to offer."

"I did not agree to that."

She raised her chin. "You are too afraid?"

Of course he was and, by God, he had every right to be. What the hell could he say to her to get her off this subject? There was no way he could allow another stranger to dictate to him sexually. He couldn't tell her that—couldn't let her know he feared losing sexual control more than he feared losing his life. He focused his attention on her face, refused to look at the instruments of diabolical pleasure around him.

"What if it was me?"

He swallowed. "I beg your pardon?"

"What if it was only me who played with you?" Her eyes were sharp, as if she could see right through to his fear.

"Why would that make any difference?"

"Because you could trust me not to hurt you?"

"You can't trust anyone not to hurt you."

"That is true. Perhaps we will discuss your participation

here when we have more time." She turned away from him and replaced the manacles on a hook on the wall. "We need to move on."

Philip remained by the wall, his breathing uneven, his mind struggling to deal with the memories she'd forced him to recall. Why had she stopped pressing him? Had she realized the depth of his aversion? It was hardly surprising; he hadn't exactly hidden it well.

Helene took one last look around the room, wrote another note in her book, and went back to the landing. Silently, Philip followed her, his boot heels echoing hollowly on the wooden stairs as he hurried to catch up. The more familiar lushness of the floor below was almost comforting after the starkness above. Even the air smelled better, fresher, less laden down with suffering and sex.

Helene was already working her way through the first of the small salons, setting things to right, retrieving lost garments, opening windows and drapes. Philip watched her, amazed at the deftness of her touch and the fluidity of her motions. How unlike the languid hostess of the evening before. Which was the real Helene? He wasn't quite sure anymore.

After they finished the last public floor, Helene waited for him at the bottom of the main staircase, a sheaf of notes in her hand. The clock struck eight times. Philip couldn't believe he'd already spent two hours at the pleasure house.

She glanced up at him. "It is time to meet the rest of the staff. Please come along."

She headed toward the back of the house, and Philip dutifully followed, feeling very much as he had when ordered around by his governess. Helene opened a door and was greeted by a chorus of "good mornings." To Philip's surprise, there were at least fifty people in the room, including the butler, the cook, and the scullery maids. Philip tried to slip in unobtrusively behind Helene, but she caught his elbow.

"This is Mr. Philip. He will be accompanying me around the pleasure house for the next month. If he has questions or tasks for you, please help him to the best of your ability."

He nodded at the murmured greetings and leaned back against the wall, for once happy to allow Helene center stage.

She consulted her notes and cleared her throat. "There are several areas that need to be cleaned more thoroughly, particularly the third level. Are we short of staff?"

Judd, the butler, stood up. "We are, madame. Two of our regulars are away caring for sick relatives."

"Do we know when they will return?"

"I cannot say, madame."

Helene sighed and took off her spectacles. "Please make sure the staff members receive their wages and something extra to help with the doctor's bills. If anyone is willing to work upstairs for as long as needed, I will offer a bonus."

Several hands went up, and she nodded. "Please see Mr. Judd if you are interested, and thank you."

Philip almost forgot his annoyance as he listened to Helene alternately praise and gently chastise her staff. He'd expected her to be more demanding, more like the typical madame of a brothel insisting her workers increase her revenues, but she wasn't like that at all. Her staff seemed to appreciate her as well. Staring at each face in turn, he hadn't seen any signs of discontent or heard any muttering. Everyone seemed happy to work for her. It made no sense. His wife had had terrible trouble keeping staff at their house, but that might have been because she was so difficult to please.

When the meeting ended, he followed Helene back to her office and waited while she sat at her desk and transferred the contents of her notebook to her daily journal.

"How is it that you don't expect your staff to create money-making opportunities for you?"

She looked up at him. "What do you mean?"

He sat down, crossed his legs, and leaned back in the seat. "I'm sure you know. Most brothels offer 'extra services' for a price."

She sighed. "I've already told you. This is not a brothel. Every sexual service my clients desire is provided for nothing."

"So you say, but nothing is really free, is it?"

Her smile was complacent, which irritated him immensely. "That is correct. My members pay a significant fee to enjoy all the activities I offer."

He raised his eyebrows. "How significant?"

"There is an entrance fee of thirty-five guineas and an annual subscription of twenty guineas."

Philip stared at her. "Are you serious? It costs only twenty guineas to become a member of White's, and their annual subscription is eleven!"

She looked interested. "Is that so? I'm surprised they charge so little."

"And how many members do you currently have?"

She shrugged. "About one hundred and fifty, I believe. I can show you last year's accounts if you care to see them."

Mentally Philip tried to calculate how much income Helene was generating from her business. After seeing the amount deposited in his new bank account last month, he should've guessed she was doing rather well. The figures made him dizzy. She certainly didn't need a man to support her at all.

"You have done very well for yourself."

She arched an eyebrow. "You make that sound like an insult."

"Well you can hardly expect me to applaud you making money from such perversions, can you?"

Her smile was calm. "I make money by satisfying rich aristocrats' fantasies. They are not necessarily *my* perversions."

"But you provide them."

"I provide a unique service. My clients trust my discretion, my high prices keep the club small and discreet, and I offer anything a man or woman could desire. What is wrong with that?"

Philip stood up. "Nothing, if you have no morals."

Helene got to her feet, too, her cheeks flushing. "I have morals. This is a business, not a statement of my beliefs." She wagged her finger in his face. "And I also offer my staff an opportunity to indulge in their sexual fantasies too. Don't forget that."

He bowed. "Of course, I'd forgotten what a philanthropist you are. The rich pay for the poor man's pleasure as well—how liberal of you."

She glared at him, her breasts rising and falling with each agitated breath. "I'd forgotten what a prude you have become. What happened to the man who learned about unchristian erotic acts in India?"

"He died, madame, along with his youth the day he got married." He headed for the door, desperate to get away from her before he said anything even more incriminating. "I'll be in the kitchen, if you need me."

13

Helene checked the time; it was past midnight and the salons were packed with her clients. Despite Philip's forbidding presence at her elbow all night, things had gone rather well. She'd taken the opportunity to flirt outrageously with every man who approached her, just to see Philip's scowl deepen.

When faced with the dubious delights of the third floor that morning, she'd thought he was going to run. But he'd managed to stand his ground. Although part of her was disappointed, her curiosity was stirred. Beneath that harsh exterior was a man who had suffered. Something deep inside her responded to that and wanted to help him. What had happened to make him fear loss of sexual control? What exactly had his marriage been like?

She blew a last lingering kiss to young Lord Blake and turned to Philip, who was scowling. "Are you ready to go?" She yawned behind her fan. "I believe I am quite fatigued."

He bowed and took her hand. "Then we shall take our leave." He walked toward the main doors and glanced down at her. "We are retiring together tonight?"

She smiled up at him. "Of course. I don't break my promises."

They arrived at her suite, and he shut the door behind him, his expression inscrutable. Helene turned to face him, realizing she was slightly nervous but also excited.

"What do you wish of me, my lord?"

"I want you to undress."

"Of course, my lord." She kicked off her soft kid slippers and presented him with her back. "If you could unlace me?"

He obliged, his fingers steady and nimble as he undid both her bodice and her corset. She pushed them down over her hips and stepped out of her single petticoat.

"Sit down on the stool and take off your stockings."

She raised her eyebrows. "My shift as well?"

"Just your stockings."

She took her time rolling the delicate silk stocking down over her calf and placing it on her dressing table. Philip retreated to the door, arms folded, gaze fixed on her legs. She finished with the second stocking and put it with the first.

"And now, my lord? Would you like me to undress you?"

He shook his head and walked toward her. "No, thank you, madame. Now I wish you to sit on the side of the bed."

"Like this?"

Helene arranged herself on the edge of the high wide bed, her legs slightly parted, her hands braced on the cream satin sheets.

He came even closer. "Open your legs wider and pull up your shift. I want to see you."

She held his gaze, aware that he was trying to objectify her, make something pleasurable into something she should be ashamed of. He had no idea that she was enjoying herself immensely. It was a long time since any man had told her what to do.

"Like this?"

She slowly raised her shift and felt the cold air against her most tender flesh. Her nipples tightened as he continued to stare at her sex.

"Touch yourself."

"Where, my lord?"

He gestured between her legs. "You know where. I want to see you slide your fingers deep. Touch and rub your nub; make yourself come."

"And what will you be doing while I . . . amuse myself?"

"Watching."

She cupped her breasts, rubbed her thumbs over her already aching nipples. "Do you wish me to touch myself here as well, sir?"

"Yes."

She slid one hand down over her stomach and flicked her already swollen clit. Philip let out his breath, one hand clenched and unclenched at his side. She watched him as she continued her slow exploration, let him see her enjoyment, refused to let him cheapen the experience.

"Put your fingers inside."

He stepped closer as she penetrated herself with two interlocked fingers. She moaned as her cream eased her way, smelled her own desire, and heard the slick wetness of each subtle motion.

"Pinch your nipples, harder."

His voice had gone husky. His tight pantaloons were now tented, and his erection pushed at the thick satin.

She glanced up at him through her lashes. "Don't you want to help, my lord?"

"I want . . . I want you to come."

She increased the thrust of her fingers, used her thumb on her clit, and felt her climax build. She arched her back and drew her feet up onto the bed to give him the perfect view of her sex.

"I'm coming for you."

She closed her eyes and gasped as her pussy clenched around her fingers and heard his answering groan as she writhed against the pleasure. How long was it since she'd focused all her attention on herself rather than on some stupid man? When she opened her eyes, he was still standing in front of her.

"Do you wish me to suck your cock now?"

He shuddered and forced his gaze away from her. "I don't need anything from you."

"Are you sure, my lord?" She slowly withdrew her fingers from her pussy and brought them to her mouth, used the tip of her tongue to clean them. "Because I am more than willing to service you. It is part of our bargain, is it not?"

"I don't need you."

She climbed off the bed and came to stand in front of him. "Why are you denying yourself release? Do you think it makes you better than me?"

"A real man should be able to resist carnal temptation."

"A stupid man, maybe. What I offer you is part of our bargain. Why, after insisting you spend your nights with me, do you refuse what is yours to enjoy?"

He stared at her, his mouth set in a grim line.

Helene's sexual glow began to fade. "Perhaps I begin to understand you. Did you ask for those thirty nights simply to prevent me from having sex with *anyone*?"

"Perhaps I did."

She smiled at him as anger rapidly replaced desire. "Then you will be disappointed." She pointed at the bed. "I can pleasure myself quite adequately, as you just saw, and I feel no shame for it."

He flinched as she reached out and swatted the front of his pantaloons. "You are the one with the inconvenient erection. If I'm not good enough to touch your cock, go and amuse yourself in the pleasure house. I'm sure you'll find somebody there who will oblige you."

"I don't need anyone to touch me."

She turned on her heel and climbed into bed. "That's right. You have a hand, don't you? Or is that too sinful as well? Self-abuse is frowned upon in many circles; I believe they even offer contraptions to stop men from attempting it."

"You'd probably know all about that, wouldn't you?" he sneered.

"*Non*, because here at the pleasure house, sex is seen as a natural and beautiful part of life—not something to be ashamed of or to fear. You are the one with the problem, not me." Helene punched her pillow, took her book from the bedside drawer, and ignored Philip.

He cleared his throat. "I am going now."

"*Bon.*"

"I will be back tomorrow."

"Don't bother."

She hunched her shoulder at him, refusing to meet his gaze. He was truly a stuffy man. Why had she even considered he would be an interesting lover? He'd obviously allowed life to embitter him to such an extent he no longer had the capacity for sexual enjoyment. She could do without sex for thirty days if it meant the end of Philip Ross's involvement in her business.

"I'm not giving up, Helene. I'll be here for the next twenty-nine days as promised."

She looked at him then. "You expect to spend the next month in the most extreme pleasure house in London without succumbing to your desires even once?"

"I'm . . . not sure."

She waved a dismissal. "We'll see, won't we? Now run along. I have a book to read."

"Helene . . ."

"Haven't you gone yet?"

He remained by the door, one hand gripping the frame.

"You are still the most beautiful woman I have ever seen. Good night."

He shut the door quietly, and Helene stared at the cream paneling. How dare he compliment her like that! It made disliking him so much harder. What would he do now? Would he run home or finally face his demons?

Behind him, the door vibrated as if Helene had thrown something at it. Philip tried to smile. At least she'd waited until he shut the door. He retraced his steps to the main servant stairway and found himself unable to go on. Here he was again in the same situation as last night, desperate for release. And this time he had only himself to blame.

He stared into the darkness of the stairwell. Watching Helene climax had been unbearable. He'd meant to humiliate her by keeping his distance, but he'd failed. Her joy in her own sexuality simply made him feel like an empty, useless vessel. God, he'd wanted to rip open his pantaloons and shove his cock deep inside her, make her climax again and again until she screamed out his name.

He cupped his balls and groaned at the heavy weight. Helene was right. If he stood any chance of overcoming his past and taking control of his sexual future, he needed the pleasure house. He needed a place where he could recapture the joy of sex, which had been so depleted by his marriage.

With a sigh, he closed his eyes and allowed his past to overwhelm him. Images of India, his voyage home, and his meeting with Helene flooded his mind. What had his most erotic desire been then? What had he craved that was utterly forbidden? He remembered the servant on the ship, the man's mouth closing around his cock.

He became aware of the hardness of the wall at his back, the happy shrieks and murmurs of Helene's clients even through the heavy doors. He knew where he needed to go and what he needed to do.

A minute later, the door on the second level marked ALL YOU DESIRE was in front of him. With shaking hands, Philip pushed it open and found himself in a small, completely dark space. He couldn't even see his own hand, so he stayed near the door.

"What is your desire?"

The voice was so quiet, Philip barely heard it. He swallowed hard. Could he go through with this? Could he salvage something from his past to help rediscover himself?

"I want a man . . . a man to suck my cock."

His words sounded so loud and shocking in the small space that he almost wished he could take them back.

"Of course, sir. We can accommodate your desire within the next ten minutes. Please move to the room on your left."

Uncertainly, Philip stretched out his left hand, felt a door-jamb, and moved toward it. The second space felt larger than the first, although he still couldn't see more than a foot around him. The wait seemed interminable, his raised heartbeat mirrored by the urgent throb of his cock. Every tense second brought him closer to fleeing, to reneging on his bet and trying to make a life with his children far away from London and the delights of Helene Delornay. But could he run from himself? He'd tried that before and it hadn't worked.

A faint outline of white, the click of a door latch, and the plunge back into darkness snapped his attention back to the present. He jumped when calloused fingers brushed his thigh and started on the buttons of his pantaloons. He fisted his hands at his sides as his cock quivered and gushed precum, soaking his underthings as the man slowly exposed his cock.

"God . . ." His hips jerked forward as his shaft was drawn into a warm, wet mouth. He forgot to think as the man started sucking, shoved his hand in the man's thick hair to hold him just where he wanted him. Within twenty desperate strokes, he was coming hard, fucking the man's mouth with all his strength, shoving his cock as deep as he could as spasm after spasm of seed shot out of him.

"God . . . I'm sorry."

He tried to pull back but felt the man's teeth close gently around the base of his now-flaccid shaft and went still. Smaller sucks now, a tongue curling over the crown of his cock, probing the slit, rimming the head, dipping down to suck his balls and caress the sensitive skin between his arse and his shaft.

His cock grew and filled the other man's mouth again. Only then did the man release him. He kissed the crown and lapped at the gathering fluid.

"You may call me Adam. May I use my hands on you as well?"

The voice was cultured, that of a gentleman, not the servant Philip had unconsciously expected. He might have met this man socially, might meet him yet and never know him. Unaccountably, his cock swelled even more at the thought.

"Yes."

Adam kissed Philip's cock again, swirling it around in his mouth as he cupped Philip's balls.

"Ah . . . that's . . ."

Philip closed his eyes as bliss shuddered through him. Adam's mouth was strong, almost rough, his hands and long fingers caressed Philip's buttocks and thighs, inviting him to drive his cock deeper into Adam's mouth.

Philip tried to stop thrusting. "I don't want to hurt you."

Adam's answer was to take him deeper, suck him harder, dig his fingers into Philip's buttocks and force him to pump as fast as he could. His second climax went on and on, his whole body convulsing in delight as he spent himself in this unknown man's mouth.

"Thank you."

Adam released his cock and gave him one last kiss. "The pleasure was all mine."

Philip cleared his throat. "What about your needs?"

"This room is for secret desires, yes? You like to have a man's mouth on you. I like to take a man in my mouth. We are even."

Adam tucked Philip's cock back into his underthings and buttoned up his pantaloons. "If you wish to see me here again, I would be more than willing to serve you. Just ask for me by name."

Philip had no opportunity to reply as Adam backed out of the room, shutting the door behind him. Philip took a deep breath. His legs were still shaking, his whole body soothed by the outpouring of his seed, the sense that he had spent far more than that. He felt more at peace with himself than he had for years, even though in most people's eyes he had allowed an immoral act. But Helene and all the clients of the pleasure house would not condemn him. They would understand his need to rediscover himself.

He turned back to the door and felt his way back into the main hall, almost collided with a couple kissing against the servant's door. The woman's leg was wrapped high around the man's thigh. Philip edged past and took the hallway back to the main salon and then down to the silent warm kitchen to collect his hat and gloves.

What would Helene think of his adventures? He put on his hat. She probably already knew what he'd done. Nothing in the pleasure house escaped her. He took a last longing look at the stairs leading to the rear of the house. Part of him wanted to go back to Helene and take her to bed. His past experiences made him want to think about what he'd done before he got tangled any deeper in Helene's nets.

Perhaps he wouldn't need to say or explain anything to her. If Helene truly believed all men and women were entitled to experiment with sex until they found their particular pleasure, she should be able to accept him just as he was. He realized he was smiling. It would be interesting to see if she lived by her own rules. So many people didn't.

"He asked me to suck his cock."

"Is that all?"

Captain David Gray shrugged and then smiled at her. "It was enough for me. I enjoyed him immensely."

Helene had been roused from her bed by Judd to deal with Philip's not unexpected request in the room of desires. She'd asked one of her favorite clients, Captain Gray, to respond to Philip's needs and had waited anxiously in her sitting room to hear how things had gone. She smiled at the young naval captain.

"I am glad you enjoyed yourself. Did he?"

"He came twice in my mouth, so I assume so." Captain Gray's smile became more hesitant. "I didn't give him my real name, but I did offer to suck his cock any time he wanted."

Helene squeezed his arm. "I'm pleased to hear it. And there is no need to report back to me if he asks for you again. I respect your privacy."

"Thank you, madame. I hope he does come back." He sighed. "But that is in his hands, not mine."

"I wish I could give you an answer, David, but I, too, am unsure of what he truly desires." She lightly kissed his cheek. "We will both have to wait and see what happens, won't we?"

David bowed and kissed her hand. "Thank you for thinking of me, madame. I promise you my complete discretion in this matter."

He took his leave, and Helene blew out the candles and returned to bed. She would've loved to see Philip with David, knew he wouldn't have been able to cope with her presence at all. She lay back on her pillows and slid her hand between her legs. Was this the extent of his sexual identity? Could he no longer perform with a woman at all? If so, she would be disappointed. Despite her need to be rid of him, she smiled slowly as she imagined Philip fucking her. The next twenty-nine days might prove to be very interesting indeed. . . .

14

_____

"So I keep a personal file on every client, their sexual likes and dislikes, the number of times they visit the house, their special requests . . . Philip, are you listening to me?" Helene glanced across at Philip, who sat beside her at her desk.

He stared at her for a long moment. "I beg your pardon?"

She put down her pen. "I asked if you were listening to me. How do you expect to learn about the pleasure house if you can't even give me your attention for five minutes?"

"I heard what you said."

"I doubt it."

"You said you have a file on every member of the club. Do you have one on me?"

"Not yet. Would you like one?"

His smile was dismissive. "I'm sure you've got plenty of information to put in there already."

She sniffed. "You've only been here five days, Philip. You haven't done anything particularly exciting."

He'd also been entitled to five nights in her bed as well, although since their second night together, he'd escorted her to her suite, kissed her hand, and left. To the best of her knowledge, he hadn't availed himself of any of the pleasure house opportunities either.

He raised his eyebrows. "I have disappointed you?"

"I didn't say that." She smiled kindly. "A man of your age probably needs his rest."

A muscle twitched in his jaw as he stared at her. Helene continued to look innocent. She had no wish to share her concerns with him. If he wanted to turn down the delights of her bed, he was a fool and not worth bothering about. Either his experience with Adam had convinced him that he really preferred men, or the immorality of the place had overwhelmed him and he had decided to retreat again.

"You are not taking our bargain seriously."

He frowned. "I spend all day with you. What else do you want?"

"What about the nights?"

He shrugged. "I take you to your room every night and see you safely into your bed. What more do you want?"

"Nothing at all, my lord. I couldn't be happier."

His smile was slow and full of male satisfaction. "You want me to stay, don't you? You want me to fuck you."

Helene slammed the book shut and put her pen away in the top drawer. "I want you to fulfill all parts of our bargain and escort me to the opening of a new room on the public floor tonight. I would like a man's opinion."

"If that's what you really want—which I doubt—of course I will." He got up and walked over to the window, one hand rubbing the back of his neck. "I'll take an early dinner in the kitchen with Madame Dubois and be ready whenever you want me."

Helene glared at his unprotected head. She held her temper, but only just. She wasn't used to her male lovers speaking to her like that. She'd grown used to being adored. A smile quivered on her lips. He really was proving to be an infuriating man.

"I want to be there for the first viewing, so about eight, then?" He turned to stare at her. "Eight it is."

True to his word, Philip was waiting for her outside the new room. He'd changed into his evening clothes and looked rather severe, the black coat and white pantaloons a perfect match for the austere lines of his face. Helene had put on one of her more daring gowns, a cream and lace confection that barely contained her breasts and clung to the outline of her legs.

His gaze flicked over her and settled on the shadow between her breasts. "If you sneeze, won't that bodice fall down?"

"Of course not. It will catch on my nipples." Helene ran her finger along the dips and curves of the lace to illustrate the point. "I'm unlikely to sneeze in here anyway."

"Let's hope not." He pointed at the door. "The writing on the plaque isn't filled in."

Helene opened the door and stepped inside. "It will be if the room is considered a success tonight. Let's find our seats."

She chose to sit at the back just to the right of the door, and Philip joined her. To her delight, the space was already full. The center stage was filled by a large bed covered in red satin sheets.

Philip nudged her. "Aren't the sheets a little too gaudy? Surely you don't want to create the image of a brothel."

She gazed at him in surprise. "Skin shows up better against the red. But if we really don't like the effect, it can be changed."

A blond-haired man appeared dressed only in his shirt and breeches. He placed a candle at the side of the bed and started to remove his shirt. A woman followed him, clad only in a thin nightgown. She carefully placed her candle on the other side of the bed and came to stand by the man. He started to kiss her, his hands roaming over her buttocks and waist as she strained against him.

A dark-haired man appeared and joined the others, kissing the woman as well, drawing her nightgown over her head to expose her small breasts and the dark hair between her thighs. Helene smiled as the two men focused on the woman, their mouths on her breasts, her lips, and her pussy. This was exactly what she'd asked for, something elegant and sensual, something that built toward a climactic moment.

The woman helped the men remove their clothes, and soon all three of them lay entwined on the bed. Helene glanced at Philip. He seemed engrossed, his attention fixed on the erotic display in front of him. He certainly didn't look like a man who wanted to leave.

The woman lay stretched out on her back, legs spread wide. The blond man on her right lapped at her sex, and the dark-haired man suckled her breasts. Helene felt her own body respond to the luscious scene; her nipples tightened, and cream flooded her sex. She jumped when Philip covered her hand with his and squeezed hard.

On the bed, the second man slid down to the woman's pussy, his tongue tangling with the other man's, their fingers interlocking as they plunged them repeatedly into the woman's sex. Even through her excitement, Helene noted with a connoisseur's eye that both men were angling their bodies to allow the audience the best view of the woman.

The spectators murmured in appreciation as the woman grasped both the men's cocks and started rubbing them. One of the men groaned, and the other kissed him full on the mouth before returning his attention to the woman's clit.

"A true ménage à trois, then." Philip's whisper barely stirred the air beside her ear.

"*Oui.* A lot of the women here are fascinated by the thought of two men together. This scenario allows them to watch and then decide if they wish to take part."

"How far will they go?"

"As far as each involved party wants to. Limits are usually agreed to before they start, although sometimes not adhered to. Some might choose to stop now; other women might want to have sex with both of the men. Some might even prefer to watch the men have sex and not participate at all."

"An interesting room with many varied options, then."

"As you can see."

She smiled into the darkness as the blond man knelt between the woman's thighs and penetrated her with his thick shaft. The dark-haired man moved up the bed and positioned his cock over the woman's mouth.

Suddenly, Philip stood up and pulled her with him, his hand hard on her elbow. No one in the enrapt audience seemed to notice their departure as the woman opened her mouth to admit the man's dripping cock. In the hall, Philip kissed Helene, one hand wrapped around the back of her neck to keep her close. She kissed him back, her body already well on the path of passion, his seductive scent as familiar now as her own.

When he finally released her mouth, it was only to tug on her hand and drag her along the hallway and down the stairs to her suite. He moved so fast that she was panting by the time he closed the door behind him. She backed away until she was standing by her bed.

He took off his coat and waistcoat and threw them on the floor. His eyes were glittering, his mouth harsh. What had happened to change his relaxed attitude? What particular thing had disturbed him? Desperately, Helene tried to think back over the performance they had just witnessed.

"Did you hate that room too?"

He glared at her as his hands moved to his throat. "My wedding night was a disaster. I tried to be gentle; I tried not to frighten her, but Anne was inconsolable. In truth, she was so distraught, I didn't even try to fulfill my marital obligations. I just lay beside her and listened to her weep all damned night."

Helene struggled to understand his abrupt change of subject as he tugged at his cravat without unfastening the pin, ripped it away from his throat and tossed it to the floor.

"For three months I tolerated her weeping and fainting and her refusal to allow me to remove any of her clothing or mine. In desperation, I even agreed to take her back to my parents' country seat, where she promised me she would be more willing to accept me in her bed."

He took two strides forward and sat down heavily on one of Helene's delicate French chairs. The chair creaked and groaned as he pulled off his boots and stockings.

"When the appointed night eventually arrived, it was, of course, a complete disaster." His smile held no warmth. "I've never seen so much blood come from a woman. She screamed and fought me with her nails, but this time I would not stop. I was determined to have her. And even then, I tried my hardest not to hurt her, tried to ease into her, kept my thrusts shallow and controlled, kept my weight off her, but still she screamed and swooned."

Helene stared at him as he got up from the chair and moved even closer to where she stood. Would he direct his anger at her, or was it simply tied to his words and memories? She was the one who had wanted him to lose his inhibitions. Perhaps she should've been more careful. He unbuttoned his breeches, shoved his hand down them, and dragged out his shirttails.

"Of course, I kept away from her after she ran screaming to my mother. I hadn't lived with my family for almost five years. They were quite willing to take her word over mine. God, the whole house treated me as if I were an uncivilized monster. What else could I do?"

He touched Helene's shoulder. "Turn around." He unlaced her with quick rough hands and spun her back to face him. His fingers moved in her hair, and it fell around her shoulders; the jeweled pins dropped to the floor. "Take off the rest."

Helene didn't argue as he stripped off his shirt and stepped out of his breeches. He was magnificently erect, his cock already gleaming with precum.

"Three months later, Anne told me she was breeding and that as I had accomplished my hateful task, I didn't need to share her bed again until after the baby was born." He shrugged. "Not that we were sharing a bed anyway."

He reached out and cupped Helene's breasts; his thumbs scraped over her nipples, making them instantly hard.

"I couldn't fuck anyone in my parents' house, and somehow, whenever I found a willing lass in the neighborhood, my wife always found out and started a scene worthy of a Drury Lane farce. So I grew well acquainted with my hand and my imagination." His mouth twisted up at one corner. "The images were all of you, even though I'd sworn never to think of you again."

She had to turn her head away as his teeth scraped her neck. His actions were exciting. Did he know she craved such directness, such caresses that gave her no choice but to submit? She shuddered as he nipped her ear and guided her back toward the bed, his gaze still distant and distinctly unfriendly.

"Two years later, I had my wife once more, and she produced our daughter. After that, she refused me completely." He lifted her onto the bed and leaned over her, his hot wet cock pressed against her belly. "Do you realize I had more sex with you during that one wild weekend than I had with my wife in seventeen years?"

Helene licked her lips. "That is scarcely my fault, is it, monsieur?"

He grasped his cock around the base and rubbed it against her clit until she moaned.

"I didn't say it was."

He shoved his whole length deep, and Helene gasped. She tried to draw her knees up, but his weight held her pinned to the bed. He slowly withdrew his cock and stared down at it before pressing hard and deep once more.

"At first I tried not to think of you when I masturbated, but after a while, you became the only thing I wanted to fantasize about, the only thing not tainted by association with my family." He pulled out again, filled her with the whole thick length of his cock in another smooth endless stroke.

"I imagined you under me, begging me to fuck you even when I took you hard and fast, begging me to fill you with my cock."

He looked down at her, his chest heaving, his heartbeat audible. "And now I'm going to make you scream for real."

Helene moaned as he slid his hands under her knees and drew her feet over his shoulders. She couldn't stop the depth of his penetration or his weight coming down onto her pubic bone. She kept her eyes open as he pumped into her, each stroke filling her to the brim, forcing her to climax again and again. He didn't stop even when she screamed his name, his face contorted with the agonies of lust as he rocked into her.

She grabbed his forearms and held on as he continued to pound away, determined to watch him at this most intimate of moments, to see his expression when he climaxed deep inside her. He started to groan with every stroke, his muscles trembling beneath his skin, his cock growing impossibly bigger inside her.

He climaxed with a roar that took her over with him. She had to shut her eyes then to hold on to the exquisite moment, to allow her body to endlessly spasm into pleasure, to clench and draw every last drop of his cum deep inside her. With a groan, he collapsed over her, pinning her to the bed, his face buried against her neck.

Helene lay still, allowing him this moment of possession, her mind already busy reviewing the intriguing story of his marriage. She was certain there was more hurt to uncover, more deceit, but did Philip even realize that himself? He levered himself away from her a little.

"I apologize. I should've pulled out."

Her sexual glow was abruptly extinguished. She shoved at his shoulders, and he obediently rolled over onto his back.

"Your apology is a little too late and a little complacent. You probably assume that because I'm a whore, it doesn't matter if I get pregnant."

He turned to look at her and frowned. "I meant what I said. I should have pulled out. That was all. Why make such a drama out of it?"

She rolled away from him until she was sitting on the far side of the bed and drew the sheet up to cover her breasts. "You also probably assume that a whore would know how to get rid of any inconvenient reminder of your passion."

"Helene, what in God's name has got into you?" Philip sat up and glared at her. "If I assumed anything, I apologize. If there are consequences to my actions, I would expect you to tell me and I'll honor my obligations."

"There will be no 'consequences,' as you call them. I can no longer have children." She swallowed hard. "I suppose you would consider that a blessing in my chosen profession."

Philip held up his hands. "What do you want me to say? If I agree with you, you'll be offended. If I don't, you'll probably be offended too."

Helene stared at him. Part of her wanted to stuff that pompous statement about his obligations right back down his throat and reveal the *obligations* he'd already given her. The rest of her simply wanted him to leave. She raised her eyebrows.

"Are you done?"

"What?"

"Are you done with me? You've had me; don't you have to leave now?"

His expression darkened. "Helene, stop acting like some poor downtrodden whore."

She gaped at him. "What did you call me?"

He met her gaze head-on. "I don't think of you as a whore. I never have, so don't pretend to be one."

"Liar."

"Helene . . ." He sighed. "I want to fuck you again. Why are you making this so difficult?"

He crawled toward her, and she tried not to look at the muscles of his thighs and the taut flatness of his stomach, where his half-erect cock flaunted itself.

"You promised me your nights. Not one quick roll in the bedclothes."

"At your age, I didn't expect you to have the stamina for more than once."

He smiled and reached down to stroke the growing hardness between his thighs.

"But then you didn't realize how much time I had to make up, did you?"

She struggled to find the words to put him at a distance again, even as her body yearned and readied itself for his touch.

"Are you seriously suggesting that after your second child was born, you never had sex again?"

He shrugged. "Not with my wife. We reached an agreement that I could have a mistress if I promised never to touch her again. I found a widow in the town twenty miles away who was content to share my bed occasionally. It was enough."

Despite herself, Helene felt some sympathy for Philip, condemned to a loveless, sexless marriage while she . . . while she had at least enjoyed her scandalous life.

"How old is your daughter?"

"Emily is fifteen."

"And your older child?"

"My son, Richard? He is seventeen."

Not that much younger than the twins. Did Richard bear any resemblance to his father or to Christian? Her anger against Philip died as quickly as it had arisen. He didn't know about the twins, so his comments about her fertility were not meant to be personal. She had to remember that. If she hoped to persuade Philip to relinquish the shares to her, she had to keep to her part of the bargain.

With a sigh, she let go of the sheet and gave Philip her most beguiling smile.

"Would you like me to suck your cock?"

He stared at her for a long moment, the suspicion in his eyes clearly at war with his rising lust.

"If you promise not to bite it off."

Helene leaned over and licked the crown. "That, I can promise. I would hate to deprive myself of such pleasure."

Philip groaned as she licked him again.

"Thank God for that."

15

Helene sat at her desk biting the end of her pen. A week had passed since Philip had agreed to her bargain, and she had not succeeded in scaring him away. In truth, he had become as familiar to her as the rest of her staff and just as efficient. At the moment, he was in the kitchen discussing the quality of the wine deliveries with Judd and Madame Dubois.

His sexual appetite knew no boundaries either. Despite his age, he was as eager to fuck as any of the young lords who had shared her bed in the past. The difference was that he liked to be the master in bed, whereas the young sprigs of nobility had allowed her to dictate every sexual move.

Helene realized she was smiling. She liked his roughness, his eagerness, and the way he tried to dominate her. It certainly made a change from all the tutoring. If she was not careful, she was going to miss him when the thirty days were up. . . .

A commotion in the hallway interrupted her thoughts, and she glanced at the door. *Mon Dieu*, the twins must have returned. How on earth was she going to keep them away from

Philip? It wasn't as if she could expect to dump them on George for another three weeks. She stood up as the noise grew louder. Would Philip even recognize his own children? Like most men, he certainly wouldn't be looking to acknowledge his old bastards.

The door opened, and George and the twins entered the room. George looked unusually harried, his hat askew, his immaculate linen crumpled. Christian looked his usual disdainful self, but Lisette had picked up some color in her cheeks.

"Your children insisted on leaving at some ungodly hour this morning and traveling at speed to get here. So here they are." George bowed in Helene's direction. "I'm off to sleep for a week. I'll see you when I wake up."

Helene blew him a kiss as he backed hastily out of the room. The twins didn't bother to say good-bye. Helene summoned a bright smile.

"Bonjour, Christian, bonjour, Lisette. How did you enjoy your visit to Brighton?"

Lisette actually smiled at her. "I enjoyed it, Maman. The scenery was beautiful, and we got to see all the fashionable people strolling on the promenade in the afternoons. Lord George was an excellent host."

"No, he wasn't," Christian interrupted.

"He was. You were just angry because he wouldn't let you gamble or join the wilder young men at their scandalous parties."

"And what would you know about it, Miss Prissy-face?"

Helene hastened to interrupt. Even during her short acquaintance with the twins, she'd realized they could snipe at each other for hours if not distracted.

"I am glad you enjoyed your stay. What would you like to do now?"

Christian frowned. "We're not ready to go back to France, if that's what you mean. We haven't seen hardly anything of London yet."

"That is true. I've arranged for a new companion to take you both around next week." She forestalled Christian with a decisive wave of her hand. "You can stay in the guest suites here as long as you keep out of the pleasure house. I won't insist you return to the hotel if you promise to behave."

Lisette's smile faded. "You cannot spare a few hours to take us out yourself?"

Helene stared at her. "I . . . assumed you wouldn't welcome my company." Had she misread the signals? Were her children trying to reach out to her?

"We don't want her with us, Lisette. She'd spoil it."

Helene turned back to Christian. "How would I do that?"

"Because you are a notorious whore. I don't want Lisette being ogled by the kind of men you deal with."

Helene sighed and sat back down. "I'm not a whore. I'm not considered completely respectable, but unless you have aspirations to be accepted by the *ton*, being seen in my company would hardly ruin you."

Christian shrugged, his color high. "*Everyone* knows who you are. You run a notorious brothel, for God's sake."

"I don't run a brothel. My clients pay a great deal of money to indulge in the sexual liaisons of their choice in the privacy of this club. I employ no professional whores, and no money changes hands." She fixed Christian with her hardest stare. "I would still like to know who told you I am a whore."

"*I'd* like to know why you lied to us for all these years."

Helene took a deep breath. The twins were almost adults. Perhaps they would finally understand her motives. Despite her concern over Marguerite, at least once she had to try and explain what she'd done.

"I lied because I didn't want you to be ashamed of me."

Christian raised his eyebrows, reminding her forcibly of his father at his most haughty. "Ashamed?"

"I was unmarried and about to embark on a new business venture. I had no idea if it would succeed or not. I thought it would be better if you were both cared for in a safe place." She risked a glance at the twins and found them both listening intently. "In the early years, it also became increasingly difficult to visit France because of the continuing chaos of the revolution and the rise of Napoléon. I contemplated trying to bring you out with me, but in the end, I truly believed the nuns had the best chance of protecting you."

"Did you ever visit the nunnery, Maman?" Lisette said.

"You know I did. I tried to come at least once a year."

"But you never really *saw* it. You only saw the pieces the nuns allowed you to see."

"Are you suggesting you were mistreated?"

Lisette stirred in her seat. "Not mistreated, *non*, but the nuns cared for a lot of children, and we were but two of many. We were separated as well."

Helene swallowed hard. *Was that true?* "I did what I thought was best for you at the time. I was working twenty hours a day to get the pleasure house on its feet. Even if you'd stayed with me, I would never have seen you nor had time to care for you."

Christian took his sister's hand. "*Non*, maman, you did what was best for yourself. That's what you've always done. You abandoned us and Marguerite for your own selfish gain."

She met his hard gaze and remembered how convinced she'd been that her choices were right. She recognized that same determined light in her son's hazel eyes.

"I was eighteen, when I made that choice Christian. The same age as you are now. Do you truly believe every decision you make is correct?"

"Of course I do or I wouldn't make them."

She smiled haltingly. "That is the advantage of growing older. I'm no longer sure I made the right choices when I was your age."

"But you made them."

"And I have to live with them." She held his gaze, trying to show him the love in her eyes, but he looked away. "As you will have to live with the choices you make now." She took a deep breath. "And before you ask, I've had no news of Marguerite yet."

There was a gentle knock on the open door, and Philip looked in. "Am I disturbing you, madame?"

She gathered her composure and managed a smile. "Not at all, my lord. We were just finished." She turned to the twins and spoke in rapid French.

"We can continue this conversation later. After your long journey, you probably need to eat. Why don't you go down to the kitchen and see Madame Dubois? I'm sure she can make you a delicious meal."

Christian looked mutinous. "I'm not a child. Don't tell me what to do." He glanced at Philip, who waited patiently in the doorway. "Who's that, your latest lover? He looks a little old in the tooth. I heard you like them young."

"I will see you later, Christian, Lisette."

The twins filed out, Lisette looking as unhappy as her brother. Helene turned to Philip and prayed his French was not as good as hers. How much had he understood of the conversation—and worse, what might he have overheard?

Philip studied Helene's flushed face. She looked truly upset, something he hadn't believed possible until she had started to shed her layers of absolute composure to reveal the passionate woman within. His French was excellent, but the speed of her delivery and the local dialect had kept him from understanding every word. Still, he was convinced he had the gist of it.

"So he thinks I'm too old, does he?"

To his astonishment, Helene simply stared at him, her fingers knitted together in front of her, her lips pressed into a tight line. He took a seat in front of her desk and continued to study her. Seeing her vulnerable made him feel uncomfortable in ways he refused to examine. What had the young sprig said to upset her so much? Was he a past lover? The thought made anger churn in his stomach.

"He is young." Helene moistened her lips.

Philip shrugged, disturbed by his instant annoyance at her defense of the young man. "He is an arrogant fool. All men are at that age. Who is he, and who is the girl?"

Silence stretched between them until he was about to open his mouth to repeat his undeniably rude question.

"They are my children."

He took his time to digest that bare statement. From the brief glimpse he'd had of the two young people, he'd seen they were blond, French, and prone to arguing, very much like Helene, in fact.

"I thought you said you couldn't have children."

She finally met his gaze. "I said I could no longer *have* children. After the twins were born, I was unable to conceive again."

"Ah, that would explain it, then."

She lapsed into silence again, and for once he let her. He swung his pocket watch idly between his fingers as he considered his options. Did he really want details of her love life after she'd left him? He found that he didn't. The thought of her body being possessed by another man was too difficult to deal with. He shoved that thought away even faster. Why should he care, after all? He was only here for the next twenty-three days, and he'd had enough emotional entanglements with his late wife to last him a lifetime.

"Judd and I have decided to try a new wine supplier."

She blinked at him. "I beg your pardon?"

"I said, Judd and I have decided to try a new wine supplier. I think you've stayed with the La Tour brothers for reasons of loyalty, not economics."

"I've known them for years. I was one of their first clients."

"They are one of the premier wine merchants in London now. I scarcely think they need you anymore, and, according to Judd, the quality of their products has been diminishing over the last year."

"Perhaps they are having a difficult time getting the best wines because of the war."

Philip was relieved to see some color creep back into Helene's face as her interest in the conversation grew.

"Where is their loyalty to you, one of their best customers? I don't see it. They don't deserve your account."

She raised her chin. "I make the final decisions about our suppliers, not you."

"Not anymore. You will soon have a partner to consider, remember?"

She stiffened. Ah, there was the fire, the determination to best him. His smile was deliberately patronizing.

"I've already told the La Tours that we wish to take our business elsewhere. We'll see how they react to that and make a decision."

"You had no right to do that." Helene stood up. "You should've consulted me first."

"I am consulting you." Philip got up, too, and moved in on her. He slid his arm around her waist and drew her close. "I'm just waiting for you to agree with me."

He kissed her and drove his tongue deep, needing to possess her, to remind her of their already deep sexual bond.

She wrenched her mouth away from his. "Don't think you can use sex to get what you want from me."

He smiled. "Isn't that what you do? Don't you tolerate me in your bed because I have something you want?"

She stared into his eyes. "I do a lot more than tolerate you."

He kissed her again, caught her lower lip between his teeth and bit slowly down. "Are you sure about that?"

"I don't fake my pleasure. Do you?"

"I can scarcely do that. The evidence of my lust fills you up and makes you so wet that sliding into you the next time is much easier."

He took her hand and placed it over his erection. "My desire for you can sometimes be inconvenient as well."

She tried to step out of his arms. "Definitely inconvenient. I have to go and meet with the La Tours and reassure them that I have no intention of taking my business away."

He kept her close, kissed the long line of her throat until she trembled in his arms. The scent of her arousal mingled with her perfume, and his cock grew harder. "Wait until tomorrow. See what their response is first. If you go running back to them now, you will look weak and indecisive."

"And you will look foolish for intervening without being asked."

He shrugged. "I hardly care about that. Judd agreed with my decision—go and speak to him." He kissed her again. "At least do that."

This time when she tried to escape him, he let her go and bowed. "Will you accompany me to the theater tonight?"

She paused, hand pressed to her breast, her eyes still wary. "Why?"

"Because I would like to take you?"

"Are you sure you wish to be seen with such a notorious whore?"

The bite behind her words could hardly escape him. Did her

son disapprove of her and her lifestyle? Did that hurt? He imagined how he might feel if his son hated him.

"I believe my reputation can stand it. How about yours? Surely I am such an elderly man that you have nothing to fear from me."

Her smile was slow in coming but breathtaking when it appeared. She sank into a low curtsey.

"Then I would be delighted, my lord."

16

_____

After meeting with the twins again and trying to soothe their ruffled feelings, Helene was quite glad to be leaving the pleasure house for a few hours. She rarely went out anymore, so intent was she on her work. Having Philip around had helped her realize she deserved a real assistant to share some of her burdens. Judd was an excellent deputy, but he lacked her intuition about people.

She studied her pale lemon gown in the mirror. It was one of her favorites. A daffodil silk underdress covered by a fine net slip adorned with tiny seed pearls. She clasped a matching set of pearls around her neck and a bracelet to complete the set.

How long was it since she had gone to the theater? More years than she wanted to count. She'd given up attending after several of her escorts had resented other men coming to pay their respects to her. That was the trouble with young men; they were so insufferably jealous. After one such occasion that had almost ended in a sword fight at dawn, Helene had decided to stay home.

Philip met her in the grand entranceway of the pleasure

house dressed in his usual austere colors—dark brown and white this time—although a diamond glinted in his cravat. He bowed low and helped her into her cloak.

"You look beautiful, madame."

"Thank you, my lord."

She allowed him to lead her out into the crisp frostbitten air to where his carriage awaited them. He settled her on the seat and sat opposite her, his emotions hidden beneath a slight frown. When they had sex, she loved to see that frown disappear, to watch the sensualist who struggled to break free of his past emerge and take over. His stamina was remarkable, the depths of his lovemaking as yet unchartered. He caught her staring at him and his frown deepened.

"What is it?"

She raised her eyebrows at him. "Am I not allowed to look at you?"

He grimaced. "Why would you want to? I am hardly remarkable."

His lack of confidence continued to surprise her. In her selfishness, his wife had done him a lot of harm.

"I think you are remarkable."

"Because I put up with you?"

She smiled. "It is true that most men fail to live up to my exacting standards."

"That wasn't what I meant. You are one of the most infuriating women I have ever met." He eyed her consideringly. "Every time I think I understand you, you surprise me."

"Isn't that the way it should be?"

"No, and I'm not sure I like it."

"Because you can't simply categorize me as a whore and consign me to the devil?"

"That would certainly make things easier." He shifted in his seat. "I believe my main problem is that the moment I see you, half my blood is diverted straight to my groin. I've never liked being led around by my cock."

"It is scarcely my fault if that happens. You should strive for greater self-control."

The carriage drew to a halt, and Helene gathered her skirts to descend. Philip got out and came around to help her down. She took his hand, gasped when he yanked hard and pulled her tight into his body. His erection grazed her stomach.

"And what if I have no self-control left?"

She smiled sweetly and shoved at his chest. "Then perhaps I will have to be careful."

The theater was already crowded as they made their way up the main staircase to the upper levels. Helene tried to ignore both the admiring looks from the men and the deliberate cuts from some of their womenfolk. It wasn't as if this was new to her; beauty brought its own peculiar advantages and disadvantages. She wasn't quite sure why so many of the ladies disliked her. She never slept with married men, and she taught the younger ones how to better pleasure women. In her opinion, the *ton* should be grateful to her, not disapproving.

But then, as her pleasure house was a discreetly kept secret, perhaps the women simply believed she was a high-class courtesan. She certainly looked like one. She refused to let it bother her, so she smiled and waved at her acquaintances as Philip settled her in his box.

"Do you know everyone here?"

"Not everyone." His abrupt question made her glance up at him. "I haven't been to the theater for several years, and I never attend social events. I'm not considered suitable."

"And yet the *ton* is happy for you to provide them with the sexual services they require."

She shrugged. "Are you feeling sorry for me? Please don't. I have no ambition to dance at Almack's."

He took the seat beside her and began to study the playbill.

"Despite you being a pariah, I expect we'll be inundated with callers at the interval."

She gave him her best smile. "If you don't want to be seen with me, I'll understand. Feel free to leave."

He scowled at her. "I escorted you to the damned place. I'm not going anywhere." He shoved the program at her. "It's Mozart. Do you like him?"

"Of course I do." She studied the closely written sheet. "*Cosi Fan Tutte* is one of my favorites." She smiled sweetly. "And so appropriate for a woman with no morals like myself. Did you choose this particular opera to make a point?"

Philip snorted. "Unfortunately, I don't have the power to tell the theater what to perform on any given night." He snatched the playbill back. "I don't even know what you're talking about."

"The opera is about two sisters and their lovers. The lovers agree to a wager to adopt disguises and court the other's fiancé to show that all women are basically unfaithful."

"Why bother to wager about something that is already proven?"

"You believe all women are incapable of fidelity? And what about men?"

He shrugged. "It is different for a man. He is expected to sow his wild oats."

Helene fixed him with a quelling stare. "You, sir, have appalling double standards. If men can 'sow their oats,' then why can't women?"

"Because a man has a right to know there are no cuckoos in his marital nest."

Helene looked out over the stalls and pit of the theater. The discussion obviously disturbed Philip on some fundamental level, and she had no wish to spoil the evening before it even started. What on earth had his wife done to him? She suspected she hadn't heard the half of it. It was becoming harder and harder to pretend she didn't care about the underlying causes of his problems and want to help him solve them.

To disguise her uneasiness, she focused on the seething masses below her. The stink of unwashed flesh, cheap perfume, pipe smoke, and alcohol created a heady brew. Glass bottles caught the candlelight and threw it back to bounce off the diamonds and precious gems of the more wealthy patrons seated above.

The orchestra struck a loud chord, and some of the lights were snuffed out by the attending footmen. The roar of conversation dimmed slightly as people turned their attention to the stage. Helene sat back and prepared to enjoy herself. Music was one of her true pleasures, although she had never learned to play an instrument properly.

Much later, she was so engrossed in the music that Philip's hand on her thigh made her jump. He'd edged his gilded chair so close to hers that there was no longer any space between them. His fingers slid up her arm and came to rest at the nape of her neck.

He leaned close until his mouth almost grazed her ear. "Do you remember that inconvenient lack of self-control we discussed?"

She nodded as he stroked his finger along the line of her jaw.

"It has returned with a vengeance and needs to be satisfied right now."

"Ssh."

She tried to show she was too interested in the music to want to have anything to do with him. His mouth traveled down her neck and settled over the pulse at the base of her throat. The delicate lick of his tongue brought all her senses alive.

"I'm thinking about when you climax under me, Helene. How your body clenches around my cock and sucks out every drop of my seed."

She shivered as the tip of his tongue traced a lazy path back to her ear. The music swelled around her, making each small sensation more intense, more exquisite, and more deeply personal.

"I'm also thinking about having you just before the interval so that when all your friends arrive, they'll see me fucking you, watch you coming apart for me, know you are mine alone."

"I am not your possession."

"Aren't you?"

She struggled to push aside the sensual haze enveloping her. "I don't belong to any man, and I never will."

He bit down on her earlobe, and she was instantly wet, her nipples aching to be touched, her sex flowering for him.

"What about the father of your children? Didn't you belong to him?"

God, she'd wanted to, but she'd had to let him go . . . hadn't she? Helene closed her eyes and wrenched away from him, her breathing uneven. She'd forgotten how tenacious he could be and how well he read her emotions. Was she ready to tell him the truth about the twins? It might serve her purpose and drive him away for good, but was it worth the inevitable consequences for her already hostile children? She yearned to find some peace with them, some middle ground where they could at least be pleasant to each other. Adding Philip to the equation would be like dropping a lighted brand into a vat of oil.

She half stood and moved her chair farther away from him until she was back in the shadows at the rear of the box. She'd have to tell him at some point, but not yet, not while he was chained to her side. The beauty of the music, combined with her sudden burst of emotion, made her want to weep. She settled back into her seat and gasped as Philip moved his chair too.

He slid his hand behind her head and leaned across her. "Don't shut me out."

His mouth covered hers, demanding entrance. She let him

in, anything to stop him talking, anything to stop her confessing her most painful and intimate secret. He groaned as her tongue met his in a fierce duel and slid his other arm around her waist to cup her breast. She gave herself to the erotic moment, the caress of his tongue, his gloved fingers shoving up her skirts and sliding inside her.

He thumbed her clit in time to the thrust of his finger and had her reaching for a fast climax. Her fingers dug into the fine fabric of his coat as she lifted her hips against his kid leather–covered palm. He pulled away from her as a burst of clapping mingled with whistles and jeers erupted through the theater.

She stared at him, realized his breathing was as harried as hers, that his white satin pantaloons were straining to contain his erection. He kissed her swollen mouth and inclined his head.

"We'll finish this later."

From the satisfied smile on his face, she knew how she must look—dazed, sated . . . a man's possession indeed. She patted her hair and straightened her gown. She couldn't stop her friends and acquaintances from noticing her arousal, but she refused to let them see her looking like a common trollop.

There was a knock on the door, and Peter Howard and Lord George Grant entered. Helene smiled brightly.

"Good evening, my friends. Are you enjoying the opera?"

Both men kissed her hand and nodded to Philip, who had taken up a position behind her chair, probably to hide his erection. His hand rested heavily on her shoulder in yet another gesture of ownership.

"Helene, aren't you going to introduce us?" George said.

Helene glanced up at Philip. "If you wish. May I introduce Lord George Grant and Mr. Peter Howard? Gentlemen, this is Mr. Philip Ross."

"Actually, darling, I'm Lord Philip Knowles now."

George flicked her a startled, speculative glance and then returned his attention to Philip. "Congratulations on your new title, my lord. I knew your predecessor, Lord Derek, rather well."

"Really?" Philip's tone didn't invite confidences. "Unfortunately, I didn't. Our families didn't get on at all. The connection was slight and my elevation to the peerage quite unexpected."

As George and Philip eyed each other, Peter winked at Helene and took the seat beside her. "Thanks for helping Anthony out this week."

Helene sighed. "I'm worried about him, Peter. I don't like the games he plays or the people he associates with."

"Neither do I, but what can we do?"

"Nothing, unless you wish to tell Valentin and let him sort it out."

Peter shuddered. "I wouldn't wish that fate on my worst enemy, let alone Anthony. It's hard enough for him having Val as a brother without creating further tensions."

"I agree, which is why I'll try and monitor his activities in the pleasure house and intervene if necessary."

"I'll do the same, and I'll also try and talk some sense into him, not that he'll listen, of course."

Helene patted his hand, aware that George and Philip had stopped talking and were both staring at her.

She summoned a smile. "The opera is wonderful. I can't remember why I stopped attending. I must inquire about renting a box."

Peter stood up, his fair hair glinting in the candlelight. "Valentin already has one. I'll mention your interest to him. I'm sure he'd be delighted to see you occupy his." He nodded at the two men. "A pleasure to meet you, but I must return to my seat." He gestured at the doorway, which was rapidly filling with people, and blew Helene a kiss. "You'll hardly miss me in the crush."

"Au revoir, Peter." Helene kissed her fingers. "Give my love to Abigail."

She glanced expectantly at George, but he seemed determined to stand his ground, his suspicious gaze fixed on Philip. She sighed. Was he going to be difficult? He sometimes seemed to believe it was his duty to drive her suitors away. In the past it had amused her, but she didn't think Philip would take it well at all.

Philip grimaced as Helene allowed herself to be engulfed by visitors. In truth, he was surprised at the variety of theatergoers who had decided to invade his box. He'd assumed they would all be young men. Although there was a fair sprinkling of obviously infatuated youths, many of the guests were fashionably dressed couples. Everyone seemed delighted to see Helene and happy to acknowledge her. His prejudices against her supposed lifestyle were beginning to fade as reality took front stage in his previously distorted viewpoint.

"So, my lord, how long have you known Madame Delornay?"

He turned from his contemplation of Helene to find Lord George Grant was still at his side. He studied the grim expression on the man's face while he decided how to frame his answer.

"I've known her for several years."

"So have I. In fact, I am one of the original trustees of the pleasure house." His smile seemed forced. "You, of course, are now a shareholder as well."

"I know that."

"And what do you intend to do with your shares?"

Philip raised his eyebrows and let his contemptuous stare speak for itself.

Color spotted Lord George's cheeks. "I apologize. That is none of my business." He tried to laugh. "As one of Helene's oldest friends, I have been accused of being overprotective sometimes. I hate to see her being put in such a vulnerable position."

"Helene vulnerable?"

"You do not see her like that?" Lord George paused. "Forgive me, but surely any woman who survived what she did deserves to be commended, not condemned."

"I'm not condemning her. I'm sure she could survive anything if she put her mind to it. She is a very strong and determined woman."

"You sound as if you do not approve. When I met her in the Bastille, I was forced to rely on her strength to save my life. Perhaps that is why we see her differently."

Philip produced his most dismissive smile. "Indeed. I can't say she's ever saved my life. Complicated it, perhaps, but that is what women do, is it not?"

Lord George blinked at him. "I suppose it is."

The crowd around Helene thinned as the warning bell sounded the five minutes to the end of the interval. Philip frowned. Would Lord George actually leave, or was he planning on joining their party for the evening? Lord George's overprotective streak and deliberate insinuations about how well he knew Helene were starting to annoy him. He *knew* Helene. He'd known her from the first moment they'd met.

Philip found he wanted Helene to himself, to continue their sexual play, and simply for the pleasure of her company. He'd seen nothing in her manner to indicate she yearned after any of the men who'd crowded the box—including Lord George.

Despite her attempts to withdraw from him, he did understand her sexually, knew exactly how to arouse her without even thinking about it. He suspected that after all her years of bedding younger men, she found it disconcerting to be faced with a man who knew what he wanted. Yet she knew him, too, didn't she? Knew what he craved and had offered him the means to enjoy it. He thought of Adam, of that secret room, of how he yearned to explore that side of his nature again.

He studied Helene, who was laughing up at Lord George. Her expression held no hint of longing or desire, no hint of the passion he could arouse in her with a single touch. He shifted in his seat and checked his watch. Would Lord George ever leave?

"I'd better be off, Helene. I'll see you tomorrow."

Lord George bowed and finally left, leaving Helene alone with Philip. She looked at him as he slipped into the empty chair beside her.

"Why are you frowning?"

"I like frowning." He gestured at the now-empty box. "How do you put up with all that flattering and fawning nonsense?"

"Is that how it seemed to you? That I enjoyed being the center of attention?"

He stared at her. "That's not what I meant. You can't help it, can you? Your beauty draws the eye. It must be something of a burden."

"How perceptive of you to realize that." She sighed. "When I was younger, I used to pray that God would make me plain. Eventually I realized that beauty has its own rewards, and I decided to exploit them for my own gain."

He looked out over the noisy theater. "Lord George said he met you in the Bastille and that you saved his life."

"Did he really?"

"Is it true?"

"That we met in the Bastille? *Oui.*"

"You were both prisoners?"

The orchestra began playing, and darkness filled the intimate space between them. The scent of raw gin and burnt candle wax drifted upward from the packed masses below. She almost felt as if they were enclosed in the intimacy of her bed, safe behind the curtains, whispering secrets to each other.

"I wasn't strictly a prisoner by then. George was. He'd been caught spying for the English and was due to be executed."

"Why weren't you a prisoner anymore?"

"I was whoring for the guards."

"Why?"

She shrugged, and her shoulder brushed his. "My family was dead. It was the only way to survive."

He caught her hands, quieted her restless fingers between his own. "How was it that you were the only one to survive?"

"Because I was beautiful. Because the guards were prepared to humor my father and offer me my life in exchange for the use of my body."

"How old were you?"

"Does it matter?"

He tightened his grip on her hands. "How old were you?"

"I was almost fourteen."

"Younger than my daughter is now . . . God. No wonder you see your beauty as a curse."

"It is strange, isn't it? At first I wished my father had allowed me to die with him. I hated him for forcing me to live like that." She tried to withdraw her fingers, and Philip slowly released them. "But I soon realized my will to live was stronger than I had ever imagined and that beauty had its benefits after all."

She drew a calming breath. How long was it since she'd talked about the past?

"Anyway, I managed to free George from his cell and contact some of the British spies who helped him to the coast and on to freedom."

"You make it sound so simple. I doubt it was."

She shrugged. "I was a young girl. None of the guards believed I had the ability to do anything except . . ." To her surprise, she realized she couldn't go on, couldn't revisit the horrors without them overwhelming her, especially in Philip's company. She got clumsily to her feet and knocked the chair over.

"I have a headache. Can we go?"

"Of course, madame." Philip stood up as well, his face still in the shadows, his voice as calm as if they'd been discussing the weather. "I'll go and fetch your cloak."

She turned blindly toward the stage, where the lovers continued to sing in perfect harmony, and shuddered. Even the perfection of the music failed to calm her. Exposing her past to Philip made her feel vulnerable, and she hated that. Had she become so adept at hiding her secrets that she had cut herself off from her true self? She closed her eyes. And what had possessed George to share his early memories of her with Philip? Didn't he realize that he was putting her in danger?

"Madame?"

Philip touched her shoulder and then wrapped her in her cloak, his hands so gentle she wanted to weep again.

"*Merci.*"

To her surprise, he went to open the door of the box without saying anything. She pulled the cloak over her head and hurried toward him.

He stopped her with a hand on her shoulder. "Helene, I'm glad your father tried to save you."

She forced herself to look at him. "Why?"

"Because as a father myself, I can understand how he'd do anything to keep his daughter alive."

"Even condemn her to a life as a whore?" she whispered.

He raised his eyebrows. "Even that if it meant she lived." He traced a tear on her cheek. "Do you still hate him, then?"

She stared at him. "No, of course not."

He didn't reply, but his attention remained on her. "My carriage should be ready by now. Shall we go?"

As they drew away from the front of the theater, Helene surreptitiously wiped her eyes. Philip's ability to see her father's dilemma had shaken her. He'd made her realize she hadn't really forgiven him at all. Despite Philip's attempts to engage her in conversation, that unwelcome revelation kept her silent and subdued for the rest of the short journey.

17

Philip glanced down at Helene as she swept past him into her suite. She hadn't spoken to him at all on the journey home, but he didn't believe she was suffering from a headache. Her revelations about her past had shaken him deeply. So much for his image of her as a coldhearted whore. He wished he hadn't allowed Lord George Grant to annoy him so much that he'd insisted on questioning Helene.

He waited as she took off her cloak and threw it over the back of a chair. Philip eyed her profile. Would she like him to comfort her? To his surprise, he wanted to very much. It would be easy to cross the small space between them, to take her into his arms and make love to her all night long. He was old enough to know he couldn't change the past, but he still believed he could provide her with some comfort.

He took a step toward her and then stopped as she spun around and gave him a dazzling false smile.

"Are you all right, Helene?"

"Of course I am. Why wouldn't I be?"

She sauntered toward him, hips swinging, breasts thrust out. His cock woke up, and he resisted the desire to readjust himself. She ran her finger down the silver buttons of his waistcoat until she reached the waistband of his pantaloons. He shuddered as she cupped his growing erection.

"Helene . . ."

She sank to her knees so gracefully, he was reminded of a swan. Her fingers worked at the placket of his pantaloons until it hung open to reveal his smallclothes. His cock was already trying to escape the confines of the fine linen.

He groaned as she licked his shaft through the fabric, making him instantly wet. His fingers curved around the back of her skull as his common sense tried to fight off the strident demands of his cock.

"You don't have to do this."

She went still and looked up at him. "Do what?"

"Act the whore for me."

Color flooded her cheeks. "I am merely amusing myself and hopefully arousing you."

He bent forward, grasped her by the shoulders, and drew her back to her feet. "No, you're not."

She met his gaze, anger and misery at war in her blue eyes. "I'm not pleasing you?"

He sighed. It was incredibly hard to be honorable when he was so very willing to drag her into bed and fuck her until dawn. But he'd learned his sexual lessons far too well to allow himself to be used by someone suffering an emotional crisis.

He dropped a kiss on her forehead. "Helene, I'm not sure I can give you what you want this evening." He paused to button his pantaloons. "I'm not even sure if you know what you want."

"I want you."

"No, you want to prove something to yourself, and I've never enjoyed playing those kinds of games."

Irritation shimmered in her eyes. "I don't know what you are talking about."

"Then go to bed and I'll see you in the morning."

"And what will you do now? Go and seek out someone who doesn't want to play games?" Her dismissive smile wasn't designed to reassure him. "Good luck with that in this house."

"Isn't this place supposed to provide anything I desire?" He bowed and turned for the door. "Then if I wish it, I'm sure I'll find it."

"Philip . . ."

"Madame?"

"If there is something else you want here rather than me, I would not deny you."

Philip paused. So she did know about what he'd gotten up to in the room of desires.

"I want you, you know that, but not when you are in this mood." He swung back to face her. "And what else I desire is surely my business."

She met his glare without flinching. "As I said, I am happy for you to explore everything that interests you."

"How gracious of you and how incredibly patronizing." He took two steps toward her. "When I came in here, all I wanted was to take you to bed and fuck you until all you could think about was fucking me back."

She bit down hard on her bottom lip as if trying to keep from speaking.

He bowed elaborately. "Now, I'll take myself off, follow your orders, and find someone who really wants me."

Her expression changed, grew softer. "Philip, I'm sorry, I didn't mean to—"

"Good night, madame." He didn't allow her to finish, afraid she'd somehow undermine his ability to leave. What the hell was it about women that they couldn't make up their minds about what they wanted?

She turned away from him. "Good night, then."

He hesitated once more and then forced himself to walk out. Was she more shaken by her confidences in him than he'd realized? Was that why she was pushing him away? His conscience reminded him that he had turned her down first, but there was good reason. She didn't have to play the whore for him to disguise how she felt; he knew her too well.

He reckoned very few people knew about her past. Was it a good time to reassure her that he'd never share her secrets with anyone? He risked another glance back at the door and grimaced. Perhaps not.

He continued up the back stairs into the main part of the pleasure house, nodded to the burly Irish brothers on guard by the staircase, and took himself to the room of desires. He stared at the door for a long moment. Was he using his self-righteous anger against Helene to justify indulging in his perversions? He frowned. Dammit, she'd been happy to let him explore his sexuality, so why shouldn't he?

He was horny as hell, and he needed some relief. Helene had no claims on him. He had a perfect right to fuck whatever or whomever he wanted. He pushed open the door and found himself in the now familiar blackness.

"What do you desire?"

"Adam. I want Adam."

"Please step to your left, and he will be with you shortly."

Philip let out his breath and made his way into the eerie darkness. Regardless of Helene, if he ever wanted to be whole again, to be able to function as a normal human being, he had to get over the ghosts of his past. He had to come to terms with what had been done to him.

He rubbed his cock, which had been semi-erect all night and now throbbed like a toothache. It seemed he couldn't forget Helene after all. She'd triumphed over her past, hadn't she? Faced far worse sexual horrors than he had and survived. His hand stilled on his shaft. Did she see through him, after all? Did she recognize a fellow sufferer and want to help him?

The door to his right opened briefly, and Philip straightened.

"Good evening, sir."

"Good evening, Adam."

"How may I serve you?"

Philip briefly closed his eyes. "I'd like you to suck my cock and then . . . I'd like to suck yours."

"Are you sure that is what you want, sir?"

Philip shuddered as Adam moved close and cupped his jaw.

"I need to do this. I need to see if there is any joy left in it for me."

Adam let out his breath. He smelled of the sea and the bracing freshness of a windy day. "If it pleases you, sir, we can lie on the bed and pleasure each other at the same time."

"I didn't know that was possible."

Adam chuckled, the sound surprisingly normal considering the circumstances. "Indeed it is, and most enjoyable too."

Philip followed him blindly to the corner of the room, where he caught his first glimpse of a narrow white bed lit by a single candle. He hesitated as Adam unbuttoned both of their plackets.

"I do not want to be held down."

Adam paused, his fingers brushed Philip's straining cock. "We can lie on our sides, or you can lie on top of me."

"On our sides, then."

Adam climbed onto the bed, and Philip followed, reversing his direction so that his head was by Adam's knees. He shuddered as Adam nuzzled his cock.

"I'm glad you asked for me. I liked taking you in my mouth."

It was enough to make Philip shove Adam's breeches down to expose his cock, which was also hard and ready. Philip groaned as Adam's mouth swallowed him whole, and gave himself up to the pleasure. He closed his eyes and tentatively licked Adam's cock, felt Adam's whole body stiffen and arch toward him. He opened his mouth and took Adam's shaft deep, groaned as he felt the pressure increase on his own cock and matched his sucks to Adam's so they eventually came together.

So strange to feel a man's cum in his throat again. So different to his last encounter, when he'd crawled away and retched to purge his body of such vile abuse. This time he swallowed gladly, eagerly even. One less horror to haunt his dreams. One new memory to replace the old.

Was that what Helene had done? Replaced each horror with a new encounter when she was in control? God, he hoped so for her sake. It helped him understand her so much more. He realized Adam was speaking.

"Are you all right, sir?"

"Yes, I am. It was . . . good."

"I'm glad." Adam stroked Philip's thigh, ran a finger down between Philip's buttocks and circled his arse hole. "I wanted to touch you here, but I didn't have permission."

Philip gently removed Adam's hand. "I'm not sure I'm ready for that."

Adam sighed. "I understand." He paused. "I would let you have me like that."

"I'm not sure I'm ready for that either."

Philip rolled into a sitting position and set about straightening his clothes. Adam did the same.

"May I ask you something personal, sir?"

"You may ask, but I can't guarantee you'll get an answer."

"Were you forced? Did some man take you without your consent?"

Philip stared down at his feet and fought off the memories. Adam touched his knee. "It's all right, sir. My first sexual encounter with a man was not of my choosing either."

"And yet, here you are, trusting me not to mistreat you. You are a braver man than I."

"This encounter is of my choosing. I can walk away from you whenever I want."

Philip stood up and pretended to rearrange his cravat. "And what if you can't walk away? What if you are bound by ties of matrimony and afraid for your children's safety if you leave?"

Silence filled the room as Adam got to his feet. "I apologize for upsetting you, sir, and I hope you will consider asking for me again. Good night."

Before Philip could reply, Adam stepped back into the shadows and disappeared through yet another door. Philip stared into the darkness and cursed quietly under his breath. His body hummed with sexual satisfaction, yet his thoughts were chaotic. Could he understand the choices Adam and Helene had made to rediscover their sexual selves? Could he learn something from them after all? Dammit, if he couldn't tell Adam, the only other person who might understand him was Helene.

He fumbled his way to the nearest door and stepped outside, used the servants' stairs to take himself back to Helene's apartment. The footman on duty merely nodded as Philip carefully opened her door. A fully lit candelabra provided enough light for him to see that Helene was in bed. He walked across the thick carpet and stared down at her.

She immediately opened her eyes. "Philip?"

He knelt beside the bed, took her hand in his, and kissed it. He slowly breathed in her lavender scent and shut his eyes.

"My wife wasn't as innocent as she seemed."

Helene squeezed his hand. "I did wonder about that."

He glanced up at her. "You are an astute woman. I was a fool. She lied to me about her virginity and her health for years."

"But why?"

"Because she'd already acquired a lover before our marriage and was terrified I would find out and separate them forever."

"I remember you told me she lied to keep you out of her bed for months until you took her home. Is that where her lover was?"

"Yes. I suspect he was the one who told her she had to bed me at least once to allay my suspicions." He shuddered. "By that point, I was too grateful to worry about her motives. I just wanted sex."

"And she conceived your son on that one occasion?"

He smiled. "I know. It sounds suspicious. When I eventually realized what was going on, I wondered if she had deliberately given in to me at that particular time to conceal an already advanced pregnancy. But my son was born later than expected, rather than earlier, so I have to assume he *might* be mine. I'm told he bears a strong resemblance to me."

"And your daughter?"

Philip swallowed hard. "No, not that she will ever know that or that I will ever treat her differently."

Helene sat up, her arms wrapped around her knees. "How did you find out?"

"I went into my wife's suite late one night to remonstrate with her about her treatment of our son. Unfortunately, I walked in on her and her lover fucking." He tried to swallow, couldn't manage it. "My wife was so terrified, all she could do was sob, but her lover . . . he was far quicker to react."

"What did he do?"

"He knocked me out. When I came to, I was tied to the bed. He forced me to watch him fuck my wife and then he"—he closed his eyes—"made me take his cock in my mouth and then he fucked me."

"Oh, Philip . . ." Helene leaned forward and cupped his face in her hands. "How horrible for you."

"That wasn't the end of it. He knew my wife was well loved

by my family, and he threatened to make her tell them he was *my* lover and that she was living in fear of me. He thought she would be able to convince them to keep me away, not only from her, but also from my son and any other children we had."

He stared into Helene's eyes. "I couldn't abandon my son. I couldn't allow him to come under the influence of that perverted monster, could I?"

"*Non*, you could not." She touched his face. "You did what had to be done to save your son."

"And suffered through a marriage from hell because of it."

"But you survived, yes?"

"Barely. When Anne became pregnant the second time and tried to persuade me back into her bed, I refused. I offered her a bargain. I would acknowledge the child and allow her to keep her lover if she never expected me to touch her again. In truth, Anne's health had deteriorated badly by that point. Even my mother urged me not to force myself on an unwilling wife who feared another pregnancy." He grimaced. "I was more than willing to oblige her."

"What happened to her lover? Did he stand by her?"

Philip grimaced. "He stayed. He was employed as a gardener on the estate. That's how they originally met. I couldn't fire him in case he resorted to blackmail. I kept myself busy on my father's estates, supervised my children's welfare when their mother grew too frail to manage them, and stayed far away from her." He hesitated. "I'm not even sure why I'm telling you this. I haven't told anyone before." He shrugged. "Perhaps it is a night for confidences."

Helene kissed him and wrapped her arms around his neck. "Come to bed."

He grimaced. "I've not washed and I've been with—"

She cut him off with another kiss and drew him down onto the bed. "Come to bed."

With a sigh, he let her take off his clothes and cover him

with the sheets and the luscious curves of her body. She pushed him onto his back and straddled him, the moist warmth of her sex against his stomach. She kissed him again and then kissed her way down his neck and used the tip of her tongue on his nipples.

"Helene . . . you don't have to do this."

He realized his words were an echo of their earlier conversation. He meant them this time, too, but Helene was different; her reaction to him was all herself and owed nothing to artifice.

He groaned as her mouth traveled lower, dipped into his navel and through the coarse hair of his groin. His cock rose to meet her, eager to be touched, to be surrounded by the warm wet cavern of her mouth. She licked the crown, her tongue curling around him until he filled out even more. So different from Adam but equally erotic. Precum trickled down his shaft, and she lapped that up as well. His hips lifted, trying to coax her to take more of him, to take him deep and hard, to suck him dry.

"God . . ."

He moaned as she swallowed him down her throat and held him there. With a shaking hand, he reached down to caress her hair, to hold her right where he needed her at the dark center of his desire. She started to suck, long hard pulls on his willing flesh that made him even harder and bigger. He planted his feet on the bed so that he could raise his hips into each stroke.

Helene cupped his balls, drawing them up against the base of his cock to brush against her pursed lips. Her fingers stroked him from arse to shaft and circled his balls in an endless pattern of bliss. Her thumb lingered by his puckered hole, pressed and retreated in a tantalizing rhythm that drove him mad.

"Yes, touch me there. Do it."

Helene sucked harder, and he closed his eyes more fully to appreciate the sensations. Her thumb slipped inside him, going farther with every stroke, creating a new sense of raw need until he was ready to plead for her never to stop.

"Please . . ." He heard himself begging, but for what he couldn't say, as all the physical feelings coalesced into one driving need to come as hard and as fast as he could. He climaxed, felt his cum shoot out of him in an endless hot stream down Helene's throat.

When he finished shuddering, he gathered her in his arms and pulled her over him. He kissed her cheek and nuzzled at her throat. She sighed and kissed him back, relaxed like a cat despite his lack of lovemaking. He slowly opened his eyes and stared up at the cream bed hangings.

"Helene?" he whispered.

"Mmm?"

"When he forced me . . ."

"Anne's lover?"

"I got hard."

"So?"

"Even though he buggered me, I got hard enough to come for him."

Helene came up on one elbow and stared down at him. Her long blond hair tickled his face. "You cannot control everything, Philip. Sometimes I climaxed when I was with a man who was just using me. It doesn't mean you enjoyed it."

He stared at her. "Are you sure? Doesn't that make me as perverted as him?"

"Because your body reacted as it should to sex? We are all designed to procreate, *n'est-ce pas*? Our creator tried to make it a pleasurable experience, despite us. Why else would we keep doing it?"

Philip frowned. Trust a Frenchwoman to be so pragmatic about the mechanics of love. "I hadn't thought of it like that."

"Then think about it now while you sleep."

Even as he struggled to do that, his body betrayed him and sent him spiraling down into blessed unconsciousness.

18

"I have some news for you."

"About Marguerite?"

Helene dropped her pen and stared up at George, hope at war with fear in her breast. George grinned as he took off his hat and gloves and tossed them on her desk.

"It's good news, I think. She and her husband were seen at Calais yesterday, purchasing passage to Dover."

"She is coming to England? Perhaps she will agree to meet with me here."

George shrugged and sat down. "I don't know about that. She doesn't even know your real address, does she?"

Helene stood up and paced the length of the room. "Yes, she does. I told her everything when she was eighteen, including my real address if she ever needed to contact me." She pressed her fingers to her temple in an attempt to soothe the sudden pounding. "I have wondered if my revelations caused her to behave so out of character and run away."

George considered her. "You might have shocked her, but I

doubt she'd react by running away with the first man who asked her to marry him."

"You don't know Marguerite. She is something of a romantic." Helene sighed. "Perhaps she thought being married would protect her from further contact with me."

George chuckled. "Then she doesn't know you very well, does she? I'll wager you'll move heaven and earth to get her back."

"That is true, George." She patted his shoulder. "I truly appreciate your help."

"Do you wish to go to Dover or wait until we get more information? I can have her followed for you. It's not as if they are trying to hide."

Helene paused. "I want to go to Dover. I can at least inquire at the posting inns if she is staying there." She sighed. "But how can I go with you when I'm pledged to stay here with Philip?"

George's gaze sharpened. "I've been meaning to ask you about that. What on earth were you doing with him at the theater? I thought you hated going out in society?"

"That's not entirely true. I just hated being escorted by foolish young men."

He frowned. "If you'd asked me, I would've taken you—or am I too foolish as well?"

She removed her hand from his shoulder. "Of course you aren't, but you are married and you know how I feel about that."

"I do, and it continues to irritate me." George stood up. "And did you enjoy your evening?"

"I certainly enjoyed the opera. My companion behaved himself quite adequately as well."

"You've succumbed to his hidden charms, have you?"

Helene frowned. "There is no need to use that tone with me. I'm not your wife."

He stiffened. "That was uncalled for."

"I'm sorry, George, but I don't have time to deal with your issues with Philip. I must find Marguerite."

He stared at her, his face expressionless. "If I may be so bold, why are you 'pledged' to Philip Ross?"

Helene focused on putting away her pen and daily journal, unwilling to meet George's gaze. She knew he wouldn't take her revelations well and decided to be economical with the truth.

"We reached a stalemate over the question of the shares, so I made a bargain with him. He has to survive thirty days working with me at the pleasure house. If he fails, I get the shares back."

George considered her, his mouth a hard line. "And it didn't occur to you to inform me of your plans? I am your business partner as well."

"It happened quite suddenly, George, when you were away in Brighton."

"Looking after *your* children."

Helene prayed for patience. "Yes, and I appreciate that more than I can tell you."

He turned abruptly to face the door. "Ah, here is Mr. Ross. Perhaps you should tell him your news, seeing as you are now so close." He bowed. "Unfortunately, I'm unable to accompany you anyway. I have a meeting with the bank. Send me a message if you need me."

Philip inclined his head a scant inch as George nodded brusquely and slipped past him. His inquiring gaze met Helene's.

"What news is that?"

Helene sat down. "Where have you been? It is almost ten o'clock."

His eyebrows rose. "I told you. Viscount Harcourt-DeVere asked me to meet with him at his house."

"Ah, yes, I'd forgotten."

He eyed her carefully as he settled into the chair George had just vacated.

"The viscount told me something very interesting about the beginnings of the pleasure house."

"Really?" Helene fussed with the remaining items on her desk as she tried to think of a way to tell Philip she needed to go to Dover without arousing his suspicions.

"He told me that Lord George wasn't the only person you helped rescue from the Bastille. In fact, he said you were quite the heroine."

"Scarcely that." She tried to smile. "He is prone to exaggerating my importance."

He held her gaze. "I sincerely doubt it. In fact, your business was funded by some of those grateful persons. Why did you allow me to think you slept your way into acquiring the pleasure house?"

"I didn't, Philip. That was entirely your suggestion."

"But you let me believe it."

"I do not have to justify myself to every man I meet."

"You relish being described as a whore, then?"

She shrugged. "To most people, I'll always be a whore, regardless of my motives. Those who bother to get to know me know the truth."

"What an incredibly arrogant assumption."

His eyes glittered as he continued to stare at her. Why was he so angry? She really didn't have time for this. She needed to find Marguerite.

"Philip, is there a reason for this conversation?"

"What in the devil is that supposed to mean?"

"I'm not sure why you are annoyed, but I don't really have time to discuss it."

His expression was now thunderous, reminding her remarkably of George earlier.

"I intended to express my admiration for you and offer my apologies for my asinine assumptions. But, please, don't let me waste your valuable time."

Helene slammed her hand down on the desk. "Will you please listen to me?"

He glared right back at her. "I thought I was. You are the one who appears to be having difficulty concentrating."

"I have to go to Dover."

"When?"

"As soon as I can arrange it."

He stood up. "I can take you in my curricle."

She bit her lip. "Couldn't you just lend me your curricle and stay here?"

"No." His smile was deliberately confrontational. "I'm supposed to be your shadow, remember? And I certainly wouldn't trust you with my horses."

"You're supposed to be learning about the pleasure house. Perhaps you should stay and take charge for the day."

"No, thank you. I'd rather come with you."

She glared at him in frustration. He didn't even flinch, just continued to stand there, wasting even more precious time.

"Come with me if you must." Helene tossed her head as she hurried for the door. "I'll go and get my bonnet and pelisse and meet you in the hall."

It was still drizzling when they set off. Luckily she'd put on her warmest pelisse and fur-lined boots. Philip had also draped a thick rug over her knees and raised the roof of the curricle to afford them some protection. To her surprise, he was supremely confident at the reins, even in the maddening London traffic.

He glanced down at her as they finally abandoned the chaos of the city and headed out onto the more open areas of the Dover Road. Rain dripped from the brim of his hat in a steady pattern onto his knees. She'd left a hurried note for the twins and their chaperone and sent one to George to ask him to forward any new information to the Mermaid coaching inn in Dover where she hoped to stay.

"Are you all right, Helene?"

"Yes, thank you." She tried to smile. "I appreciate your help."

He snorted, his keen gaze already back on his horses and the road. "Not that I'd noticed."

"I *am* grateful. You didn't ask for details; you just took me at my word that I needed to go."

"I'm still expecting an explanation. I was just concentrating on getting us out of the city before I asked."

She sighed. "Do I have to tell you everything?" He didn't immediately reply as his gloved hands shifted on the reins to steer the horses around a large pothole. She stared out at the gray, clouded sky. "Could you at least wait until we arrive in Dover?"

"I can wait that long."

Helene let out her breath. If there was no trace of Marguerite and her husband in Dover, she wouldn't have to say anything to Philip at all. She cast him a quick glance; well, perhaps she would, but at least she could decide exactly what she could get away with.

The sun appeared briefly through the massed clouds, illuminating the harshness of the early winter landscape. She couldn't help but remember her last journey with Philip—the coach accident that had changed her life, their passionate encounter at the snowbound inn. She gave a sudden reluctant laugh.

"Let's hope it doesn't snow."

"You are worried about being trapped in another inn with me?"

"*Non*, this time I wouldn't be so frightened."

"You were frightened of me?"

"Not of you." She leaned closer as the curricle tipped to the right and caught a faint hint of cigar smoke and sandalwood, felt his arm muscles bunch beneath his coat as he fought the reins. "I was frightened of how you made me feel."

"I believe I felt the same," he said slowly. "Neither of us was equipped to deal with such a grand passion at that age, were we?"

She bit her lip. "I've always believed that a person has to stick by the choices they make, but sometimes I wish I'd known then what I know now."

"And what is that?"

"That grand passion does not come along very often."

She lapsed into silence as they approached a tollgate, waited while Philip tossed the gatekeeper some coins, and they moved on. The rain stopped and bright sunshine struggled through the few remaining clouds. He used his whip on his horses, upping the pace, making Helene seek a safer handhold.

He glanced down at her. "Make yourself comfortable, madame. We still have a long way to go."

It was dark by the time the horses clattered into the cobbled stable yard of the Mermaid Inn. Helene's teeth were chattering, and her feet felt like blocks of ice. Apart from a red nose, Philip seemed remarkably well. He jumped down from the curricle with all the agility of a man who'd been for a drive in the park rather than a bone-grinding journey of eighty miles.

He didn't bother to hand Helene out of the curricle. He just picked her up, strode to the door, kicked it open, and deposited her on the tattered rug within.

"Landlord!"

His imperious shout bounced off the low plaster ceilings and drilled through Helene's head. She glared at him as he went back outside to converse with the ostler. The curricle was driven away, and by the time Philip rejoined her, the landlord was bowing to them both. Helene opened her mouth, only to be fore-stalled by Philip.

"We need a room for the night. Can you accommodate us?"

"Yes, indeed, sir. Please come this way."

Helene traipsed up the narrow staircase and allowed him to show her into a charming room facing the front of the house. The landlord lit the fire and chatted to Philip about the weather while promising a good dinner before the hour was up.

With a sigh, she took off her bonnet and gloves and sank into the nearest chair. She pressed one hand to her aching head.

Philip gave her a sharp glance. "My good man, perhaps you could also provide my wife with a hot brick for her feet and maybe something for her headache."

At once the landlord stopped talking and bowed his way out of the door, promising all sorts of delights in but the blink of an eye.

Helene sighed gratefully as he finally left the room. Philip took off his hat, coat, and gloves and held his hands out to the fire. After a while, he came to kneel beside her chair.

"Are you all right?"

She forced a smile. "I'll be fine once I sit still for a while. I've never been a good traveler."

He patted her hand. "I'm sorry if we traveled too fast. I assumed you wanted to get here as quickly as possible."

"I did and I thank you for your efforts." She wrinkled her nose at him. "Although these days I'm not used to having a man direct my travel arrangements."

"Did you expect me to sit back and let you take charge?"

She studied his affronted expression. "I suppose not. You do not strike me as the kind of man who would ever be comfortable with a woman telling him what to do."

"Disappointed?"

"Not at all. You are far more of a challenge."

"I'm glad to hear it." He got to his feet as there was a knock on the door. He opened it to admit a buxom young maid.

"Good evening, sir, ma'am." She smiled at Helene. "I've got a hot brick for your feet and an herbal tisane from the missus, who says you should drink it while it is hot."

"Thank you. Do you know if there have been any messages for me?"

"I'll check, ma'am." She bobbed a curtsey. "If there is one, I'll bring it up with your dinner."

Helene grimaced at Philip as he shut the door behind the maid. "I should imagine that if George left me a message, it will be in my own name. Perhaps you shouldn't have told the landlord we were married."

Philip shrugged. "I'm sure we can think of a plausible explanation."

"I'm sure you can." She sipped at her tisane and inhaled the soothing scents of honey and chamomile. "I've heard many a married man make excuses for appearing to forget he had a wife. Some of them were even quite imaginative."

"You needn't worry, then. Just tell me the best one and leave it to me."

Helene briefly closed her eyes as her headache started to ease. "If George has left me a message, I might need to go out after dinner."

"Surely that can wait until morning? It is far too late to be wandering around the streets of a notorious seaport."

"I didn't ask you to accompany me."

He went still. "You don't think I would allow you to go out unescorted?"

"It's not a question about what you 'allow.' I'm not your wife, remember?"

"But you are a vulnerable female."

"I'm quite capable of taking care of myself."

A knock on the door interrupted them. Philip got up to open the door.

"We haven't finished this discussion, Helene."

She smiled sweetly. "Yes, we have."

The maid who had brought the tisane placed a large covered tray on the sideboard and turned to Helene. "There was a message came for a blond-haired lady. Would that be you?"

Helene nodded encouragingly as Philip pretended to inspect the steaming plates of food on the tray.

"Here you are, then."

"Thank you."

Helene took the sealed note and slipped it into her reticule. The maid bobbed another curtsey and took the covers off the food. The succulent smell of roast lamb and chicken filled the room. To her surprise, Helene realized she was hungry.

"I'll bring up some more plates and some nice cheese and port as well, sir." This time the maid addressed Philip.

"That would be excellent."

Helene allowed Philip to serve her a plate of food and took it to the chair closest to the fire. She balanced the plate precariously on her knees as Philip joined her. For a while, there was silence as they both ate. Helene didn't manage much, but her stomach was definitely steadier. Philip continued to eat, washing down his food with copious amounts of a fine red wine. Her fingers slid into her reticule and touched the note.

"Aren't you going to open it?"

She almost jumped as he fixed his gaze on her. "I suppose I should. If we are lucky, this might prove to be a wild goose chase."

He removed their plates and sat back in his chair, his hazel eyes considering. "You still haven't told me what or whom we are chasing."

"I might not have to." She opened the seal on the letter and quickly scanned the contents. "Ah . . ."

"Well?"

"She is here."

"Who is?"

"My daughter."

"I thought your daughter was safely ensconced in your house in London. What happened? Did she run off?"

"This is my oldest daughter."

Surprise flared in his eyes. "Exactly how many children do you have?"

"Three, my lord, that is all. My eldest daughter recently married, and I need to speak to her."

"How recently did she marry?"

"Why should that matter?"

"Because I've lived in your house for over a week, and not one female has mentioned a wedding. That must be unheard of."

Heat blossomed on Helene's cheeks. "She is of age. Her decision to marry was her own business."

"How old is she?"

"One and twenty." She watched the puzzlement on his face deepen and resigned herself to yet more explanations.

"You had a child when you were fifteen?"

"*Oui.*"

"Before you even met me?"

Helene inclined her head. Philip sat forward in his seat and linked his hands between his knees.

"I have to assume she married without your consent." He frowned. "Did she marry unwisely?"

"It depends on your point of view. In most people's eyes, she has done remarkably well. I believe her husband is a peer of the realm."

His eyebrows rose. "Yet you are not happy."

"I . . . am her mother. I wish to speak to her to make sure

everything is all right and that she was not coerced or forced in any way."

"Why would you think that?"

Helene got to her feet and went to the window overlooking the street below. "Because I have a vague recollection of the man she married from the pleasure house."

"You assume that anyone who has been there is in some way suspicious?"

She rounded on him. "Of course I don't. I would just like to see my daughter and reassure myself that all is well."

He rose to his feet and looked down at her. "Then let us be off."

"You are not coming with me."

"Then you are not going."

"Philip Ross, you have no right to order me around."

He shrugged. "I have every right. No lady under my protection goes out alone at night. It is far too dangerous."

She stamped her foot. "I am not a lady!"

"You wish to be mistaken for a prostitute again? Because if you go out alone, I'm certain that will happen."

She glared at him as he moved to block her exit by leaning against the door. Her fingers itched to pick up the fire tongs and bash him hard on the head.

"If you come with me, you wait outside."

He bowed. "I'll wait outside the room you occupy. I refuse to compromise more than that."

"You refuse to compromise?" Helene grabbed her bonnet and placed it on her head. "You are the person behaving like a complete bully."

"Take it or leave it, Helene."

She stared at him for a long fierce moment, imagined his lifeless form stretched across the hearth.

"All right. Marguerite and her husband are staying at the Royal Dover Inn."

"The Royal Dover?" He paused as he shrugged into his coat. "That is the best accommodation in town. It hardly sounds as if she is anxious to avoid detection."

"As I said, she is of age. I can't simply steal her back."

Helene tied the ribbons of her bonnet and reached for her pelisse. Philip plucked it out of her hands and helped her into it. He kissed her throat, making her shiver.

"I'm sure everything will be fine."

"Easy for you to say," she muttered as she drew on her gloves.

He held the door open for her. "That is true, but I do understand, Helene. I have children of my own."

More than you know. Helene kept that sour thought to herself as she went down the stairs and out into the unwelcoming darkness of the night.

19

When they entered the Royal Dover Inn, Helene was almost grateful for Philip's commanding air and instant expectation of being attended to. Within no time at all, she found herself whisked away into a private parlor to await Marguerite while Philip stood discreetly on guard outside the door.

Helene spent the long minutes of waiting in a fruitless attempt to marshal her arguments for Marguerite. But nothing seemed to help. What on earth could she say? Their relationship was far too fragile to risk saying the wrong thing.

The door opened and Helene swung around to face Marguerite. She was dressed in a fashionably low-cut blue silk dress that matched her eyes. Her dark hair was drawn back from her face and piled high on her head. Two ringlets brushed her olive-tinted cheeks. In stature, Marguerite resembled Helene, but her coloring was all her own. She looked as apprehensive as Helene felt.

"*Maman*? Is something wrong?"

Helene tried a smile. "No, my dear. I just wanted to wish you happy and make sure that everything was well with you."

Marguerite paused by the door as if expecting an ambush. "How did you know I was in Dover?"

Helene shrugged. "A friend of mine told me you and your husband had booked passage for England."

Marguerite frowned. "Are you saying you had me followed?"

"How could I do that? I'm not working for the government, nor am I that wealthy."

"But you have many clients who could help you."

Helene sighed. "That is true and I confess, I did want to know when you returned to England."

"Why?" Marguerite gathered her black silk shawl closer to her breasts. "I told you I was safe, and I asked you to leave me alone."

"I know." Helene sat down and gestured to the seat opposite her. "Will you sit a moment so that we can talk?"

Marguerite glanced uncertainly at the door. "I have to get back soon. Justin is coming to eat dinner with me."

Helene took a deep breath. "Are you all right?"

"I am fine, *Maman.*" She smiled radiantly. "I am in love. Isn't that the best feeling in the world?"

"It is, my dear." Helene couldn't help but smile back. "I'm just glad to see you are happy."

"How could I not be? Justin makes me feel like the most precious woman in the world. He says he worships me."

"Then you are indeed a lucky woman."

Marguerite sighed, her expression blissful. "I know. And what is even better is that I've told him all about my life, and he doesn't care that I'm illegitimate."

"Did you tell him about me?"

"He knows who you are. In truth, he thinks it is highly amusing that you are my mother. He also seems to think that is why we rub along together so well."

Helene wasn't sure she liked the sound of that. Did Justin Lockwood believe Marguerite had the same wide sexual tolerances as her mother? Was that why he had married her?

Marguerite sank down onto the seat beside Helene. "I'm sorry I didn't tell you I was going to get married. It all happened rather quickly. I met Justin in the village while I was running some errands for the nuns. His horse had thrown a shoe, and he was having some trouble getting anyone to understand his terrible French."

Helene managed to smile. "I don't intend to intrude on your marriage, my dear. You need have no fear of that."

Marguerite looked at her, her expression relieved. "I'm so glad to hear that. This is a wonderful opportunity for me to share my life with a man I respect and love."

There was no sign of strain in Marguerite's words. No hint of coercion. It was obvious that she didn't need to be rescued after all. Despite her misgivings, Helene had to believe everything would work out for the best.

She clasped Marguerite's hand. "You will write to me?"

"Of course, *Maman*. And when we're settled, we can meet more regularly."

"I would like that."

Marguerite hesitated. "You must not think me ungrateful for everything you have done for me. I know how hard it was for you after I was born."

"I wish I'd done more. I wish I'd kept you with me through it all."

Marguerite looked earnest. "You did your best, didn't you? You kept me alive, gave me an education and opportunities you were denied. What more could any child want?"

"You might want to ask Christian and Lisette that question." Helene sighed. "They still hate me. Did you know they have turned up in England?"

"The twins have? How did they know where you live?"

Helene watched Marguerite intently. "You didn't tell them?"

"Of course I didn't. I promised not to." Marguerite smiled. "That is so typical of them. When I was younger, I hated you for a while too. Then you had the courage to come to me and tell me the truth. Now I am proud to be your daughter."

A tear slid down Helene's cheek. Just as she resolved to let her daughter make her own choices and be happy for her, Marguerite had given her the greatest gift of all—forgiveness. Was there anything sweeter than that for a mother?

"Thank you, Marguerite." Helene hugged Marguerite hard. "I truly wish you happy."

For a moment, neither of them spoke, just held each other in an all-encompassing, crushing embrace.

"*Je t'aime, Maman,*" Marguerite whispered.

"*Je t'aime, aussi.*"

"I'll write to you. I promise."

"I'll write too."

Marguerite disengaged herself, wiped at her cheeks, and jumped up. "I have to go now. Justin and Harry will be waiting for me."

Helene stood up, too, her smile dying. "Sir Harry Jones is traveling with you?"

Marguerite nodded, setting her ringlets bobbing as she opened the door. "Yes, isn't that wonderful? He has certainly enlivened both our spirits and our journey through Europe. I'm not sure what we'll do with ourselves when he has to go home."

With a last kiss, Marguerite skipped lightly up the stairs, her dark satin gown quickly blending with the gloom. Helene repressed an urge to call her back, to warn her—but of what? Married couples often took other people along on their honeymoons. If Justin Lockwood had truly meant his marriage vows, it wasn't as if Sir Harry represented a threat to Marguerite. She started for the door and found her way blocked by Philip.

"Where are you going?"

She gazed up at him, wondered if her doubts were clear on her face as his grip tightened.

"What is it? Is something wrong?"

"I'm not sure." It was hard to resist the desire to run up the stairs after Marguerite and beg her to come home, but she had no choice. "Can you take me back to the inn?"

"Of course." He took her arm and guided her toward the rear of the inn. "I've heard rumors of a prize fight in one of the taverns on the waterfront. If it's true, we'll have to watch our step."

Outside, the narrow cobbled streets seemed to be full of men of all ages and classes intent on finding the rumored site of the fight. Their excitement generated a frisson of danger in Helene, a sense that violence could erupt at any moment. Philip drew her closer to his side and kept to the inside edge of the walkway.

A roar and the crash of breaking glass ahead of them sent more waves of energy pulsing through the crowd. Philip swore as a gang of sailors started to run through the center of the milling crowd, forcing everyone else to the sides. Helene gasped as Philip was knocked into her, shoving her up against the bow window of a milliner's shop.

"I'm sorry, Helene. Are you all right?"

She caught her breath as the crowd surged around them. It reminded her of her family's capture during the revolution, of the sense of being caught up in something she could not control. The mob had swarmed over her parents' carriage, brought it crashing onto its side, and dragged them out like sacrificial animals to appease their bloodlust.

"Hell and damnation!" Philip caught her around the waist and pulled her back into the comparative safety of an alleyway between two of the shops. The crowd roared past them like a mighty river in flood, unstoppable and uncaring about the damage caused in its wake.

"Helene, say something."

She looked up into Philip's worried face, saw his fierce determination to protect her mirrored in his hazel eyes. She reached out a trembling hand and touched his cheek, desperate for something to connect her with the present, to tear her thoughts away from the horrors of the past.

"Helene . . ."

She managed a shaky smile. "I'm fine now. For a moment, I feared myself back in France during the terrors."

"God, I didn't even think about that. I swear I won't let anyone hurt you."

She went up on tiptoe and kissed his mouth. "I know." She kissed him again, harder this time, nipped at his bottom lip. He needed no further invitation to kiss her back, his body pressing her against the uneven stone wall as he devoured her mouth. She slid her hand between them and cupped his balls.

He groaned and stepped away from her. "Not here. It's not safe. We're almost at the Mermaid."

Helene squeezed him once more and then let go. She would have let him take her right then up against the wall but discovered her fear of being found by the mob was even greater.

Philip grabbed her hand and stuck his head out of the alley. "Most of the crowd had disappeared. Let's go."

He yanked hard on her hand and started off down the street. Helene barely had time to grab a handful of her skirts to prevent herself from tripping and was grateful she wore flat-soled walking boots. Her breathing became uneven, but she kept on running as the sign for the Mermaid Inn came into view.

Philip pulled her into the hallway and on up the stairs, slamming their bedroom door shut behind him. Still fighting for breath, she faced him, held his gaze, let him see the lust in her eyes. He leaned against the door, his breathing as ragged as her own.

A muscle flicked in his cheek as he stared at her. "Are you going to tell me what happened?"

She shook her head.

"Don't you think I'm entitled to an explanation?"

She concentrated on the hard planes of his face, needed him to touch her so badly that her whole body started to shake.

"I want you to fuck me."

His expression tightened. "Is that all I am to you? Someone to fuck?"

"Isn't that what I am to you?"

"You are more than that, and you know it."

"Because I understand you?"

He took off his coat and hat, and tossed them onto a chair. "Are you suggesting you don't? You are the first woman I've ever told about my wife and her lover."

She shrugged. "I'm a whore. We're supposed to be good at listening."

"You are a liar."

She fed off his anger, encouraged it, fanned it even higher. "How so?"

He advanced toward her. "You use sex to hide your true feelings and to turn men into slavering fools."

She tossed her head. "And you are such an expert about sex."

"I'm experienced enough to know the truth when I see it."

She lowered her gaze as she struggled to assimilate what he had said. How dare he try to tell her why she did anything at all!

"So you don't want to fuck me."

His fingers slid under her chin, and he forced her head up until their eyes met.

"Of course I do, but tonight it will be on my terms, not yours. I intend to make love to you until you beg me to stop."

"No one man has ever managed to satisfy me all night."

"Then tonight will be a first for you, won't it?"

His cold lips closed over hers, and she gasped as his tongue filled her mouth. His hands worked on the buttons and ribbons of her gown and stays, ripping and tearing when he couldn't get access fast enough. With a muttered curse, he backed her toward the bed and sat her on the edge.

He used his broad shoulders to shove her legs apart and slid two fingers right inside her, using his thumb for her clit. Helene moaned as he bent his head and added the torment of his tongue and teeth to her wet, swollen sex. She lifted her hips, seeking the delights of his stabbing tongue, felt her body gather itself for a climax.

He pulled back, his mouth and chin gleaming with her cream, his expression feral. She tried not to writhe and beg for him to let her finish as he stripped off her gown and light stays, leaving her in silk stockings and garters.

"Such a beautiful body, Helene. So easy for a man to lose himself in it and in you."

He slipped one finger inside her, watched as he slid it in and out. The soft wet sucking sounds excited her even more. With his other hand he cupped her breast, used his thumb to bring her nipple to a hard aching point.

She was trembling now, her nerves stretched tight, anticipating his next caress, needing it more than she needed to breathe. He kissed her, his tongue coated in her juices, which she eagerly lapped up.

"You're going to take my cock in your mouth and make me hard now. I want you to do it quick, like a man."

"Like Adam?"

"Yes, like Adam."

To her annoyance, he seemed unsurprised by her knowledge of his sexual activities. Had he come to terms with his needs, then? Had he realized what he truly desired?

He helped her down from the bed and slowly undid his breeches. His shaft already tented his underclothes. He shivered as he pulled them down to reveal his cock.

"Do it."

Helene sank to her knees at his booted feet and licked the dripping crown of his cock. His hand tightened in her hair.

"Take it all."

She opened her mouth wide, and with a surge of his hips, he fed his cock between her lips. She had little time to prepare as he began to push himself deeper with each hard thrust. Not that she minded. She'd wanted to be overwhelmed and dominated, to not be allowed to think of anything but pleasuring him. And he knew that. Despite his irritation, he still knew what she wanted and was more than willing to give it to her.

"Stop now."

She held still as he carefully disengaged his shaft from her mouth and sat heavily into the nearest chair. He patted his knees.

"Come here."

"I'm not your dog."

"You are, however, in need of my cock."

He didn't smile, just continued to stare at her. With a sigh, she complied. He lifted her onto his lap, her thighs straddling his, soft buckskin leather against her naked skin. His thick wet shaft was wedged between them. His fingers and thumbs closed around her nipples and pinched hard, making her moan.

"Do you want my cock?"

"If you want to make love to me until I swoon, then I would say it was a necessity."

He squeezed her nipples again, bent his head to nuzzle the

exposed tips with his tongue and then his teeth. She couldn't help squirming closer to him, her already swollen clit rubbing against the root of his shaft.

"Do you want it, Helene?"

She tried to shake off the waves of intense desire shuddering through her, to find a clever riposte, but she couldn't. He fingered her nipples again tugged at the tips until they ached. She writhed against him again, every coarse hair on his groin a separate torment against her clit.

"Yes."

He considered her, his eyes narrowed, his lush mouth curved up at one corner. "Tell me exactly what you want."

Helene closed her eyes as he placed his hands around her waist and set her farther back on his thighs, away from his cock. He slipped his hand between her spread thighs and rubbed his palm against her sex.

"You're certainly wet enough, so tell me what you want."

His tone was commanding enough to annoy her, but she was too in need of relief to argue about that now.

She sighed. "I want your cock inside me."

"Just my cock?"

She blinked at him. "What else is there?"

"Whatever I want, surely?" He stretched out his arm and retrieved her hairbrush, measured the length of the handle against his cock. "For example, this would work well."

Helene simply stared at him as her heart rate kicked up. Beneath that harsh exterior, he truly was an exceptionally sensual man. She kept her expression neutral, her voice even more so.

"Do you wish me to use it on you?"

His eyebrows rose. "What?"

She touched the bristles, stroked her fingers over his on the handle. "I can spank you with it." She watched him carefully through her lowered lashes. "Or oil the handle and insert it in your arse." His cock jerked, dripped more precum in a sudden slippery rush. "Perhaps now that you've had Adam, that is really what you prefer."

"I haven't had Adam. I'm not sure I could ever become that intimate with a man."

"Ah, I see. You allow him to pleasure you and give nothing in return—such a gentleman."

He held her gaze and smiled slowly. "I wouldn't say that."

She stared at him, tried to picture him pleasuring a man, and found the image not only believable but highly arousing.

"Perhaps you'll let me watch next time."

"Perhaps." He smoothed his fingers over her hairbrush. "But for now, let's concentrate on you."

Before she could utter another word, he flipped her over onto his lap. Her hair fell over her face as she struggled to right herself, but he was too strong. She shuddered as his hand smoothed over her buttocks.

"Gossip in the kitchen insists that you have never experienced the joys of the top floor yourself. Is that true?"

Helene stopped moving and lay still, trying to catch her breath. She stiffened as Philip caressed her flesh with the flat wooden side of her brush.

"Answer the question, Helene."

"If you are asking if I have never allowed a man to dominate me, then you are correct."

"And why is that?"

"I would think it is obvious."

"You are afraid you might enjoy it too much?"

"Don't be absurd. I've had enough of being forced by men to last me a lifetime."

"I'm not intending to force you."

"Then why won't you let me sit up?" She wiggled in another attempt to get free and felt the swell of his cock jerk against her hip.

"Because I wish to play with the luscious curves of your

arse, of course." He moved the brush around, slid his other hand between her legs, and cupped her sex. "You told me you wanted to be fucked all night. Don't you trust me to do that?"

Helene opened her eyes and stared at the worn red pattern on the fireside rug. What did she want? And could she really trust him enough not to hurt her?

"Helene?"

She jerked as he tapped the brush five times against her right buttock and then her left, felt warmth pool in her groin. Each small slap of the brush pushed her against Philip's hand, which covered her already aroused sex.

He did it again, harder this time, then paused to fondle her breasts and tug hard at her nipples. Heat coalesced in her sex, and she shuddered as he resumed his attentions to her buttocks, alternating from left to right. A suggestion of pain shimmered in her mind and was transformed into raging desire.

She sensed she was about to climax without him even penetrating her and pushed shamelessly against his hand. With a muttered curse, he dropped the brush, grabbed her around the waist, and righted her. She screamed as her world revolved, and he impaled her onto his cock in one demanding thrust. She came hard, biting at his mouth as he tried to kiss her, fighting his iron grip on her hips that held her down on him.

Grimly Philip held on, let her pulse and writhe around his cock until she collapsed against his shoulder. He prayed he wouldn't inadvertently make himself come as he lifted her off him and put her back over his lap.

"What are you doing?"

Helene sounded dazed and most unlike herself. He liked that.

"What I want."

He picked up the brush again, studied her now slightly reddened arse. He'd spent some time on the top floor watching the clientele perform outrageous sexual acts. Seeing someone being spanked made him hard as hell. By God, he was hard now, so eager to fuck Helene that it hurt to breathe.

With great care, he stroked the bristled side of the brush over her skin, enjoying the way she trembled at the subtle touch. Her breath hissed out as he applied a little pressure to the figure eight he was making across both her buttocks. He slipped one finger inside her wide wet passage and curled it around to probe that especially sensitive spot.

Helene obliged him by coming again, her sharp cries a siren call to his oversensitive cock. He knew he couldn't wait any longer. With a harsh groan, he picked her up, backed her against the nearest wall, and shoved his cock home. She didn't stop coming as he pounded into her, her heels dug into his buttocks as she held him deep, taking every inch of him.

He started to grunt with every long stroke, felt his cum gather in his balls and force its way up his shaft.

"Helene . . ."

He could only groan her name as he came inside her, his seed filling her as she climaxed with him, wringing every last drop from his still pulsing shaft. There was no finesse, no gentle loving; this was sex at its most powerful and raw. The way it should be between them, the way it always had been and always would.

He didn't bother to pull out, just carried her over to the bed and fell on it with her wrapped in his arms. When he opened his eyes, she was staring at him, her expression belligerent.

He sighed. "What is wrong now?"

"You didn't give me a chance to decide whether I wanted you to spank me or not."

"You wanted it. You screamed so loudly when you came I thought I'd be permanently deaf."

"You are a conceited oaf."

He levered himself up on one elbow to look down at her properly. Her nipples were tight red buds, and their bellies were meshed together with a combination of his seed and their sweat. He loved the way they smelled together. Experimentally, he moved his hips, heard her bite off a gasp.

"Do you need more, madame?" His cock thickened at the thought of having her once more. He angled his hips against her pussy again, slipped his hand between them to locate her clit, found it slippery with his cum and very sensitive to his touch. "Of course you do. You are insatiable, are you not?"

He slipped out of her and kissed his way down her belly and through her fair thatch. He used the tip of his tongue to titillate her clit until she writhed against him, and then set off on a leisurely tour of her pussy lips and slick opening. She was so wide for him now, he could stick four fingers in without her feeling too tight.

She came suddenly against his mouth, and he stuck his tongue deep inside her to feel her muscles clench, enjoyed the rush of her cream. He reckoned if he really did intend to satisfy her all night, he needed to pace himself and pleasure her in as many ways as he could devise to save his cock from drooping.

He knelt up to look at her. She lay sprawled on the bed, legs open wide, breasts heaving, blue eyes softened with desire. No wonder every man in London wanted to be in his position. He could hardly blame them. Helen of Troy resurrected. No wonder men fought over her. If she belonged to him, he'd fight for her too.

Helene watched as he palmed his cock and drew it away from his stomach. He held her gaze, glad she enjoyed looking at him, eager to bring her to that gasping screaming plateau of sexual perfection once more. He wanted to crawl up the bed and place his cock between her perfect lips, but he wasn't ready to come again quite yet.

He climbed off the bed and retrieved the brush. Showed it to her before he coated it in her thick cream and his seed and slid it inside her. Her hips bucked as he worked it in and out of her wet fuckable pussy. He bent his head, delicately set his teeth on her clit, and waited until she climaxed again before releasing her.

Idly he knelt back and fingered her nicely swollen clit, collected his seed on his finger, and headed for her arse. There were plenty of candles in the room, and oil was easy to come by. He'd always wanted to use two dildos on a woman at the same time. While he worked her pussy and arse, she could pleasure his cock with her mouth. If he wanted to last the night, it was definitely time to become more creative.

20

Helene lay sprawled bonelessly over Philip's body, her cheek pressed to his chest, her arm around his waist. His heart thumped steadily, comfortably, along with hers. Faint streaks of gray light penetrated the half-open, moth-eaten bed curtains. Birds were singing, and the rumble of cart wheels over the cobblestones below made the diamond-paned windows vibrate. She turned her head slightly to kiss his nipple, and he groaned.

"God, Helene, you really are insatiable."

She smiled against his chest. In truth, she was worn out and completely satisfied, but she wasn't sure she wanted Philip to know that yet. He nuzzled her ear and bit down gently.

"As I have gratified your lust, are you now going to tell me what happened with Marguerite?"

Helene kept her eyes closed. "She was worried that I meant to interfere with the marriage."

"You were going to interfere."

Helene sighed. "I know, but she was so happy; I couldn't bring myself to ruin everything purely on unproven suspicions and my instincts."

"From what I've seen and heard, your instincts are usually correct. What exactly is worrying you?"

"Marguerite's husband, Lord Justin Lockwood."

"I don't believe I've ever met him. Is he known to be a violent man or a drunkard?"

"Not that I know of." She rolled over onto her back and stared up at the low-beamed ceiling. "It's more a question of where his sexual tastes lie."

Philip frowned. "Do you think he's perverted?"

"No, just that he might prefer the company of men."

"Then why would he bother to marry?"

"Most men of his persuasion do. It's the only way they can avoid the rumors about their sexual inclinations and activities. Often, they feel obliged, for family reasons, to provide the next heir."

"You have proof of her husband's tastes?"

Helene turned to smooth a lock of hair back from Philip's face. "If I did, do you think I would have left Marguerite with him? I've simply seen him with the same man on several occasions at the pleasure house."

Philip came up on one elbow and considered her, his hazel eyes narrowed. "Doing what?"

"Nothing remarkable, just sitting very closely together."

"Not in bed, then?"

"*Non*, as I said, it is just a feeling I have that they are more than just friends."

He reached out and traced the outline of her mouth with one lazy finger. "Now Lockwood is married, perhaps the friendship will reach its natural conclusion."

Helene held his gaze. "That is what I hoped until Marguerite said that Sir Harry had accompanied them on their honeymoon too."

Philip's eyebrows rose. "Well, damn."

"Indeed. But there is nothing I can do unless she asks me for help, is there?"

"No, not a thing." He stroked her cheek. "It's devilishly hard being a parent, isn't it?"

"You have no idea. Just wait until your children reach their twenties." She kissed his roving fingers. "At least Marguerite doesn't blame me for all her ills, like the twins do. Last night she even thanked me for bringing her up."

"And that meant a lot to you, didn't it?"

She tried to laugh. "I've never forgiven myself for allowing others to care for my children when they were growing up."

"But you were only a child yourself, and you could scarcely have allowed them to live with you in a brothel."

She slapped a hand over his mouth. "It is not a brothel." His tongue tickled her palm, and she whipped it away.

"I know, but you were wise not to have them with you. Most upper-class parents send their children off to the care of wet nurses, nannies, and boarding schools. I hardly ever saw my mother when I was growing up, and it did me no harm."

She studied his relaxed features, saw no hint of condemnation in his gaze, and kissed his mouth.

"Thank you."

"For what?"

"For making love to me all night and for understanding me."

"I wouldn't claim to understand you at all; you're a woman. But I do *know* you."

"In the biblical sense?"

He grabbed her, rolled her onto her back, and pushed his knee between her thighs. "Definitely, and the night isn't quite over yet."

Helene clutched at his forearms as he braced himself over her. "You don't have to prove yourself anymore. You are definitely the best lover I've ever had."

The crown of his cock nudged her swollen sex and slid in an inch. He groaned and slowly rocked his hips, each motion pressing him farther inside.

"God, you feel as tight as a virgin. Are you sore?"

"Of course I am. I might be insatiable, but I'm still human."

"You'll take me once more; I know it." His balls pressed up against her buttocks as he slid all the way to her center. "I promised to satisfy you all night long, and it isn't morning yet."

Helene closed her eyes and relaxed, allowed Philip to direct her movements and play her as he wished. He took his time, his movements slow and unhurried compared to the night's first fierce couplings. Warmth engulfed Helene's belly and flowed lower to her sex. He changed his position, slid his hands under her buttocks, and continued his long regular strokes.

She hadn't expected to climax, was almost surprised when the pleasure crashed over and through her, leaving her shaking and clinging to Philip. His mouth covered hers as he continued to thrust, faster now, each motion sharper and shallower. He froze over her and came in long pumping jets of seed deep inside her womb.

"I hope you're satisfied now, Helene." Philip's voice was a mere thread. "Or else a good man died for nothing."

With a sigh, she took his weight on her, curled her arms and legs around him, and drifted off to sleep. Her last thought was that she was glad she didn't have to ride a horse all the way back to London but could relax in the comparative luxury of the curricle.

By the time they reached London that night, Helene regretted the necessity of having to leave her bed at the inn at all. At times during the journey, Philip had provided her with his lap to lie across and the support of his body, but she was still sore. Perhaps she really was getting too old to indulge in such prolonged and exciting sexual antics. She smothered a smile against

Philip's shoulder as she recalled some of the details of his love-making. Well, maybe not quite yet.

Philip patted her gloved hand.

"We are almost there, Helene. Do you want me to come in with you, or should I take this opportunity to go and see if my staff have deserted me and my lodgings are still standing?"

Reluctantly, Helene straightened. "Yes, go home, and I'll see you in the morning."

She certainly needed time to consider their journey, to understand why she had allowed him to treat her as he wished. Why she felt so safe confiding in him.

He raised his eyebrows at her. "Am I being dismissed?"

She retied the ribbons of her bonnet and settled it back in the middle of her head. "Why do you sound so annoyed? I would imagine you would be grateful for a night in your own bed."

"You think I'm not up to another night like the last?" Helene merely looked at him until the corner of his mouth kicked up in a reluctant smile. "Perhaps you are right." He elbowed her in the side. "There's no need to make excuses, darling. If you can't bear the thought of being mastered again, I understand."

Helene opened her mouth and then shut it again. She would not allow this infuriating man to get the better of her. She smiled sweetly. "You are right; I do need my sleep."

He chuckled. "I'm always suspicious when you smile like that and agree with me."

The curricle leaned dangerously to one side as Philip maneuvered around a tight corner and slowed the horses to a walk. One more deft turn and they were in the elegant square of houses where Helene's was located. One of the footmen stationed at her front door ran out to hold the horses while Philip got down to help her out of the curricle.

He lifted her onto the flagstones in one easy motion and kept hold of her, his hands firmly around her waist.

"Are you sure you don't want me to come in?"

She smiled up at him. "I really am very tired."

"Then I'll see you in the morning." He kissed her forehead, released her, bowed, and got back into the curricle. She watched him drive away, his form impeccable as he turned out of the square. With a sigh, she trudged up the steps to the house, every muscle in her body protesting. A nice hot bath, a quiet night's sleep and she would be more than ready to face Philip in the morning.

Judd met her at the top of the stairs, his chubby face flustered. "Welcome back, madame. I hope your trip was successful."

"It was. Thank you, Judd." She noticed he still didn't look happy. "Is there something you wish to tell me?"

He cleared his throat as he shut the front door behind them. "Well, actually, madame, there are a couple of things that have gone, shall I say, slightly awry."

"Are the twins all right?"

Helene removed her bonnet and coat, and Judd handed them to a footman. From the resolute expression on his face, she knew she wouldn't be climbing into her bed for quite a while.

"They are fine, madame, and happily ensconced in the guest suites with Mrs. Smith-Porterhouse."

Helene headed for her study, Judd at her side. She halted as she saw a fashionably dressed woman pacing the hallway outside her door.

"Is this one of those little problems you mentioned, Judd?"

"Indeed, madame. I can only apologize. The lady entered the house under false pretenses and insisted on waiting to speak to you."

Helene fixed a smile on her face and advanced upon the younger woman. "Good evening. May I help you?"

The woman turned to look at Helene, her gaze dismissive, her tone even more so. "I'm waiting to speak to Madame Delornay, not one of her bits of muslin."

Helene lifted her chin and allowed a silence to fall between them before she spoke. "I am Madame Delornay. How may I help you?"

"You can't be! I've heard that hag is almost forty, and you"—she gestured wildly at Helene—"you are far too young and beautiful to be her."

Helene set her jaw, sent Judd for some tea, and ushered her unwanted guest into her study. She took a seat and waited until the woman settled herself fussily in the chair opposite her.

"I'm afraid I can't help you if I don't know who you are."

"I'm Lord George Grant's wife, Julia, although you must already know that."

Helene shrugged. "Why should I know you? You are obviously far superior in rank to me, and we do not share the same set of acquaintances."

"Although we apparently share my husband."

"I'm not quite sure I understand you."

Julia raised her head and glared at Helene through the unshed tears glinting in her eyes. "You are sleeping with my husband. Is that clear enough for you?"

"But that is untrue. I never sleep with married men, and I've certainly never slept with George. I consider him one of my oldest and dearest friends."

"As if a woman like you was going to tell me the truth anyway," Julia sneered. "I just came to warn you that if you go through with your plan to marry him, I will not go quietly. I will fight for my daughter's rights as well."

Helene raised her eyebrows. "I have no plans to marry anyone. I don't need a husband or a protector, and I'm wealthy in my own right. Why on earth would I choose to give all that up for one man?"

A hint of uncertainty showed in Julia's brown eyes. "George said you want to marry him."

"Then George is mistaken. Forgive me, perhaps he merely shouted out such a nonsensical thing when you were fighting? Men often make empty threats when they are enraged."

"George and I never fight."

"Then you are to be congratulated. I've never met a married couple who doesn't have the occasional disagreement."

There was a knock at the door as Judd returned with the tea and a selection of cakes. Helene took her time pouring the steaming liquid as her tired brain scrambled to deal with George's irate wife. It wasn't the first time she'd been accosted by a jealous woman, but it was never pleasant. Julia refused to touch her tea—perhaps she thought it might be poisoned.

Helene put down her empty cup. "I can assure you, my lady, that I have no intention of marrying George."

Julia glared at her. "You lie. I can see I made a mistake in appealing to your better nature. A woman like you obviously doesn't have one."

Helene stood up and walked across to open the door. "When you have finished insulting me in my own house, perhaps you'd like to take your leave?"

"I'll leave when I have your word that you don't intend to seduce George away from me."

Anger surged through Helene's already battered defenses as she stared at the younger woman. "If I wanted him, I could've had him any time in the last eighteen years. Why would I suddenly change my mind now?"

"Because you are getting older and losing your charms?"

"And I secretly yearn to be a nobleman's wife?" Helene smiled. "I've turned down wedding proposals from every tier of the nobility. Why on earth would I settle for the fourth son of a duke?"

Julia seemed to have run out of things to say. Her gaze remained fixed on Helene as if she was desperate to deny the truth of Helene's words.

"One last word of advice, my lady. Perhaps if you took better care of your marriage, you wouldn't need to seek to justify your adultery by attacking me for my supposed indiscretions with your husband."

Julia stormed toward Helene, her cheeks red, her breathing uneven. "How dare you speak to me like that?"

"How dare you march into my house and treat me like a scullery maid?"

To Helene's amazement, Julia's face crumpled.

"You don't understand. I only did that to make him notice me again. Now that I've seen you, I realize I can never compete."

"What utter nonsense." Helene sighed and stared into the other woman's eyes. "Please believe me—I have no desire to steal your husband, and I shall certainly tell him off for upsetting you so."

Julia grabbed her hand. "Oh, please. Don't tell him anything. He'd be so angry with me if he knew I'd been in this horrible, sinful place."

"If I don't tell him, you must forget this ridiculous notion that I want to marry him."

"I'll try."

"The only reason George comes here is to help me with my accounts. As a shareholder in the business, he is obliged to ensure that it is running smoothly and that his income is protected." She smiled. "And I wouldn't be so sure that George doesn't notice you. He was extremely upset when he found out you had taken a lover."

"He was?"

"And he loves your daughter. I doubt he would do anything to upset her."

Julia let out a shaky breath. "That is true. Perhaps all is not lost after all."

Helene patted her shoulder. "Good, then why don't I get Judd to escort you to your carriage or call you a hackney cab?"

Julia nodded docilely. "My carriage is in Barrington Square. It won't take me a moment to walk around the corner."

Helene curtsied and allowed Judd the honor of escorting Lady George Grant off the premises. She sank down in the nearest chair and groaned as her headache returned. What on earth had George been up to? How dare he drag her into his marital quarrels? She'd promised Julia she wouldn't tell him outright, but she certainly meant to make it clear to him, yet again, that marriage was completely out of the question.

She bit her lip. Had she been too hard on the woman? Having to defend herself against such ridiculous accusations had drained the last of her sorely depleted strength. This was why she never slept with married men. It was far too complicated when other people's feelings were involved.

With a sigh, she got to her feet and headed back to her private apartment. It would be strange to sleep alone after her nights with Philip. She'd grown used to him in her bed in a way she had never experienced with a man before. She paused by the kitchen, heard the twins muted laughter behind the thick door. Should she go in and say good night? No doubt if they saw her, their laughter would instantly be replaced by sullenness.

The twins could wait to hear about Marguerite in the morning. She nodded at the footman stationed outside her suite and went inside. Fresh hothouse flowers from Viscount Harcourt-DeVere's conservatory sweetened the air, and a fire burned brightly in the grate. For a long moment, Helene studied the flames as she recognized a vital truth: She would have to tell Philip about the twins. He deserved to know he was their father. It wasn't as if she wanted anything from him in return.

She was also very aware of the malicious unknown "friend" who had written to the twins to disclose her address and supposed profession. If that person had access to such private information, perhaps he also knew who the twins' father was?

Another even more unwelcome thought gripped her. As Lord Derek's heir, had Philip come across any private correspondence between her and Angelique that mentioned the twins and their whereabouts? It was certainly possible. Perhaps Philip had already worked out that he was the twins' father and for reasons unbeknownst to Helene was keeping that information to himself.

Helene rubbed her aching temple and decided to take all her problems to bed. At least that way she might be able to sleep between her worrying.

21

Philip arrived at the pleasure house just as the kitchen clock struck six times. He'd slept well, reassured his staff that he was neither dead, pursued by debt collectors, nor rolled up with grief, and answered all his outstanding correspondence. His bed had seemed empty without Helene in it, and he'd missed the simple pleasure of her acerbic company more than he had anticipated.

He took off his cloak and hat and hung them in the dark hallway. Helene's revelations about Marguerite followed by the erotic night they'd shared seemed to have complicated their relationship even further. Helene was the only woman he'd met who seemed to instinctively understand him and, more importantly, accept him for what he was.

What the devil would he do with himself when the thirty days were up? He'd be adrift again, unless Helene kept her promise and allowed him some say in the business matters of the pleasure house. He realized he'd like that. Not that he didn't have a whole new set of responsibilities to worry about and more possibly to come if the Earl of Swansford died without a son.

He slowly pushed open the door of the kitchen and found it surprisingly full of people. All the kitchen staff were busy polishing the silverware under the direction of Judd. Helene's twins sat at the table eating Madame Dubois's famous croissants. He paused to watch them, smiling indulgently as the boy teased his sister by withholding the mug of hot chocolate madame had also placed on the table. It reminded him of watching his own children at the breakfast table.

Philip forced himself to breathe. It was *just* like watching his children at the breakfast table. He turned abruptly to his left and bumped into Helene.

"Bonjour, Philip."

God, he couldn't speak to her now. With a sharp nod, he blundered his way across the hall into the wine cellar and clattered down the steps into the welcoming darkness.

"Damnation!"

He grabbed the first bottle his hand connected with and threw it at the brick wall. The glass shattered with a satisfying crash, and the strong smell of brandy stung his senses. He didn't bother to light a candle, just fumbled his way to the nearest wall and sat down, knees drawn up to his chest, his head in his hands.

After a while, he managed to control his breathing and open his eyes, not that he could see much. And truly he might as well have been blind. He'd been misled by the twins' fair coloring and his own deliberate decision to ignore any offspring Helene had created with another man. And what sensible man went around looking to see if he'd fathered any bastards anyway?

But he should at least have considered it. They'd been young and impetuous, and despite his best efforts, he'd obviously gotten her pregnant. He gripped his knees even more tightly. Why the hell hadn't she told him then or now?

"Philip?"

He looked up; saw the flicker of candlelight descending the stairs and a woman's distorted shadow on the wall. He shielded his eyes as Helene spun slowly around trying to find him.

"Philip, are you all right? Did you fall?"

He still couldn't speak, became aware of a growing ball of anger settling somewhere between his chest and his gut. She knelt down beside him, the soft muslin of her dress floated over his fingers and her flowery scent replaced the acidic tang of bottled wine. The angle of the candlelight kept their faces in the shadows, which was something of a relief.

She touched his arm, and he flinched away. So much for knowing her. So much for his strange belief that they shared a common soul. He took a deep breath, which was difficult when all he could inhale was her beguiling familiar essence.

"How old are they?"

"The . . . twins?"

"Yes."

"They have just turned eighteen."

He took his time to absorb that, worked out that they were indeed what he thought they were. Yet another woman lying to him about his own children. Did she take him for a fool like his wife had?

"Why didn't you tell me?"

Her sharp intake of breath sounded loud in the echoing confines of the cellar. "Who told you?"

He frowned into the darkness. Why did she sound so defensive? He was the one who had been deceived—again.

"Nobody had to tell me. I worked it out for myself."

"How?"

"Why does it matter?"

"Because I have taken great care to keep the twins away from you. I foolishly hoped you would be too preoccupied with other things to worry about something that happened such a long time ago."

"Too preoccupied with fucking their mother, you mean."

She didn't reply. He relished the harried sound of her breathing and the subtle trembling of her limbs where she almost touched him.

"I know you won't believe me, but I did intend to tell you."

"When? On my deathbed?"

"After the thirty days were up. I didn't want to use such an important and personal piece of information to make you leave."

Damnation, how dare she sound so reasonable and yet so vulnerable at the same time? He wanted her to hurt as much as he did, to make her feel as betrayed as he felt.

"That's very sporting of you. Perhaps it didn't occur to you that I might be able to handle a discussion about my own children without storming out in a huff?"

She hesitated again as if trying to choose her words with great care. "I wasn't sure if you would wish to know you had more children."

"Because they are bastards? I'm already accustomed to having to deal with that because of my wife and her lover. And if you had married me the first time we met, they wouldn't be bastards, would they?"

"That is unfair."

"But it is true, isn't it?"

"I didn't know I was pregnant until after you left me."

"You were the one who made me leave."

"I seem to remember you were more than willing to go after I told you I was a whore."

"That is a lie."

Silence fell between them again, and Philip closed his eyes to avoid staring at Helene's perfect profile. She eased down beside him, her back against the wall, knees drawn up to her chin.

"When I came to London, I fully intended to ask Viscount Harcourt-DeVere to help me find you so that I could at least tell you I was pregnant. It wasn't that I expected you to marry me or anything—I knew I wasn't of the right class for that—but I at least wanted you to know."

"But you didn't tell me."

She sighed. "How could I when I read in the newspaper that you were already married?"

Philip stared into the gloom, trying to piece together the sequence of events he'd tried so hard to forget.

"I had no choice. Did you think I did it out of spite? After I left you at the inn and returned to the city, I spent several days drinking and whoring to force myself to forget you. By the time I appeared before my father, I was determined to tell him to go to the devil. Unfortunately, he threatened to disinherit me, and that brought me to my senses."

He tried to laugh. "You were right about me. I was a coward. I couldn't imagine living my life without all the costly trappings I'd become accustomed to. He also threatened to marry Anne off to a notorious aging lecher, and I couldn't allow that either. So we were married by special license the next day."

He shuddered as her fingers brushed his. He took hold of her cold hand and held on tight.

"Even if I had known I was pregnant, Philip, I still would've sent you away."

"I know." He squeezed her fingers hard. "I'm not sure if I would've gone, though."

"You would've had no choice in the end. Your father was determined you should marry Anne."

"And if I had wanted to support you and the twins, I had to marry Anne to claim her inheritance. How ironic."

She stirred beside him, and her skirts made the candlelight flicker. "The twins were well cared for. Viscount Harcourt-DeVere ensured that they were boarded at the same private school as my older daughter, Marguerite. I missed watching them grow up, but at least I knew they were safe."

"Of course; you weren't able to keep them with you, were you?"

"I would've loved to keep them all, but unfortunately, my lifestyle did not allow it. As I said, I could scarcely bring them up in a pleasure house, however exclusive it was."

He could hear the raw hurt behind her light tone and realized he wasn't the only person who had suffered. The hot glow of anger inside him subsided. The older he grew, the more he realized life wasn't black and white, that there were many hues of gray in between. Helene's decisions about the twins had little to do with his wife's deliberate deception and her subsequent lack of interest in the results of her adultery.

"Some women simply abandon their children to the foundling hospitals."

She sighed. "I couldn't have done that. I never knew which man in the Bastille fathered Marguerite, but she was still my child. And the twins were doubly special, because they reminded me of you."

He swallowed hard. "If you had come to me, even after I was married, I would've helped you, supported you, set you up in your own house . . ."

"I know, but what would've happened to me then? I'd be beholden to you for everything, at your beck and call, simply existing between the moments you could snatch away from your wife. After my elderly French lover died, I swore that I would never be a kept woman again."

He thought about that. Allowed his mind to consider her words, even realized he could accept her logic, despite his hurt. "And your life has been better without me?"

"My life has been different. I have achieved a level of independence and success that few women manage. I have three

healthy children and enough money saved to know I will never
have to depend on anyone for anything in my old age."

"That is certainly an achievement." He let go of her hand.
She was right. She didn't need him at all. "Do the twins know
I'm their father?"

"*Non*, I haven't told them. I assume you would not have
been amused if they'd suddenly decided to seek you out and
confront you."

Philip stood up and brushed at his breeches. "Are you going
to tell them now?"

Helene picked up the candle and got up as well, shielding
the flame with her cupped hand. "That is for you to decide,
surely?"

"Will you let me think about it?"

"Of course. I know this has been an unpleasant surprise for
you."

"A shock, certainly." Why were they being so polite and
reasonable to each other? What had happened to his desire to
throttle her for deceiving him? It had faded away, pushed into
the background by the sense of their shared pain.

He started for the stairs, aware of her close behind him.

"Philip . . . I am sorry."

He half turned, saw her face illuminated by the light for the
first time, the tears glinting on her cheeks.

"You are sorry? You were faced with the burden of bearing
my children alone. You do not have to apologize to me."

He started up the stairs and emerged into the narrow scullery.
The kitchen door was open, and there was no sign of the twins,
a small thing for which, in his present disordered state, he was
profoundly grateful. He doubted he could face them yet without betraying something of his chaotic feelings. He'd already
guessed they were no fools.

The scent of roasted coffee caught at his senses, and he walked into the kitchen. Madame Dubois nodded to him as he helped himself to some coffee and a slice of freshly baked bread. To his relief, his stomach settled and he realized he was capable of functioning again.

Helene hadn't followed him into the kitchen. He wondered where she'd gone. He doubted she would let their agonizing exchange of confidences affect her as much as it had affected him, but she had been crying. . . .

Philip put down his mug and headed for Helene's office. She wasn't there, so he started up the back stairs and worked his way down through all the floors of the pleasure house. Where in God's name had she gone? There was only once place left to look.

He knocked on the door of her private suite and was surprised when she told him to enter. He found her sitting on the floor, surrounded by bundles of letters.

"Helene, are you all right?"

She nodded as she gathered up some of the stacks of letters and placed them into one of the kitchen baskets. He wasn't deceived by her businesslike manner—he had learned that it concealed so much more.

"I wanted to give you these. They are all the letters I have received from the nuns and the twins since they were taken to the nunnery school." She smoothed one of the faded ribbons. "I kept the twins with me for their first year. After that . . . I had to send them away."

Philip stared at the basket, almost afraid to reach for it. Helene was watching him closely.

"Of course, if you do not wish to read about them, I will understand. . . ."

He picked up the basket, surprised at the weight, and realized he held a lifetime of love.

"Thank you. I promise I will return them to you when I'm done."

She smiled. "There is no need." She clenched her fist to her breast. "I think I have them all by heart."

He studied her face, savoring the strength beneath the fragile exquisite beauty. Strength that had made sure his children survived to adulthood despite the odds stacked against them. He wished he could've seen her body swollen with his seed. . . . With a start, he realized he wanted to bind her to him in the most primitive and possessive ways a man could.

She raised her eyebrows. "Why are you staring at me?"

He managed to shrug. "Because you are beautiful?"

"You have only just noticed that?"

She collected the rest of the letters, put them back into their box, and locked them away in her bedside cabinet. Her self-possession continued to alternately enchant and confuse him.

"I noticed it the first time we met; don't you remember?"

She shrugged. "It was a long time ago. I can hardly be expected to recollect exactly what happened."

He advanced toward her and pulled her into his arms, wanted her attention completely focused on him, wanted to see that famed icy beauty dissolve to reveal her desire for him and him alone.

"You don't remember that I was as hard as a rock for that entire coach journey and that all I could think about was pulling up your skirts and fucking you in front of the other passengers?"

"I don't recall that at all. In truth, you behaved like a perfect gentleman."

"Until I did back you up against a wall and have you."

He suited his actions to his words and maneuvered her up against the nearest wall, shoving her skirts around her waist. At this particular moment, he needed to be inside her more than anything. He hastily undid the buttons on his breeches to reveal his eager cock and lifted her over him.

He held her gaze as he slowly lowered her down over his shaft, groaning as each thick inch was enclosed by her tight wet passage. She gripped his shoulders and dug the heels of her jeweled slippers into his arse.

With a groan, he shifted his grip and allowed her to move on him until he couldn't stand it anymore. He took control of her hips, pressing her down onto his engorged cock as he thrust upward, creating a fast grinding rhythm that drove them both toward a climax. Helene came first, moaning his name, and he swiftly followed, his cock pulsing endlessly as she milked him dry.

He pulled out and let her legs slide down to the floor, pressing her to the wall with his weight.

"I still get hard every time I see you, Helene."

"And I still let you back me up against walls and have your way with me."

A curious sense of peace invaded his limbs, and he struggled with a strong desire to take her back to bed and forget about all their problems in the joy of lovemaking. In the two weeks since he'd seen her again, his life had changed in extraordinary ways. Whatever happened between them, he would never forget her.

He kissed the top of her head. "If you wish to stay here and rest, I'll do the inspection for you."

She pushed at his chest. "I'm not an invalid, Philip. I'm quite capable of following my usual routine, despite your attentions."

He smiled at her businesslike tone. How like her to emerge from his lovemaking with renewed vigor when he felt like taking a long luxurious nap.

"Perhaps I'll stay here and rest instead."

She fixed him with a glare from her fine blue eyes. "You will not. You will accompany me."

"Still hoping to see me chained up on the top floor, then?"

"I would like that." Her gaze turned speculative. "Are you ready to submit to me yet?"

Despite its recent activity, his cock twitched and started to thicken. "Like you submit to me?"

She bit down on her lush lower lip, and his shaft grew even more.

"You seemed to like it when I spanked you with your own hairbrush."

Her color heightened, and she turned toward her dressing room. "I'll be ready in a moment. Perhaps you might straighten your attire."

He glanced down at his unbuttoned breeches, saw the crown of his cock thrusting through his wet shirttails, and grinned. "As I said, I don't need any of those fancy instruments of torture to get me hard, just you."

She didn't reply, but she did slam the door. Philip smiled, sauntered over to the door, and knocked.

"I'll wait for you upstairs."

He picked up the basket of letters and left, amazed that he could find Helene incredibly alluring and profoundly moving at the same time. His discovery of the twins' identity had shocked him to his core, and yet it seemed that his attraction to Helene was still as strong, if not stronger. He paused in the scullery to hide the letters under his cloak and continued on up to the top of the house.

22

"Is there something wrong, *Maman*?"

Helene jumped as she realized Lisette was staring expectantly at her again. What on earth had they been talking about? She was supposed to be enjoying her daughter's company over lunch, not staring into space worrying about Philip. There were less than seven days left of their bargain, and she was no closer to knowing what he was going to do than she had been at the beginning. She knew he'd see it through now, but after that? Could she actually work with him after all?

"I'm sorry, Lisette, I didn't quite hear what you said."

Lisette gave a long-suffering sigh. "I was asking if you wanted to go shopping with me this afternoon while Christian is busy at the races."

"I would like that, my dear. Where exactly do you wish to go?"

"To Bond Street and all the most fashionable places to watch the crowds." Lisette's excitement faded, and she bit her lip. "If you are comfortable with that, *Maman*, of course."

Helene tried to look animated. "Why wouldn't I be? We'll

take Mrs. Smith-Porterhouse with us as well. I'm sure she'd enjoy it."

Lisette fiddled with the lace cuff of her new blue muslin morning dress. "Christian says I shouldn't go out in public with you, because you are a notorious *fille de joie.*"

"And if I assure you that he is wrong, will you believe me?" Helene patted her daughter's hand. "I would like to go out with you."

Shyly, Lisette met her gaze. "I would like that too."

Helene smiled at her daughter. "See? I am not quite the ogre Christian would like me to be. I truly wish to start again and be a better mother to you."

Lisette shifted uneasily in her seat. "It is hard to know what to believe anymore. Christian says you can't be trusted, because you lied to us for years."

"I know that I lied to you, Lisette, but I don't intend to deceive you any longer. It's true that I own and operate this pleasure house, but it is not a brothel. And I certainly haven't been a kept woman since I left France eighteen years ago."

"The letter said you'd had more lovers than any other woman in London." Lisette got up and moved to stare out the window overlooking the back garden. "Is that true?"

Helene stared at her daughter's back. Perhaps this was a good opportunity to be honest with Lisette without Christian's interference. "I might have taken a few lovers over the years, but that was by choice. No one paid me or forced me. I simply enjoy sex."

Lisette spun around, her hand over her mouth, her eyes huge. "*Maman*, what a thing to say! Ladies aren't supposed to indulge in that sort of thing without the sanctity of marriage!"

"Is that what the nuns taught you?" Helene repressed a smile. "Perhaps I should've entrusted your education to a less spiritual school. I'm surprised you are so shocked. The French are usually known for their practicality about matters of love."

Lisette made a worldly dismissive gesture with her hand. "The nuns knew nothing. We girls learned everything from the kitchen staff and the novels that were smuggled in."

Helene rose to her feet and smoothed down her skirts. "One day, when you meet the right man, you will understand about love."

"Did you ever meet the right man, *Maman*?"

An image of Philip flashed through Helene's mind. "My life has been very different from yours. I wasn't able to make the same choices you will have."

"Do you mean you met the right man and lost him?"

Helene smiled. "I suppose I did, although sometimes fate can play tricks on you. If you are lucky, sometimes you cross paths with a loved one more than once." There, she'd admitted her lasting feelings for Philip to herself, even if she never intended to admit them to his face. He would enjoy it far too much.

"Like Lord George?"

Helene went still. "What about him?"

"Only that Lord George said that you'd met when you were very young and that he'd loved you ever since."

Helene managed a smile. "Lord George meant something different, I believe. We have been friends for so long, I regard him as a brother."

"I don't think that was what he meant at all."

Helene studied Lisette's speculative expression. Despite her youth, her daughter was highly observant and a shrewd judge of character.

"He is married, you know, and he has a daughter."

"I know." Lisette sighed blissfully. "I thought maybe that was what you meant when you said sometimes things don't work out the first time but might in the future."

Helene opened the door to her suite and ushered Lisette out in front of her. "I have no desire to marry George. In truth, I have no desire to marry anyone. Now go and find Mrs. Smith-Porterhouse, get your bonnet, and meet me in the hall as quickly as you can."

Lisette disappeared in a swirl of muslin skirts, and Helene gave orders to Judd to find them a hackney cab for the relatively short journey into town. She hurried back in her suite to put on her bonnet and pelisse and to change into stout walking boots.

It sounded as if she needed to have another talk with George. She couldn't have him telling her children she was pining after him when there was the very real possibility that she was pining after someone else. The twins were wary enough of her for her not to want to complicate it any more. She stopped tying her laces as a truly horrible thought occurred to her.

Because of George's insinuations about their relationship, did the twins now think he was their father? And what on earth would happen if Philip decided to tell them the truth?

Helene shuddered as she headed for the main hallway. Philip was out visiting wine merchants, so at least she didn't have to worry about him for the next few hours. He'd promised to return before the evening crowd arrived. She could only hope he didn't sample too much wine and was actually able to be useful.

George would have to be faced, but she wasn't quite sure how. Ever since Philip's arrival, it had become difficult to talk to George. All the ease in their relationship seemed to have disappeared. In truth, she was worried that his infatuation for her had spiraled out of control. Perhaps it would be best to consult with Viscount Harcourt-DeVere and see if he could intervene or speak to George instead.

"Good afternoon, madame."

Judd opened the door and bowed to her. At least it had stopped raining. She was looking forward to her shopping trip with Lisette, without Christian. He was proving much harder for her to reach than her daughter, who at least gave her the benefit of her attention when Helene tried to explain about her past. Christian, of course, being male, hated the idea of his mother having a sexual thought, let alone a series of lovers. But she wished he'd stop sneering at her and being so patronizing. The temptation to shake him until his teeth rattled was becoming hard to resist.

"We're ready, *Maman!*"

Lisette appeared, charmingly attired in a *gros de Naples* colored pelisse and a matching bonnet lined with white satin. Mrs. Smith-Porterhouse wore her usual chestnut brown cloak, which matched her kind brown eyes and hair.

She smiled when she saw Helene. "Good afternoon, Helene."

"Good afternoon, Sylvia. Is my daughter behaving herself properly these days?"

"She is indeed. I enjoy her company almost as much as I enjoy yours."

Helene had met Sylvia and her husband at the pleasure house several years before. Sylvia had continued to visit both Helene and the pleasure house since her husband's death. She'd been delighted to accept Helene's request to act as Lisette's chaperone, declaring she was so bored as a respectable widow that she could scream.

With a satisfied nod, Helene took Lisette's hand and headed out of the door to the waiting carriage. At least shopping would take her mind off her other problems for a while.

Late that night, Helene sat opposite Philip in the kitchen, their attention on the account books. The rest of the staff had long since gone to bed. As their discussions had grown more heated, Philip had discarded his coat and rolled up his shirt-sleeves as if preparing for fisticuffs.

"Helene, all I'm saying is that just because you have done something one way for the last eighteen years doesn't mean it can't be improved upon."

She glared into his hazel eyes, aware that he might have a point but reluctant to concede anything.

Philip cursed under his breath. "For God's sake, woman, I'm not trying to ruin your business; I'm trying to improve it. I do have a stake in its success, remember?"

"How could I forget?" she snapped back before she could stop herself.

He thrust a hand into his hair. "One of your most irritating faults is that you always think you are right."

Helene opened her eyes wide at him. "One of *my* irritating faults? And you are much better?"

The kitchen door crashed open, and Christian stormed in. "It won't work, you know."

"What won't?" Helene asked as calmly as she could.

"Trying to turn Lisette against me by buying her things."

"I have no interest in turning her against you. We merely spent some time together. I'm sorry if you feel threatened by that."

She was aware of Philip sitting across from her. His intense interested gaze fixed on Christian's face.

Christian shrugged. "I have no need to worry about that. There is no way you could ever buy her love."

Helene got to her feet. For the first time in her life, she had no desire to stand her ground. Perhaps Christian would never come to care for her. She was tired of fighting him for every scrap of approval, for every smile or simple acknowledgment of her right to exist.

"I'm quite aware of that. Now, have you anything else you wish to say to me, or are you finished? I have work to do."

"You always do, don't you? Work has always been the most important thing in your life. Lisette needs to remember that before she starts telling me how nice and kind you are. It makes me want to puke."

Helene averted her face, pushed past Philip, who had risen

to his feet, and ran for the door. It was bad enough when Christian was rude to her in private, even worse when he spoke to her like that in front of Philip. She couldn't bear for Philip to see how badly she had handled her relationship with his son.

Philip stared at Helene's back as she escaped the kitchen. He couldn't help but notice that Christian watched her, too, the expression on his handsome young face a combination of disgust and puzzlement. Unexpected anger blossomed in Philip's chest. How dare Christian behave like that to his mother?

Before he could stop himself, he began to speak. "Sit down."

Christian looked at him and openly sneered. "Are you talking to me?"

"I said sit down."

"I prefer to stand."

Philip shrugged. "Then stand. It makes no difference to me."

"You have no right to tell me what to do," Christian muttered as his scowl deepened.

"I believe that it is the duty of any adult male to tell a young fool off when he is being disrespectful to his mother."

"She doesn't deserve my respect. Do you know what she is?" Christian glared at Philip. "Oh yes, of course you do. You're the latest of her endless list of lovers."

"I'm also her friend, and I still maintain that any man who speaks like that to his mother deserves to be horsewhipped."

"For telling the truth?"

"What truth is that?"

"That my mother is a notorious whore."

Philip smiled. "She is indeed notorious but not for being a whore. She is notorious for owning the most exclusive private house of pleasure in London."

"That means the same thing."

"Not at all."

Christian walked away from him, his shoulders set, his hands clenched at his side. "She has lovers."

"Why shouldn't she?"

"Because she is my mother! Because she told me she was a housekeeper and lied to me for years."

"She lied to protect you."

Christian hunched a shoulder. "Now you sound just like her. If I hadn't read that letter about her real life, I—"

"Would still love her?"

Christian swung around. "No! I've never loved her. She abandoned us, whatever the reasons were, and you can't change that."

"She hardly abandoned you. You weren't thrown onto a garbage heap, left to starve in the gutter, or taken to a foundling's home—the fate of many bastard children. You and your sisters were expensively cared for and educated in a safe and pleasant environment, an environment your mother worked hard to pay for."

"On her back."

"And who gives you the right to judge her? You have never had a child. You have no idea what a good parent will do to keep a child alive."

Philip sat back down at the pine table. He had no idea who had disabused the boy about his mother, but he was wise enough to realize what a shock it must have been.

"Did your mother ever speak to you about her life before she came to England?"

"Why would she? She started whoring young enough to have Marguerite when she was only fifteen. I doubt there was much to tell."

Philip considered the young man in front of him. Perhaps

this story wasn't his to tell, but he doubted Christian would ever allow Helene close enough to tell him the truth.

"Your mother and her whole family were prisoners in the Bastille during some of the worst atrocities of the revolution."

"So?"

"So your grandfather, in an effort to save at least one of his family from the guillotine, made a bargain with the prison guards."

Christian went still, his hand on the kitchen door, and slowly looked over his shoulder. "What kind of bargain?"

"He gave them your mother to use as they wanted. I assume she was just as beautiful then as she is now. The guards agreed to the bargain and your mother was forced, not only to watch the rest of her family die, but to submit to anything those monsters demanded of her. She was barely fourteen."

He glanced up at Christian, who was swallowing convulsively. "You can imagine what they wanted from her. And she endured it for almost two excruciating years. Of course, being your mother, she didn't simply give up. She used her abilities to help several other prisoners escape the Bastille and flee to England."

Christian attempted a nonchalant shrug. "She told you this, I suppose? And you believed her?"

"No, she told me almost nothing. In truth, she let me assume she had used her body to establish this amazing business rather than funds from grateful aristocrats she had helped save." Philip leaned forward. "Your mother isn't the kind of woman who sees her own worth, and she certainly doesn't advertise how many people she helped rescue."

"Why not?"

"Because she doesn't believe she did anything particularly extraordinary."

Philip allowed silence to develop between them. He was reluctant to labor the point in case Christian started to feel defensive.

"If you doubt my story, I can provide you with the names of at least two respectable gentlemen who can tell you more."

"That won't be necessary." Christian shoved at the door and left.

Philip sighed as his oldest son slammed out of the room in a manner very reminiscent of his mother. Had he helped or hindered Helene's cause? It was difficult to judge yet, but at least Christian had listened, if reluctantly.

Philip gathered up the account books and went in search of Helene. Because of Christian's interruption, he hadn't had time to voice his other concerns about the state of the books. If he was going to meddle, he might as well finish the job.

He found Helene in her study, staring into space. Her expression was strained, her hands twisted together in a knot.

He dumped the books on her desk and shut the door. "Why do you allow him to talk to you like that?"

"What?"

"Your son—why do you allow him to treat you so disrespectfully?"

"I don't know." She stared at him, her blue eyes troubled, her shoulders already slumped in defeat.

"If anyone else spoke to you like that, you'd cut out their tongue!"

She sighed. "It's not quite that simple."

"Because you are scared of him?"

"I'm not scared. It's just that our relationship is . . . difficult."

Philip glared at her. "He treats you like a whore."

Helene flinched as if he'd struck her. "And telling him I'm not a whore when I run a pleasure house will make everything right?"

"At least you should tell him the truth about your life."

"Philip, he can barely stand to be in the same room with me, let alone share confidences."

He took a deep breath. "Perhaps you should make the time to tell him. You keep saying that you regret your past relationship with the twins, and then you refuse to set it right. It's not like you to be a coward."

She stood up, her cheeks flushed. "I am not a coward!"

He shrugged. "You are, but I think I can understand why. I have no intention of telling my children about the deception surrounding their births. My only fear is that someone else will tell them. Is that what happened with the twins? Christian mentioned a letter."

Helene shivered and wrapped her arms around herself. "Someone sent them a letter telling them the 'truth' about my supposed profession and giving them my real address. I wasn't expecting the twins to descend on me this summer. I intended to go over to the nunnery at Christmas and tell them the real story, and deal with the repercussions from there."

"Do you know who sent the letter?"

"No, I don't. I've thought about it endlessly, and I still have no idea who would want to do that to me."

He studied her defeated posture, suppressed a desire to take her into his arms and promise her that everything would turn out right.

"Don't worry about Christian. I set him straight about a few things."

"You did what?"

He frowned. "I merely told him that he had no right to speak to you as if you were a trollop, and explained why."

"How dare you interfere?" She stormed around her desk to glare up at him.

"I did what I thought was right."

"Without consulting me first?"

"As you said, it's been hard for you to communicate with Christian. I merely tried to make things easier."

She shook her head, as if words were beyond her, and then poked him in the chest. "How would you feel if I approached your children and explained a few home truths to them?"

Resentment and awakening anger crowded through his sense of righteousness.

"You can't compare the two situations."

"I certainly can. They would both be examples of high-handed, unnecessary interference."

"Not quite. I'm Christian's father."

Her hands clenched into fists. "You've known that for less than a week, and you think that gives you the right to interfere?"

"Yes."

"You have to earn that right, Philip. You can't just march in and take over after being an absent parent for eighteen years." Her smile was bleak as she retreated behind her desk and sat down.

"Surely that's up to me? I do have some experience. I have two children from my marriage."

"Are you suggesting you would make a better parent than I do?"

He frowned. "I'm not suggesting that at all. I simply decided Christian needed to hear the truth for once, rather than being coddled and indulged by you, because you are too afraid to have an honest conversation with him."

"I am quite capable of having that conversation! I have already made my peace with Marguerite and have started the process with Lisette."

"But it's harder with Christian, isn't it? Is that because he is a man?"

"What on earth do you mean?"

Philip crossed the room to the door. He was far too angry to discuss the accounts with Helene now.

"Work it out for yourself. You've spent your whole life using your beauty to bedazzle the male sex, to stop them prying into your real life, to keep them from ever getting to know you. But you can't do that with Christian, can you? You can't seduce your own son."

23

In the dim dawn light, as she worked her way through the rooms of the pleasure house's top floor, Helene kicked out at a bloodied riding crop that lay in her path. She had no energy or patience to stop and pick it up. Her staff should be doing that. She glanced around the disordered rooms. Where was everybody?

A groan caught her attention, and she headed to the last of the salons. One of her most difficult and demanding clients, Lord Minshom, stood behind a naked man draped over one of the leather chairs, his hips pumping, one hand wrapped around the other man's cock. He frowned at her, and Helene sighed. No wonder no one was cleaning. Lord Minshom wasn't the sort of man who appreciated being interrupted.

In truth, after her last argument with Philip, she wasn't in a confrontational mood herself. She retreated through the silent rooms back to the servant's staircase. How dare Philip insinuate that she couldn't handle her own son? And how dare he suggest she deliberately set out to seduce every man she met? She was quite out of charity with him and had spent the last two days avoiding him whenever possible. He still shared her bed, but when she pretended to sleep, he hadn't bothered her.

She bit her lip as she descended the stairs. That bothered her more than she could've imagined. She was used to him making love to her, wrapping her in his arms and holding her close all night long. She'd never felt as safe as she did with Philip. True, they might argue, but she'd always believed that at heart they had begun to trust each other.

But since their disagreement over Christian, Philip had emotionally distanced himself from her. Despite her resolve not to beg his pardon, his withdrawal still hurt.

Judd appeared at the bottom of the stairs, his round face peering up into the gloom. "Madame? A note just arrived for you. It says 'urgent.' "

Helene immediately thought of a thousand things that could be wrong and raced down the stairs to meet Judd. She plucked the note from his outstretched fingers and turned toward the light streaming in one of the big windows at the front of the house. She recognized Marguerite's distinct handwriting and ripped open the seal.

Maman, I need you. I'm at Grillons Hotel.

Helene reread the almost illegible scrawl several times to try and make better sense of it. The paper fell through her suddenly nerveless fingers, and she whirled around to find Judd still watching her.

"I have to go out. Get me a hackney cab."

"Madame, are you all right? Shall I call Lord George or Mr. Philip?"

"No, please tell anyone who inquires that I'm out on business and I'll be back as soon as I can."

Helene ran toward her study to pick up her reticule and to retrieve the bonnet she'd left there the night before. She had no time to change out of the old gown she wore on her morning rounds or rearrange her hair. Marguerite needed her, and there was no time to waste.

The clerk at Grillons gave Helene another condescending look and sighed. "Ma'am, for the last time, I scarcely think anyone lodging in this fine establishment would be a 'friend or relative' of yours. Are you sure you have the correct address?"

Helene raised her chin and studied the young man until he started to blush.

"If you do not tell me which room my daughter, Lady Justin Lockwood, is occupying, I will make sure you are no longer employed here or in any of the finer hotels in London."

The young man rallied. "And how would a woman of your class accomplish that?"

Helene looked around the crowded lobby. There had to be a client of hers here somewhere. Ah, yes, the perfect man. Her gaze alighted on an elderly gentleman reading a newspaper. She walked over to the man and tapped on his shoulder.

"Good lord, Madame Delornay! What a pleasure."

Helene smiled and pointed at the hapless clerk. "Lord Crenshaw, would you be so kind as to tell this young person that I am a perfectly respectable woman?"

Lord Crenshaw stood up, his florid complexion darkening as he glared at the clerk. After a quick glance around the lobby, he came to join Helene at the desk.

"Is there a problem, Madame Delornay?"

Helene fluttered her eyelashes at him. "I'm not sure, Lord Crenshaw. The clerk seems to believe I'm at the wrong hotel."

"Why on earth would he think that?"

"I have no idea. Perhaps you could vouch for my character, my lord?"

Lord Crenshaw scowled at the clerk. "Of course I can. What a ridiculous notion. Madame Delornay is one of the finest and most upstanding women I have ever met!"

"I apologize, my lord. Madame, I'll find that room number for you immediately and someone to show you up."

Helene smiled sweetly. "There is no need. I'll find my own way." She dropped a curtsey to Lord Crenshaw. "Thank you, my lord."

He winked at her. "Delighted to help, my dear."

Helene listened to the number the clerk gave her and headed for the stairs. Philip's remarks about her using her beauty to get what she wanted from men resonated in her head, followed by a rush of anger. What else was she supposed to do when the odds were constantly stacked against her?

She knocked on Marguerite's door and waited, then knocked again harder before finally trying the knob. The door swung open, and Marguerite stood there. Her face was ashen, and her unbound hair fell in thick dark waves around her face. She stared at her mother and started to cry.

"*Maman*, I'm so glad you are here. Justin is dead."

Philip fixed Judd with an accusing stare.

"Where did Madame Helene say she was going?"

"She didn't, sir. She simply said she would be back as soon as she had completed her business."

Judd left and Philip slumped back into Helene's chair. He drummed his fingers on the blotter and stared at the empty desk. Had Helene broken the terms of their bargain by disappearing without him? Or was he the only one who had to remain at the pleasure house for the thirty days? He suspected that was the truth of it and that he couldn't even use that argument to start a fight with her when she got back. And by God, he was spoiling for a fight.

In some ways it would be a relief to break their bargain, to walk away from the increasingly tense situation and ignore the feelings she stirred in him. But there was the matter of the accounts and the mess about the twins to clear up before he left. He groaned. Now he was trying to fool himself. He had no intention of leaving at all.

"Ah, good morning. I expected Helene to be in here. I do beg your pardon."

Philip looked up to see George Grant hovering at the door. "Good morning, Grant. Judd informed me that Helene has disappeared on a mysterious errand."

"Really? I wonder what that can be?" George strolled into the room and took the seat opposite Philip. "Perhaps she has a new lover."

Philip faked a smile, refusing to give George the satisfaction of looking as annoyed as he felt. Helene belonged to him for the next few days. After that was another story.

"But then again, perhaps not. I've noticed, of late, that she seems to be curtailing her amorous activities." George nodded sagely. "Yes, mayhap she has realized she needs to focus her considerable skills on one man."

Philip didn't comment. If George was fishing for information about his relationship with Helene, he'd have to try a lot harder than that. George took out a cigarillo and offered one to Philip, who declined.

"Seeing as we are all alone, Mr. Ross, perhaps I might offer you some advice?"

"About what?"

"Dealing with Helene Delornay."

"I hardly think I need advice from you, sir."

George's smile deepened. "I've known her for eighteen years. I would like to believe I've picked up some pointers as to how she thinks."

Philip simply stared at him, his eyebrows raised until George sighed.

"Look, I'm trying to help you. I've seen many men make

fools of themselves over Helene, and I can see why. She is beautiful, intelligent, and has the ability to draw men to her like bees to honey, but she can be cruel."

"I'm sure she can."

George looked relieved. "You have noticed that about her? Most men never see beyond her beauty to the steel beneath." He shuddered. "I've seen her discard men like used handkerchiefs and move onto the next without a thought for the consequences."

Philip sat back and crossed his legs at the ankles. "For a man who considers himself a loyal friend of Helene's, you do not paint a pretty picture."

George met his gaze. "I'm trying to be honest with you, Ross. She has confided in me about what she really intends to do concerning the shares you currently own."

"Has she really?"

"I think you should know that even if you stay for the allotted thirty days, the moment the agreement is at an end, she will use any weapons necessary to get those shares from you."

"What kind of weapons?"

George shrugged. "Blackmail, perhaps? That is her favorite."

"She will find very little to blackmail me about. I've led an exemplary life."

George hesitated. "I apologize for having to repeat this, but Helene told me she has sworn statements from the servants and one of her clients that you have performed unlawful sexual acts with another man on these premises."

Philip went still. "I beg your pardon?"

"Didn't you know that she documents everything? Why do you think this place is so successful? Helene knows more about the *tons* sexual depravities than anyone in England." He sighed. "I'm almost certain she's bolstering her income by running some minor extortion schemes on the side."

Philip slowly unclenched his hands. "And what does all this have to do with me? I still doubt she'll try blackmail."

George sat forward, his expression earnest. "If you sell your shares to me, you won't need to worry about that. I'll have a bigger say in the business, and I'll be able to stop Helene's more illegal activities and perhaps restrict her overall influence to the minimum."

"Even with my shares, you'll still own only thirty percent of the business."

"Not for long."

"I do not understand."

George grinned. "Don't spread this about, but Helene has agreed to marry me once my divorce comes through. I'll own all the shares then."

"My felicitations."

It took all Philip's best efforts to stay in his chair and not leap forward across the desk and strangle George Grant. Betrayal was a bitter pill to swallow, and this one bit deep.

He got to his feet and bowed. "Thank you for your honesty. It seems I should take advantage of Helene's absence and go and talk to my solicitor about those shares."

George also rose to his feet, his expression rueful and concerned. "I apologize if I have given you a bad taste for Helene's character. She is not to blame for her coldheartedness. She has many reasons to treat men badly."

Philip merely nodded as George departed, whistling merrily. After a deep breath, Philip snatched up a pen and wrote two notes. One was to Helene, which he left on her desk. The second he sealed and went in search of Judd.

"I have to go out for a short while, Judd. But I'll be back for dinner. Give madame my apologies." He held out the note. "And can you make sure this note is delivered to the man who goes by the name of Adam? I believe you'll find him through the room of desires."

Philip put on his hat and gloves and walked out of the door, determined to do what he should have done well before this damn-fool charade had even started.

"What do you mean, Justin is dead?"

Marguerite turned listlessly back into her room and sank into a chair by the meager fire. "He was shot."

"By highwaymen or thieves?"

Helene perched on the arm of the chair and held her daughter's cold hands between her own. A convulsive shudder went through Marguerite.

"No, by his friend, Sir Harry."

"What on earth happened?"

Marguerite sighed and reached for her handkerchief. "I'm not quite sure. I heard Justin and Harry arguing one evening when we were still in Dover, and Harry stormed out."

"Do you know what they were arguing about?"

Marguerite buried her face in the handkerchief. "About me. Harry seemed to believe Justin was spending too much time with me and not enough engaged in more manly pursuits."

"But you had just gotten married. Of course his focus should be on you."

"That's what Justin said when I questioned him about Harry's sudden departure. He told me not to worry and that Harry would be back. But he didn't come back, and Justin decided we should come to London to find him and demand an explanation." Marguerite sighed. "So we came here, and two nights ago Justin went to his club to meet with Harry, and he didn't come home to me. Yesterday morning, a man I'd never met before banged on my door to tell me that Justin had been killed in a duel by his best friend." She shook her head. "I didn't want to believe him, and I insisted he take me to see Justin's body."

Helene came down on her knees and wrapped her arms around Marguerite's hunched form and gently rocked her.

"It's all right, my darling. It's all right."

"No, it isn't, *Maman*, because the man was right—Justin is dead." She choked back a sob. "And the worst thing was that they didn't bring him back to me but to his family home. His parents had already decided that I was an unsuitable match for their son, and now they refuse to let me see him."

Helene closed her eyes and hugged Marguerite even tighter. "If you want to see him, I will arrange it; have no fear of that. I will also make sure that the Lockwood family treats you with the respect you deserve."

"They probably blame me for his death."

Helene held Marguerite by the shoulders, away from her. "*Non*, he chose to fight a duel. You had nothing to do with it."

"But if he hadn't married me, Harry wouldn't have fought with him."

"Sir Harry would've been jealous of anyone Justin married. Surely you realized that?"

Marguerite stared at her, a blush rising on her cheeks. "I'm not sure what you mean."

Helene studied her daughter's distraught expression and realized she was not willing to further disturb Marguerite's peace by adding a whole new layer of potential sexual duplicity to the tragedy.

She patted Marguerite's shoulders and stood up. "Never mind, my dear. Just remember that you are not to blame. I'll ask Viscount Harcourt-DeVere if he can arrange for you to see Justin's body and to deal with any other matters arising from the funeral and your husband's estate."

Marguerite stared up at her. "How can you think about such practical matters when my heart is breaking?"

"Because somebody has to." Helene started to pick up Marguerite's clothes and other luggage and stuff them into one of the empty trunks. "Do you want to take Justin's things or leave them here?"

"Sometimes, *Maman*, I think that Christian is right and that your heart really is made of stone."

Helene dropped the pair of boots she was holding into the trunk. "Marguerite, if you wish me to sit and cry with you, I will, but I'd far rather have you safely packed up and at home with me before we did it."

Marguerite got to her feet, still wiping at the tears that streamed down her cheeks. "I will come with you, then." She glanced around the hotel room. "There is nothing left for me here anyway."

Helene continued to pack as Marguerite managed to put on her bonnet, cloak, and boots. She rang for a maid and gave orders for the bags to be carried out to a hackney cab. While she waited, she did her best to console Marguerite, who seemed incapable of responding.

Helene sighed. Why was she always at fault for being practical in a time of crisis? If everyone simply sat down and cried, nothing would ever get done. Emotional outbursts were a luxury she had never been able to afford.

When the cab arrived, she helped a weeping Marguerite inside and took her home.

24

Helene guided Marguerite down the basement steps and into the kitchen. She wasn't surprised to find the twins and Mrs. Smith-Porterhouse there. Despite her best efforts to keep them occupied, the twins seemed to gravitate back toward her house at every opportunity.

"Marguerite, is that you?" Lisette shot to her feet and hurried around the table, swiftly followed by Christian.

Helene stepped back to allow the twins to hug their sister. Marguerite started sobbing again, and Lisette hugged her hard. Helene wondered bleakly if she was even necessary to Marguerite's comfort now since her siblings were there. Watching them together made her feel like an outsider again.

"*Maman?*"

Helene pasted on a smile as Marguerite turned to her.

"*Oui?*"

"Can I go and rest for a while?"

"Of course, my dear. I'll take you up myself."

"There is no need, *Maman*," Lisette said, her arm around her older sister's shoulders. "Marguerite can share my room."

"If that is what you want, Marguerite." Helene nodded at her daughters. "Perhaps you will come and see me in my study when you feel better."

Marguerite reached out to squeeze her hand. "Thank you for coming for me."

Helene shrugged. "I am your mother. What else would I do?"

Lisette led Marguerite toward the stairs, chattering all the time. Christian loitered at the door and then cleared his throat. Startled, Helene looked up.

"Thank you."

She tried to smile. "For what?"

"For finding Marguerite. I . . . didn't think you would."

Helene fought a sudden urge to cry. "I didn't do anything; Marguerite found me. Now, if you will excuse me."

Christian didn't move. "*Maman* . . . is it true, what Mr. Ross said?"

"As I have no idea what he said, I can scarcely answer you."

"About the Bastille . . . about your family."

Helene briefly closed her eyes. She didn't want to have this discussion now, so close to finding out about Marguerite's appalling tragedy.

"He told you the truth. Now, I really have to get back to work. There are many arrangements that need to be made on your sister's behalf."

Christian stepped back, his face as suddenly shuttered as hers. "If I have distressed you, I apologize."

She forced herself to meet his eyes. "No, you haven't. It all happened a long time ago, and I rarely think about it."

She prayed he wouldn't see through that lie, hoped he'd never realize that despite her best efforts, she'd allowed those events to dictate and distort her entire life.

Christian gave her an awkward smile. "I'll go and see Marguerite, then."

Helene nodded, unable to speak, and watched him leave. When the door swung shut, she followed Philip's example and found her way to a dark corner of the wine cellar. At least here she could let down her guard and sob to her heart's content. That had always been her way. Survive the crisis and then fall apart discreetly in private.

She wiped her eyes with her handkerchief and blew her nose. At least Marguerite was safe. Helene would do everything in her power to make sure her daughter received her dues as a widow. She didn't care what the Lockwood family said. That was one way she could ensure that Marguerite never wanted for anything again.

And Christian had spoken to her voluntarily. He'd even thanked her for helping Marguerite. Perhaps she ought to be thanking Philip instead. Whatever he had said to Christian had obviously affected him. It seemed Philip was a better parent than she after all.

God, everything was such a mess. She was tired of having to present a calm exterior to the world when inside she felt like crying. The temptation to lean on Philip beckoned, but it still scared her. Did she have the courage to trust him?

With a sigh, Helene stood up. Her moment of weakness was over, and she now had to move on. Her business wouldn't run itself, and in a matter of hours, she needed to become the sparkling, slightly wicked hostess the *ton* expected to see at her salons.

It was going to be hard to pretend she was a scintillating woman tonight when all she wanted was to stay with Marguerite and simply be a mother. She climbed back up the stairs and found her way to her study. Someone had lit a fire in the grate, and a pile of letters sat on her desk.

A note in Philip's now familiar handwriting caught her eye, and she frowned. He was supposed to be at the pleasure house. Where had he been when all the family drama was taking place?

She scanned the note. Urgent business with his solicitor? Considering the hours he worked, she supposed it was difficult for him to see the man without inviting him to the pleasure house, and she could see that would never do.

Philip had better be back soon, though, or their agreement would definitely be over. Helene stared at the stack of unopened letters. There was nothing else for her to do but get on with the day's business, start helping Marguerite, and hope that Philip Ross didn't abuse her trust.

"Good evening, my dear."

Helene looked up to find George, attired in his evening clothes, smiling down at her.

"George, what time is it?"

He took out his pocket watch. "It's almost seven. Aren't you dressing for dinner tonight?"

Helene took off her spectacles and rubbed at her eyes. "I can't believe it is so late. I had a lot to catch up on today. Have you seen Philip?"

"Ross? Yes, he was in the kitchen when I passed by, chatting to Judd. Do you want me to get him for you?"

"No, I'd rather talk to you, George. It seems ages since we had the chance to chat."

"What a nice thing to say." George grinned and sat down.

Helene studied him carefully, realized she had the perfect opportunity to disabuse him of a few of his more outlandish ideas.

"How are your wife and Amanda?"

His smile faded. "They are both well. Why do you ask?"

"Because I heard a rumor that your wife had gotten rid of her lover and that you were reconciled."

"Who told you that?"

Helene smiled airily. "Oh, you know how it is; people tell me things all the time. I rarely believe them."

"Then don't believe that nonsense. It's true that my wife has discarded her lover, but it hasn't changed things between us at all."

"That's a shame, George. I'd like you to be happy."

He stared at her. "You know what would make me happy. Marry me."

"You know that is not going to happen. You are one of my oldest friends. I made a rule even before I met you that I wouldn't go to bed with men I liked."

He got up and started pacing the carpet, all the good humor leached from his face. "You seem to like Philip Ross well enough and yet you let him fuck you."

"That is a completely different situation. And it is also none of your business."

George swung around. "Did you know he likes to fuck men?"

"I know that my clients' sexual tastes are their business. I'm not here to judge anyone."

Although she kept her tone light, her mind was working furiously. How had George known what Philip had been up to in the pleasure house both with her and with Adam? He'd either been snooping or reading her private files; neither action spoke of a rational man.

"Philip Ross isn't a client, though, is he?"

Helene got up and walked across to the fireplace as if to warm her hands. When George started pacing again, she took the opportunity to ring the servant's bell when his back was turned.

"Philip owns the same amount of shares as you. I consider him to be as much a member of the club as you are."

George shoved his hand through his hair. "If we are the same, why don't you fuck me?"

"George, you are married! I don't sleep with married men. You know that."

"But again you make an exception for Ross. He said he's known you for years, so you must have had him when he was married."

"I met him just before he was married and didn't see him again until a few weeks ago when he turned up here with Gideon Harcourt."

George stared at her, an arrested expression on his face. "Exactly how long have you known him?"

"That is none of your business." The faint sounds of footsteps outside in the hallway bolstered her courage. "All I wish you to understand, George, is that I will never marry you."

"You will after my divorce comes through."

"What divorce?"

He raised his eyebrows. "Didn't I tell you? I'm going to divorce my wife for adultery. When I'm free, we can marry."

Helene shook her head. "But I don't want to marry you."

He halted in front of her, an indulgent smile on his face. "Don't be silly, my dear. Of course you do."

Helene opened her mouth to reply and then closed it again as someone knocked on the door. After a wary glance at George, she said, "Come in."

Philip poked his head around the door. "Are you ready for some visitors?" His smile dimmed when he saw George. "Or perhaps I should tell them to come back later."

"No, please come in. George and I have finished our discussion anyway."

George bowed and kissed her hand. "We haven't quite finished, but I understand you have a lot to think about, my dear."

Helene glanced at Philip, whose expression had chilled as he observed George. He opened the door wide, and Marguerite and the twins came in. To Helene's relief, Marguerite looked slightly more composed, although there were dark circles under her eyes, and her lips were bitten raw.

"*Maman*, I just wanted to tell you I've decided to have dinner with the twins and Mrs. Smith-Porterhouse and then go to bed. Can our business wait until the morning?"

"Of course, my dear." Helene smiled encouragingly at her daughter. "I've already sent a message to Viscount Harcourt-DeVere, who is willing to help us deal with the Lockwood family. We can talk about what you want to do tomorrow and make our decisions from there."

Helene noticed that Marguerite was studying George with great interest. "I apologize, Marguerite. You haven't met Lord George Grant before, have you? Lord George, may I introduce my eldest daughter, Lady Justin Lockwood."

Even though Marguerite winced at the title, she curtsied and nodded at George.

"Actually, *Maman*, we have met, although I don't recognize that name." She smiled at George. "He visited the nunnery just before I left. I thought he was looking for a school to place his children."

Helene frowned. "Are you sure?" She turned to George. "Why didn't you tell me that you had visited Normandy?"

George shrugged. "I was there on diplomatic business, and I stopped off to visit a few potential schools for Amanda. It was complete chance that I happened to end up at the place where your children were at school."

Philip spoke from the open doorway, which he blocked with his body. "I've never been a big believer in coincidences or chance." He looked at Christian. "Do you still have that letter?"

Christian nodded and shoved his hand into his coat pocket. Helene scarcely breathed as he brought out a much folded and crumpled piece of parchment.

"I couldn't bring myself to throw it away. I tried but . . ."

"We understand." Philip nodded at Helene. "Take a look at it."

She reached out to take the letter with trembling fingers and recognized the handwriting in an instant.

"George, why did you write this?"

George flushed and shoved his hands into his pockets. "Damnation, Helene, you know why!"

"Because you wished my children to hate me?"

"Not at all! Because I love you, and I wanted to get your attention."

"By telling my children I'm a whore?"

"Helene, don't be silly; it's not like that. Recently I realized that the reason you wouldn't marry me was because of the pleasure house. I decided that if your children needed you, you might find someone else to run the place while you enjoyed some well-deserved time with them."

Helene sat down heavily in a chair by the fire. "*You* decided I needed to become a better mother and a less obsessed business-woman."

"Exactly. I know how hard it was for you to give the children up all those years ago. I thought this might be a way to bring them back to you."

"By telling them about my 'real' life so that they would have no option but to try and find me and voice their disgust?"

George nodded. "I know it sounds ridiculous, but it worked, didn't it? You have all your children around you now."

Helene met his gaze. "And I certainly have my hands full trying to care for them, don't I?"

"*Maman*"—Christian cast an anxious look at Helene—"I didn't know who sent the letter. It was delivered to the school by hand."

"It's all right, Christian," Philip said from the doorway. "Your mother would never believe you conspired with George to deceive her." He smiled at the boy and then at Helene. "George is right about one thing. You are doing an excellent job of looking after your children, Helene. But perhaps it is time for them to withdraw from this discussion."

Christian looked as if he wanted to protest, but Marguerite took his hand and Lisette's and drew them toward the door.

"We'll be in the kitchen if you need us, *Maman*."

"Thank you, Marguerite."

Philip's dry intervention drew Helene's attention to his expression. He wasn't smiling anymore, and his attention was focused on George. God, what was he thinking? Could he believe what a fool she'd been? Philip shut the door behind the twins and leaned back against it.

"I don't think George is being quite honest with you, Helene."

George's head snapped around. "And I don't think this is any of your business, Ross. Helene understands, don't you? I did it for love."

Philip started to laugh. "If you believe that, you'll believe anything."

Helene tried to keep her voice calm. She didn't appreciate being talked over by two men. "What are you trying to say, Philip?"

"If George truly loved you, he wouldn't have behaved like this. He sent your children a letter that not only revealed your address, but called you a whore. What kind of man does that to the woman he claims to love?"

George glared at Philip. "A man who has reached the end of his tether. A man who has waited patiently for the day when *that woman* decides to mend her ways and settle down."

"And you think Helene is stupid enough to believe that?"

George's face flushed. "Don't imagine that because she shares your bed, Helene will agree with you. She's told me many times that the men she fucks are as stupid as sheep."

"I'm not stupid, am I?" Philip turned to her.

"No, you are not," Helene snapped.

George scowled. "I have to agree with you, Helene. Ross

isn't stupid at all. In fact, he's already decided to sell his shares to me and get out of my way."

Helene stared at Philip. "Is this true?"

He shrugged. "I did visit my solicitor today."

Helene stood up. "Even if Philip did sell you his shares, I still own the remaining seventy percent of the business."

"But when you marry him, he'll have it all, won't he?"

Helene locked gazes with Philip. "I don't intend to marry him."

Philip smiled. "Have you told him that?"

Helene turned slowly to look at George. "Many times. Like you, I don't quite understand why he suddenly insists on marrying me now."

"I think I do," Philip murmured.

George sat down and buried his head in his hands. "Don't listen to him. Ross is like all the other fools in your life who have deserted and deceived you. For God's sake, he even fucks other men!"

"I don't care who he fucks. He is perfectly entitled to find out and enjoy what pleases him."

George lifted his head, his gaze pleading. "Helene . . . we've been friends for eighteen years. You have to believe me. I love you, and I want you to marry me. I see that my methods might have been a little high-handed, but they have achieved their aim. You are now free to love me, and that's all I want."

"Apart from a controlling share in my business."

"That's not true. I'd never stop you from running this business as you see fit. I would only hope that with your family now around you, you would allow me to share the burden."

Philip started to laugh. "That's not what you suggested to me."

"Ross, if you don't shut up, I'm going to plant you a facer."

Philip shrugged. "I doubt it." He turned to Helene. "Do

you remember that evening in the kitchen when we were going over the account books?"

"When Christian came in and interrupted us?"

"Yes, that one. Our conversation ended in an argument, and I failed to share my concerns with you about the books."

Helene grasped the back of the chair and held on tight. George remained in his seat, his head down as Philip continued.

"I first noticed the discrepancies when we decided to change wine merchants. I suspected the La Tour brothers were cheating you, but on further investigation, I realized that wasn't the case. The money was disappearing well before it reached the wine merchants' pockets."

George stirred in his seat but said nothing.

"I began to notice other recent discrepancies. Extra payments from some of your clients, small amounts perhaps, but added together, they represent a tidy sum every month."

Helene nodded. "I'm not stupid, Philip. I noticed something was wrong, but with all the upheaval around here recently, I hadn't managed to discuss my concerns with the trustees or the bank."

Philip nodded at George. "I think George's sudden desire to marry you stems more from his fear of being exposed as a cheat and possibly a blackmailer than from any notion of love."

George shot to his feet and pointed a shaking finger at Philip. "I do love her, you bastard! How dare you suggest otherwise!"

"I'm sure you do, but your notion of love is not quite mine or, I suspect, Helene's."

Helene ignored Philip and walked across to George. She touched his arm. "What is going on, George?"

His face crumpled at her soft tone. "God, you do understand, don't you?"

She squeezed his shoulder. "I will when you explain it to me."

He sighed, and the desperate sound shuddered through his entire body. "I have debts—gambling debts—that I have to pay."

Helene frowned. "I've never known you to be a gambler. You certainly don't play here."

George shook off her hand and started pacing again. "I've made some unwise investments over the years and used up all of my savings and my wife's inheritance. I needed the money to support my family."

"But why didn't you ask me for help?"

"Ask the woman I admire more than anyone else in the world to help me? Admit that I'd made a fool of myself and almost beggared my family? It seemed easier to take a little from the books."

Philip snorted. "Easier to steal from your friend than to ask for her help?"

George swung around. "You wouldn't understand. When have you ever wanted for anything?"

Philip's smile was bleak. "I've wanted many things in my life, some more than others." His gaze met Helene's. "But I've also learned that you can't force someone to want you or to love you."

Helene stared back at him, unable to look away from the pain in his eyes.

George groaned. "Damnation, he's the father of your twins, isn't he? I never stood a chance of marrying you after he turned up, did I?"

Philip ignored George, his attention all on Helene. "What do you want to do with him?"

"With George?" She sighed. "I don't know. Perhaps I need to talk to the other trustees and see if they will help me resolve his financial difficulties."

George cleared his throat. "You intend to help me, despite everything I've done?"

"Of course. You are still my friend."

George dropped his head into his hands, and his shoulders started to shake. "I don't deserve this."

Helene knelt in front of him and patted his knee. He grabbed hold of her fingers and held them tight. "But you will. Once the worries over your debts and supporting your family are cleared up, everything will seem different." She glanced up at Philip. "Will you escort him home?"

"If that is what you want."

She nodded. "I doubt he'll do anything foolish, will you, George? His daughter, Amanda, needs him, and I suspect his wife does too."

George got slowly to his feet, his eyes bloodshot, his mouth a thin line. "I'll pay you back, Helene. I promise, even if it takes a lifetime."

"Don't worry about that now, George. Just go home and get some rest."

He nodded and turned obediently toward the door, where Judd awaited him. She hoped he would be all right. Despite his actions, it was hard to stop caring for a man who had been a constant in her life for so long.

Philip waited until George went past him and then turned back to Helene. "I'll see George home and return here as soon as I can."

Helene shrugged listlessly. "There is no need to come back."

"Dammit, Helene, why do you do this? Why do you constantly push me away?"

She felt the hot sting of tears on her face and tried to blink them away. "Because I am afraid of breaking down completely, afraid of you seeing me like that."

He took a hasty step toward her. "Why?"

She shook her head and reached out to steady herself with a hand on her desk. "Because I have to be strong. I have to be strong for everyone."

"Not for me. You can be anything you want for me. I'm quite capable of withstanding a few tears."

"And maybe that is what scares me the most."

He stopped moving. "That I'll use your weakness against you, that I'll overpower you and stop you from being strong?" His smile was bitter. "Helene, no one can do that to you but yourself. I don't want to own you."

"Then why did you offer to sell your shares to George?"

His expression darkened. "If you really think I would do that, we have nothing more to say to each other. There's no chance in hell that you'd ever trust me with your heart if you can't even trust me with your business." He bowed abruptly. "I'll be back tomorrow to say my good-byes to the staff. I'll try and keep out of your way."

Helene struggled to breathe, to frame the words that would set them both free of the tangle she'd created, but it was too late. Philip had already left.

25

Philip had been as good as his word. Helene hadn't seen him all day. He'd plotted his route around the pleasure house so as not to cross paths with her at all. She resisted the urge to go and find him yet again and returned to her desk. Another pile of correspondence littered the surface, demanding her attention. She might as well get on with it.

During her sleepless night, she'd realized she didn't believe Philip would sell his shares to George. He'd probably used them as a lure to get George to expose his true plans for her and the business. That would be much more like Philip than to plot behind her back.

But how on earth was she going to get him to believe her? He'd obviously decided she was incapable of trusting anyone. Her thoughts spiraled around in an unending loop. She didn't want him to leave. She wanted him to stay.

With a sigh, she opened the first letter and tried to read, but the words kept bouncing all over the page. When she did manage to read one, it made no sense. She found her spectacles and tried again.

"*Maman*? Can we speak to you?"

She lifted her head and found the twins at the door, their expressions serious.

"Of course. Is Marguerite all right?"

"She is sleeping," Lisette said. "And much calmer now."

"I'm glad to hear that. It will take her a long while to get over this terrible tragedy, and we will all have to help her."

Christian crossed his arms and slouched against the wall. "Are you going to send us back to France?"

"Not unless you wish to go back."

He glanced at Lisette. "We'd prefer to stay here . . . with you, I mean. We'd like to learn about the business."

Helene smiled for the first time that day. "You are both a little young to be involved in that, but in a few years you may certainly assist me if you still wish it." She pretended to rearrange the letters on her desk. "I'm hoping that you will spend the next few years completing your education and enjoying the delights of London. Mrs. Smith-Porterhouse has agreed to stay on as your chaperone for as long as you want, Lisette."

Lisette smiled happily at her mother and then at Christian. "See? I told you she'd be pleased we wanted to stay." Her expression sobered. "Mr. Ross told us about what happened with Lord George."

"Did he? That was kind of him."

"I'm sorry Lord George hurt you, *Maman*. But Mr. Ross did say that you weren't in love with Lord George and that it was all in his mind. Is that true?"

"Yes, Mr. Ross was right, as usual."

Lisette shared another anxious glance with her brother. Helene wondered if she had sounded as bitter as she felt.

"Don't you like him?"

"Mr. Ross? I like him well enough. Why?"

"Because last night, after Marguerite took the laudanum, she said something funny."

"What did she say?"

"That when she blinked really fast, Christian and I looked just like Mr. Ross."

Helene stared at the twins' expectant faces and tried to keep her expression under control. "Perhaps you should be having this conversation with Mr. Ross rather than with me."

Christian frowned. "What does that mean?"

"It means that Mr. Ross is the only one who can answer you. He is here today. Why not ask him?"

"Do you think he would mind?"

"Why should he?"

Christian grabbed Lisette's hand. "Let's go and ask him, then. *Maman's* right, what's the worst he can do to us?"

Helene watched them go, their hands still linked, and prayed she had done the right thing. Hopefully Philip would too. She returned to the mail on her desk and opened another letter.

> *Dear Madame Delornay, our client, Lord Philip Knowles, had instructed us to inform you that the shares in your pleasure house, which were included in the estate of the late Lord Derek Knowles, revert to you as of this day.*
>
> *We would appreciate it if you could come to our offices and sign the final documents to complete this transfer into your name.*
>
> *Yours sincerely,*
> *Fotheringay, Smallwood and Smith, solicitors.*

Helene stared at the letter, noting that it was dated for the previous day and that Philip had arranged the transfer before the altercation with George. Tears pricked at her eyes. He had every reason to be disgusted with her lack of trust. He'd done everything to show her she was safe and loved, and she'd still distrusted him and shut him out.

She placed the letter on the desk and flattened it with her

fingers. What on earth was she going to do? For the first time in her life, if she really wanted something, she was going to have to take a risk. Philip's decision to tell the twins about him was his own to make. Her decision as to how to show him that she had come to love and depend on him was entirely up to her.

She stared down at the letter. When had Philip become so important to her? Or had he always been there in the back of her mind, the perfect lover, the one who all the rest of her many lovers failed to live up to? An ideal, certainly, but the reality—with his painfully gained experience, erotic sensuality, and true contrariness—was even better.

After a deep breath, Helene rang the servants' bell and Judd appeared.

"Good morning, madame. What can I do for you?"

"Can you find out if Mr. Philip intends to stay here this evening?"

Judd frowned. "I believe he does, madame. He mentioned something about seeing Mr. Adam. Do you wish me to ask him or find out in a more subtle way?"

Helene smiled. "I'd prefer to know without him knowing, if you understand what I mean."

"Perfectly, madame. I'll see what I can do."

By the time the evening came around, Helene was beside herself with nerves and unable to face visiting the regular salons at all. To add to her anxieties, the twins had disappeared all afternoon, as had Philip. For all their sakes, she hoped that even if her relationship with Philip didn't work out, the twins would have some semblance of a connection with him. They deserved to be happy, even if she had forfeited that right for herself.

It was time to decide whether she had the strength to let Philip Ross walk away from her again. *Non*, it was worse than that. She had to find the strength to accept him and ask him to stay. At eighteen, her choices had seemed irrevocable, but now she knew differently. She would not make the mistake of turning away from love again.

He'd grown into a man she could respect. A man who was not afraid to tell her that she was wrong, even when he knew she would be angry. She couldn't use her beauty to get what she wanted from him either. He expected far more from her than that.

Judd knocked on her door as the clock struck nine, and bowed. "Madame? Mr. Philip is in the main salon, and the twins are safely ensconced with Mrs. Smith-Porterhouse in the adjoining house. Miss Marguerite has eaten a light dinner and retired to bed. Is there anything else I can help you with?"

"Thank you, Judd."

The old man bowed deeply. "You are welcome, madame. You must know I would do anything for you."

"Thank you." Unaccustomed tears threatened and Helene tried to smile.

Judd's face softened. "Madame, you have saved so many of us from the gutter, from the most appalling of brothels, and from the guillotine. We owe you so much, and you take so little in return." He patted her shoulder. "We all like Mr. Philip very much; just you remember that."

She glanced at him in surprise and he winked. "He is the first man who has ever gotten away with telling you off and lived to tell the tale. It was obvious from the beginning you cared for him."

Helene could do nothing more than nod and start up the stairs after him. It was easy to forget that in a household as small as this, nothing was private or sacred. And perhaps that was as it should be. She'd created her own family around her over the years without even realizing it.

She bypassed the main salons and headed for the room of

desires, then paused at the door to gather her courage. She had to do this. She had to let down her guard, offer herself to Philip, and beg him to stay.

After the subtle pastels of the hallway, the sudden thick darkness was disorientating.

"What is your desire?"

Helene closed her eyes. If she said this, everyone in the pleasure house would know exactly what she wanted. Although, judging from her conversation with Judd, perhaps they already knew.

She took a deep breath. "I want Philip Ross."

Philip paced the main salon, glancing at the doorway every time someone came in. He'd spent the afternoon with Helene's twins—his twins now, seeing as he'd admitted he was their father. Lisette had been shy but delighted, Christian a little more wary. But even he had come around when Philip described his new country seat and the quality of his horseflesh, and proffered an invitation for them both to visit him there.

Since his accession to the title, he was moving away from neighbors who knew him intimately to Sudbury Court, the principal home of the late Lord Knowles. If he brought the twins down with him from the first, no one there would know any different. He'd have to decide with the twins exactly what they wanted made public about their relationship before he made any more decisions. He frowned. It wouldn't be easy to make up for all the time he'd missed, but he intended to do his duty whether they appreciated it or not.

His duty to their mother was another matter. When George had explained his various schemes to control Helene, Philip was barely able to contain his rage at such a betrayal. No wonder Helene felt that every man in her life took advantage of her and that she had to stand up for herself.

It had also been a revelation. Helene didn't need to be tamed or owned; she needed to be appreciated and loved for exactly what she was—an amazing woman. And he was definitely the man who could do it. He *knew* her. He'd always known her, and yet he'd almost blundered into the same trap all the other men in her life had by trying to overprotect and control her. In truth, she didn't need him or any man, but he hoped to God she wanted him to stay around anyway.

"Sir, are you waiting for Adam?"

Philip swung around and faced a tall man in his early thirties wearing a naval uniform. His blond hair was tied back into a tight black bow, and his skin was slightly bronzed, making his blue eyes reflect all the colors of the sea.

"Are you Adam?"

"I am." The man bowed. "I'm also Captain David Gray, an officer in the Royal Navy."

Philip held out his hand. "I'm delighted to meet you."

David's smile was surprisingly sweet. "Really?"

Philip moved toward a corner of the large room where they would have more privacy before he replied. "You gave me great pleasure. Why would I not want to admit that?"

"I appreciate the compliment. Many men are reluctant to admit that pleasure can arise in the most peculiar of circumstances. Now, what can I do for you? Your note sounded urgent."

Philip admired David's ability to switch from lover to professional military man in one sentence.

"In truth, the initial problem has disappeared. I was threatened with blackmail because of my involvement with you."

"Blackmail?"

Philip watched anger flow across David's face and bloom in his cheeks. This man had no more been party to George's plans than he and Helene were.

"That threat is over, but I'm hoping you will help me with another problem I have to deal with tonight."

David bowed. "I would be delighted to be of service. What can I do for you?"

Philip smiled. "I want you to tie me up."

David's mouth opened and he blinked hard. Before he could say anything, Judd appeared at Philip's elbow, his face flushed.

"Mr. Philip? Madame won't be coming to the salons this evening."

"Why the devil not? I need her! Don't tell me she has gone out."

Judd broke into a smile. "No, sir, even better. She just went into the room of desires, and she asked . . . for you."

Philip grinned at Judd and David as if his favorite horse had just won the Derby. "Then we will need to change our plans a little, but I think we can still make them work. Judd, go ahead and reserve that room for us. David, after you've tied me up, you can go and get Helene."

"Step into the room on your left, and we will fulfill your desire."

Helene felt her way through the even darker doorway into what felt like a relatively small area. After what seemed like hours, she heard a door opening on the opposite side of the room and the sound of soft breathing.

"Madame?"

Her heart almost shuddered to a stop. That wasn't Philip's voice. Oh God, perhaps he didn't want her after all.

"Madame Delornay? Will you come with me please?"

She opened her eyes to find Captain David Gray right in front of her, a smile on his face. Whatever was going on, she had to follow it through. David held out his hand, and she took it. He paused by the door.

"One moment, madame."

He let go of her hand and stepped behind her. The next thing she knew, he slipped a blindfold over her eyes.

He took her hands and led her slowly out into the hallway. She knew they were using the servants' stairs because of the hollow sound of their feet on the uncarpeted surfaces. She allowed him to help her navigate to another door, along a short cold passageway, and then waited as he stopped again.

"Please come inside, madame."

She stepped forward, waited as David removed the blindfold, and found herself staring at Philip. A large black candle illuminated the small room on the top floor of the pleasure house. Philip was naked, except for a fine coating of oil, and his wrists were manacled above his head to a wooden frame. His ankles were chained to each other but not fixed to the structure.

Helene stared at him, drinking in the sight of his shadowed muscles, the delicate curve of his hips, and the thrust of his erect cock through the dark hair at his groin.

"I promised you I would try everything the pleasure house had to offer." Philip inclined his head. "So here I am, bound for your pleasure."

Helene licked her lips. "You do not have to do this for me, Philip. I—"

"Yes, I do." He cut through her faltering attempt to speak. "I want you to understand that I am yours to do what you want with and that I trust you not to hurt me."

She almost stamped her foot. "That is what I should be saying to you! I'm the one who's shown a complete lack of trust, not you."

His smile was gentle. "Perhaps we have both been at fault. But here I am, willing to be used as you will."

Helene wrung her hands together. "I want to believe you . . . but it is so hard for me to have faith in anyone except myself."

"Then try. Use me, see if you can make me beg, understand that I'll do anything you ask of me."

Helene took a deep breath. "I should be chained up there. I want to show you that you can trust *me*."

"Then trust yourself with my body. And, if you wish it, later we'll change places and I'll make you beg."

She held his gaze, saw the calm acceptance of his vulnerability in his hazel eyes, and slowly nodded. Did it really matter which one of them was prepared to take that vital step when the end result would bring them both so much happiness?

Behind her, David Gray still leaned against the door, his interested gaze trained on them both. She half turned to look at him.

"I'd like to see David suck your cock."

Philip's expression subtly relaxed as if he sensed her complete capitulation. "That's why I asked him to help me tonight."

Helene smiled at David. "Will you do that for me?"

"Of course, madame. It will be a pleasure."

He walked across to Philip and fell to his knees. Philip inhaled sharply, displaying the tight flat muscles of his abdomen.

"How would you like me to suck him, madame? Hard or fast, soft or rough?"

Helene considered Philip's lean torso, the already wet crown of his cock thrust toward David as if eager to be swallowed whole.

"Hard, I think, and definitely rough."

Philip's throat muscles worked as David took him into his mouth. God, Helene was watching him, and it made him so hard he wanted to come straightaway—and with the suction David was using, he'd be coming fast anyway. He groaned and thrust his hips into the motion, shoving his cock as deep as he could. David's teeth grazed his shaft, sending him into an even more intense frenzy of lust. He opened his eyes and saw the top of David's head and then Helene staring right at him. He let her see his need, his imminent lack of control, and his joy in sharing it with her.

He came hard in big shuddering waves, arching his back to

shove as much of himself into David's mouth and throat as David could take. Would Helene like what she saw? Would it make her want him?

David released Philip's cock and sat back, wiping his mouth. He looked up at Philip. "Did you enjoy that?"

"Couldn't you tell?"

He leaned forward and licked Philip's cock again. "More importantly, did you enjoy it, madame?"

"Yes." Helene's reply was soft and intimate, but her expression was blissful. "Would you like Philip to suck you, now?"

David got to his feet and palmed his tented breeches. "No, madame. I think the rest of his efforts should belong to you tonight." He winked. "And probably for the rest of his life."

Philip opened his mouth to speak, but Helene was quicker. "I think he'll still need you occasionally, David, if you are willing. I would love to see you together again."

David raised his eyebrows and looked at Philip, who nodded and said, "Definitely."

"Then I shall hold myself in readiness." David winked and bowed. "Good night to you both, and I hope you survive it."

After the door shut behind David, Philip waited to see what Helene intended to do next. She came up close to him and started to remove her brown satin gown. His throat dried up as she revealed a tight black satin corset, black stockings, garters, and high-heeled shoes. Her lush breasts practically sat on the shallow cups, revealing her tight nipples through the soft black lace.

He watched as she strolled across to the rack of whips and other sex toys, his whole body tensing in anticipation. She selected a riding crop and came back to him. He shuddered as she trailed the tip of the whip over his chest and then his nipples until they were two hard points of aching sensation.

"Have you let David fuck you?"

"No."

He almost forgot to breathe as she moved the crop lower and circled his navel. The oil David had covered him in now glinted on the black leather.

"Why not?"

"Because I'm not ready to be taken by a man like that."

She ran the crop over his cock, rubbed it against the wet crown until the leather grew damp and created extra friction against his rapidly expanding flesh.

"What if I asked you to take him now?"

He closed his eyes as the crop slid over his balls and the soft skin behind them.

"Then I'd do it."

He jerked as she bent to kiss the tip of his cock.

"What if I fucked you instead?"

It was suddenly hard to breathe, so he concentrated on that as she continued to torment his cock and balls with the now wet leather crop.

"I don't understand what you mean."

She laughed and lightly flicked the crop against his thigh. "You've seen what goes on here on the top floor. You know there is more than one way to take a man."

He tensed as she circled him, aware that she was studying him. He couldn't help clenching his arse cheeks when she lightly tapped them with the whip. The head of the crop nudged between his buttocks.

"There are women who strap on fake cocks to take men who like to be used like that. Have you seen them?"

"Yes." He groaned as the crop slid farther down and nudged his balls from the rear.

"And then there are the fake cocks or dildos that mimic the same full sensation but not the excessive movement. Both men and women can use those." The crop went still. "Which would you prefer?"

God, she expected him to choose? Philip gritted his teeth. "Whatever you want, Helene, I'll do it."

She dropped the crop and went back to the cupboards and pulled out a drawer. She brought it across to the bed so that he could see the contents. He already knew what it contained from his daily visits to the floors. Cocks of all lengths, widths, colors, and substances—leather, stone, glass, and wood, all intricately crafted for pleasure.

His cock grew harder just looking at them. What would she choose, and how would it feel to allow her to stuff his arse full? He stifled a groan as she pondered each object, stroking them with her fingers, weighing them in her hands until she finally made a decision.

She picked a thick carved wooden cock that was about the length of his own when erect.

"Will you take this for me?"

He nodded, unable to speak as he braced himself for the intrusion. Helene smiled for the first time, and he realized she was enjoying herself, was trusting him to enjoy it too.

"It's big," he managed to murmur.

She fingered the wooden cock, brought it around to compare it to his. "About the same as yours. I think you'll like it."

She disappeared behind him again, and he smelled a hint of lemon and spices and felt the coldness of oil between his buttocks. Her hand slid over her hip and grasped his cock at the base. She squeezed and relaxed until he forgot about what was to come in the pleasure of her hand on him. Forgot until she eased an oiled finger inside him and then another.

He tried to ignore the strange invasion, succeeded so well that he grew almost accustomed to it, welcomed each subtle play stretching his flesh. Three fingers now and the pressure increased. His breathing grew labored. He no longer knew how much time had passed as she worked him, widened him, and soothed him with soft kisses on his back.

Oh God, that wasn't her fingers anymore; that was the harder press of the wooden phallus. But it was too late to expel it as she worked his cock into a frenzy. It felt like his shaft had expanded to fill his arse as well. The stiff aching, stuffed sensation turned into a stab of pure lust as she probed deeper and found something inside him that responded eagerly and desperately to the demands of the wooden cock.

"Helene . . ."

He wanted to see her, yet wanted her never to stop doing whatever it was she was doing, because he'd never felt so aroused before in his life.

"Wait," she whispered.

He almost cried when she stopped touching him, thrust his hips blindly in protest until she reappeared on her knees in front of him, took his cock in her mouth, and continued to slide the phallus in and out with her other hand.

"God, Helene, I want to come down your throat right now," he growled. "Don't stop."

She sucked him harder, and everything became a blur of sounds and sensations, taking him to a blizzard of ecstasy that he would not be denied. His cum exploded into her mouth as she rammed the wooden phallus home one final time, leaving him gasping and moaning and calling her name.

When he was able to breathe again, he glanced down at her. Her cheek was pressed to his thigh, and her arms were loosely around his hips.

"Helene, you know I love you." She kissed the soft skin above his hip bone. "I don't want to control you. I thought I did, but I realized that wasn't what you needed at all."

She sat back and looked up at him, her expression careful. "I'm quite capable of taking care of myself."

"That's true, but I'd like to be the kind of man you can respect, a man who respects you. Someone to share your burdens and support you, not add to them."

She smiled up at him. "There is something you have forgotten."

"What is that?"

"I need someone who understands where I came from. Someone who *knows* me."

He held her gaze. "I know you, love. Sometimes I don't always like you, but I'll always try to understand you and love you regardless."

"Yes," she whispered, her eyes full of tears. "If only I'd trusted myself all those years ago and gone with you . . ."

"I'd have let you down, and you would've ended up resenting me. I'd much rather have you now, as the man I am today than the young fool I was then." He paused. "And truly, aren't you proud of the woman you have become?"

Helene wiped a tear from her cheek and stared up at Philip. He was right, damn him, as he increasingly was these days. She got to her feet.

"Do you think we could continue this conversation without you being chained up?"

"I would like that."

She released the manacles on his ankles and then stood on tiptoe to attempt the ones around his wrists.

"You must promise me, Philip, that you will still be amenable when the restraints come off."

"Too late, my dear. I never promised you anything."

She shrieked as she released him, and he grabbed her around the waist and held her tightly to his bare chest.

"Do you know that you have been in my head and my heart for the last eighteen years?"

She touched his cheek. "You have been in mine too. None of my other lovers ever measured up to you."

He shifted her weight, bringing her throbbing sex into line with his fast-growing erection.

"That's good, because you won't miss them, then."

She opened her eyes wide at him. "What do you mean?"

He carried her over to the black-silk-draped bed and dropped her on the center of it, pinned her down with his body before she could protest. He grabbed her hands and brought them over her head. Before she could protest, she heard the metallic click as he chained her wrists together.

"Philip!"

"You did say I could make you beg, didn't you?"

He rotated her onto her stomach and slid several pillows beneath her stomach so that her back was arched, her bottom raised up and available to him. She gasped as he smacked her buttocks and then reached over her to investigate the collection of dildos in the drawer.

"Something nice and thick for your arse, I think."

Helene tried to relax as oil trickled between her buttocks, followed by the urgent press of a thick leather dildo against her rear passage. She moaned as the dildo slid slowly home. Moaned harder when Philip raised her even higher and slid his cock into her pussy.

She was so aroused from watching him that she climaxed instantly, her body clenching under the twin penetration, the flick of his fingers over her clit, his teeth biting into her shoulder. There was no sense of being forced or of being afraid. Only a wish to please him and please herself in whatever sexual way they devised.

Even as she climaxed again, he pulled out and turned her onto her back. As he looked down at her, his hazel eyes filled with lust and determination.

"No more lovers for you, Lady Knowles."

"I didn't agree to become your wife!"

He shoved his cock deep inside her and held still. "But you will. Think about our children."

She tried to wiggle out from under him, but it was impossible. "I will not! I will agree to have no other lovers if you desist in this ridiculous notion that we can ever marry!"

He reached between them and roughly fingered her clit, sending her over the edge into a sea of pleasure. She resurfaced to find him smiling down at her.

"I'm not giving up on that ridiculous notion, Helene. We'll share our children, and you'll occasionally take my advice about the pleasure house, so why shouldn't we marry?"

She held her breath. "Don't you want me to give it up?"

He frowned. "Why would I? You make more money per year than my old estate did. I realized George was on to something. If I marry you, I'll own the whole thing."

She stared at him, her breasts crushed against his chest, her legs spread wide by his hips and the deep throbbing penetration of his cock.

"I'll never marry you if you take control of my business. I'll kill you first."

"That's my Helene."

He smiled then and bent to suck hard on her breasts. She moaned as he rocked his hips, sending tremors of joy through her entire body. She struggled to retain a coherent thought, let alone a whole argument. All he had to do was kiss her and she simply wilted.

He raised his head and kissed her lips. "We can have a quiet wedding with everyone who attends sworn to secrecy."

"We are not getting married!" His grin was lascivious and full of sexual promise. "Philip Ross, stop it, right now."

"Stop what?"

"Distracting me with sex."

He bent to kiss her nose and trailed his lips over hers. "But I've learned from an expert."

"Philip . . ."

He kissed her again, this time more deeply, his cock still buried deep inside her, his heart beating hard and fast next to hers.

"All right, I'll stop, but you have to promise to consider everything I've said."

Helene stared into his eyes. Saw nothing to fear and everything to play for. With a sigh, she kissed him. "It would have to be extremely private."

His smile was slow and full of smug male satisfaction. "Our wedding? That can certainly be arranged."

She grabbed his shoulders, still unwilling to concede completely in case he thought he'd won. "But I still want to think about it."

He slid his arms under her knees and rose over her. "There's a sensible woman. I've waited eighteen years to get this far. I'm sure I can wait a little longer."

Helene gasped as he started to thrust faster and harder. Whatever happened, she had been given a second chance, and she intended to enjoy every glorious second of it.